IT TAKES A WOMAN

SCORNED WOMEN'S SOCIETY BOOK #4

PIPER SHELDON

WWW.SMARTYPANTSROMANCE.COM

COPYRIGHT

This book is a work of fiction. Names, characters, places, rants, facts, contrivances, and incidents are either the product of the author's questionable imagination or are used factitiously. Any resemblance to actual persons, living or dead or undead, events, locales is entirely coincidental if not somewhat disturbing/concerning.

Print Edition
ISBN: 978-1-959097-54-9

To J.R., always

And, to the #VIPeeps

PROLOGUE

GRETCHEN

"Hungry Like the Wolf" by Muse

Champagne was one of those drinks that always seemed to go from a great idea to a terrible decision in the span of a couple sips. I had just crossed that threshold … two glasses ago.

Skip paced the room, whispering to himself as though practicing a speech. The SWS and their partners were giddy with excitement for the upcoming engagement. They'd quickly paired off to canoodle and give each other heart eyes. Suzie and Ford. Kim and Devlin. Roxy and Sanders. Sigh. I mean, I get it. I was there once upon a time, but this was all a little too much. I half expected fat little cherubs to plummet from the sky and shoot hearts out from their bows.

I needed a distraction. Take the edge off. The champagne gave me ideas. Lonely, horny-lady ideas.

Like a rabbit smelling a wolf, my nose pricked to attention.

Designer cologne. With notes of maturity and fancy-pants.

I glanced up from where I hid in the corner of the room nursing my bubbly to find that I was in fact being watched by Vincent Debono. He glanced away quickly but he'd definitely been checking out my rack. I mean, I couldn't blame him. I looked *chef's kiss* tonight. The LBD—little black dress—hugged my healthy curves like a pinup model and my red curls were on point. I would want me.

He stood there, leaning casually against the wall, one hand in his pocket as he pretended to watch the awaiting drama. His dark eyebrows and thick black-framed glasses looked sharp with the designer suit, fitted perfectly to his body. His hair was slicked back with product just begging to be all mussed up. This wasn't New York, this was Donner Lodge in Green Valley. What was he trying to prove? And that trimmed beard that accentuated his perfectly square jaw? Ugh.

What was this guy's deal? Why was he even here? To see Roxy? Didn't he get that her and Sanders were a done deal? Anybody with eyeballs could see it. I'd interacted with him a few times and got a quick read on him: stuffed shirt, married to his job, no sense of humor. But damn fine. Damn, damn fine.

I shoved off the wall and made my way across the room to talk to him. As I crossed, I took extra care to sway my hips from side to side. I rolled in my lips to smooth my fire engine red lipstick. He glanced up, did a double take to see me approaching, and straightened up off the wall.

"Gretchen," he said with no intonation, his New York accent hardly noticeable.

I leaned against the wall next to him purposely mirroring his previous stoic body language. "What do you even do here?"

I hadn't meant for it to come out so accusatory, but something about him wanting Roxy when she was so clearly in love with Sanders ruffled my feathers.

"Nobody really knows," he said flatly.

My head whipped to him. Was that a joke? His face was as passive as ever as he glanced around the room.

I narrowed my eyes at him. It couldn't have been sarcasm. I had already decided that this suit didn't have a sense of humor.

Before I could push him further, he said, still without looking at me, "I wanted to tell William that I found a tent with his name on it hidden in a back room. This place is a mess but I'm not sure how it ended up here."

I turned away and stilled. Shit. I forgot about that. "Oh. That is strange." Why did I sound like a robot?

His gaze burned the side of my face. "I don't suppose you know anything about that?"

Had Sanders unwittingly helped me "accidentally" lose Skip's tent a few months ago? Maybe. Hard to say. Nobody needed to know. "Of course not."

He made a sound like he didn't believe me. When I peeked at him, he scratched at his beard. "Doesn't look like right now is the best time to talk to him."

He shot a glance to Jack and Skip making their way to the outside terrace. Jack was visibly stressing, and Skip had a half-hidden smirk on his face. It was go time.

I had a few minutes. The decision was made. Gretchen LaRoe once decided was impossible to dissuade.

I crooked a finger. "Follow me."

He frowned. "Excuse me?"

I walked away, his gaze on my ass as tangible as if he'd smacked it. "You can't just command me and expect me to follow," he said.

As he followed me.

I looked over my shoulder to raise an eyebrow at him. Busted. His gaze moved to my face and then twisted into an annoyed frown.

I pulled him into a nearby closet by his silk tie. One light bulb swung above us, like an interrogation room in a cop drama. There was hardly any space and immediately his amazing heady scent engulfed me. The heat of him sent goosebumps up the back of my neck. God, I needed some. I was fairly certain he was single. I was many things, but "the other woman" wasn't one of them.

"Attached?" I asked.

"No, but I—"

"Into women?"

"Yeah, but—"

"Wanna make out?"

"Gretchen, can we—Wait, what?"

I didn't repeat myself, I just raised my eyebrows as I licked my lips. His gaze went to my mouth. He swallowed. I'd short-circuited him. I pulled him closer, still gripping his tie as I thrust my hips against his.

His eyes widened.

This was what I needed, the familiar thrill of control. I could do this. I could own him for a few minutes. Get out of my head for just a bit.

"Gretchen. Are you okay?" he asked, resting his hands on my shoulders. His face was twisted with worried concern. Not quite the reaction I had been hoping for.

I blinked up at him. Now I needed that hard reboot. "I'm fine."

How had I missed how handsome he was? He had such a strong, well-shaped nose. I didn't even notice noses normally. And those little crinkles at the edges of his eyes were disarmingly charming. Was this champagne brain? His gaze moved over my face, catching again on my lips. It roamed lower to the ample cleavage of my sweetheart neckline. His thumbs rubbed the exposed skin of my shoulders. As if he were fighting himself, trying to push me away. Or maybe pulling me in?

"Totally fine," I repeated.

"Because you seem …" He tilted his head to study me instead of finishing the thought. There was no need for all that. Looking into my mind with those soulful eyes.

I rolled my eyes, flipping out my hair, intentionally knocking his arms off me in the process. "If you don't want to make out, that's fine, but don't make me the excuse. I just thought it would be fun."

I shrugged and glanced around unconcerned. Fine. He didn't want to kiss me, what did I care? I'd find someone else to kiss. No harm, no foul.

He stepped closer, his gaze locked on my cleavage before slowly dragging up to hold my focus. "I never said that." His voice rumbled through me, hardening my nipples.

I looked up at him, my lashes tickling my eyelids. He lowered his head. Right before our lips met, he said, "I just don't want to be the reason you avoid whatever you're feeling."

"I wouldn't worry about it."

Our mouths clashed and a surprising bolt of electricity shot through me. If I thought he was gonna kiss like a dead fish, I was wrong. But I hadn't thought that, had I? There were plenty of hot people in Green Valley I could've chosen to lock lips with but there was something about this guy that intrigued me. He managed to push my buttons and he didn't even know he was in the cockpit.

Ephram could always push my buttons. My late husband had a way of riling me up like no other, good or bad. Sometimes I think he worked me up just so we could have make up sex.

Vincent groaned and deepened our kiss.

So the guy had style. He could kiss. Did it make up for his stuffy attitude and … New Yorkness? No, but—

His mouth pulled off mine with an annoyed grumble. "Hey." He leaned my head back, hand tangled in my hair to command my attention. "If we're doing this, then I want you here with me."

My mouth fell open.

"I can practically hear you thinking. Whatever it is can wait. Don't waste my time."

Hot damn! Was his voice always that raspy? Was he always that bossy? Momma likey.

I grabbed his face and brought it back to mine. Right before our mouths met, I whispered, "Yes, sir."

His pupils widened right before his mouth found mine again. This time there was a lot less thinking. More hands groping. Hard cock pressing against my hip. Hands at my breasts. He grunted and nuzzled at my neck, trying to push the capped sleeves of my dress down.

I threw my head back and blinked at how good this felt. So good. Like unsettling good …

"Gretchen?" Roxy called with a knock at the door. "Are you in there?"

In between kisses, I managed to call out, "Hi. Yes."

Vincent wasn't deterred by my sudden stiffness. He pawed at me like a greedy teenager.

"It's almost time," she said louder.

"Uh, coming," I shouted.

"Not yet, you're not," Vincent whispered in my ear as a giant shudder shook my body.

Shocked—and more than a little impressed—I shoved Vincent off me.

"Have you seen Vincent?" Roxy asked. "He told me he'd swing by but I can't find him."

The man in question wiped his mouth and seemed to come back to his body with a dazed shake of his head.

"I'll, uh, help find him," I said.

"What're you doing in there?" Roxy's voice grew suspicious.

"Nothing," I called.

Vincent came close and whispered in my ear, "Fixing your dress."

I fought another shudder as I shouted, "Fixin' my dress. Be right out and I'll fetch him. I think I saw him head to the kitchen."

"Thanks. And hurry!" Her footsteps stomped away.

I let out a long breath.

Just what had she interrupted? How far was I about to go? I hadn't lost control like that in some time.

"Go ahead. I'll be out right behind you." He tugged at his pants. I raised an eyebrow, again, more than a little impressed. "I need a minute."

"Okay." I hesitated. How did one handle a hookup like this? Did I want this to continue? Nah. There was no point. "Well, I guess I'll see you around."

"Yeah, see ya." He didn't look up but there was tension in his shoulders.

That had been weird. A little more intense than I would have liked.

I shook my head, fixing my dress and headed back toward the group.

Oh well. All's well that ends well.

Glad I got that out of my system. No need to ever think about that kiss or Vincent Debono ever again.

CHAPTER 1

GRETCHEN

"Don't Stop Me Now" by The Regrettes

Barely a step off the stoop I froze in awe. My bag dropped to the floor along with my jaw.

Roxy, Kim, and Suzie shoved in behind me, pushing me farther into the entryway of the Brooklyn brownstone like a loaded-up pinball machine until we were lined up shoulder to shoulder.

"Well, stuff me in a turkey and call me thankful," I said.

Suzie let out a low whistle. "Holy cluck."

"This is amazing," Kim said.

"He's rich enough to buy a new boat when the last one gets wet," Suzie whispered.

"I had no idea," Roxy mumbled.

The Scorned Women's Society, SWS for short, stood slack-jawed taking in the beauty of the home around us. Over the years the shape and size of the SWS shifted to accommodate the various exes of the infamous Jethro Winston, providing what they needed before they drifted on. These three besties and I made the "core four," as I called them in my head. We were here in New York at the end of summer looking to celebrate our friendship, shop for Suzie's bridesmaid's gowns, and take advantage of a free place to stay provided by one Vincent Debono, Roxy's coworker at Donner Lodge.

A friend's coworker and nothing more than that.

The four of us shuffled forward in a tandem of tiny steps, as our heads swiveled left to right like the Sanderson sisters on the prowl, taking in every captivating detail. And there were many. From the delicately tiled black and white flooring where an antique mahogany coatrack stood, to the elegant styled staircase leading to the next story, to the living room showcasing a blend of fine furniture and even finer art. My greedy eyes soaked up as much detail as possible.

This house was like no other I had ever seen, certainly not those I was familiar with back home in Green Valley, Tennessee.

I turned to Roxy. "How serious is this whole thing with Sanders?"

She tilted her head and pretended to think about it. "I think it's gonna stick."

"Damn."

Sanders and Roxy had worked through some pretty heavy shit and had been going strong almost a year. "But if I had known Vincent was hiding all this …" she added dryly.

For being such a button-up typical suit, the style and personality in Vincent Debono's Brownstone was … unsettling. I was unsettled. Like the time I saw my fourth-grade teacher wearing jean shorts at the Piggly Wiggly. How dare someone have a life outside the one they occupied in my head?

After sliding off our shoes—I honestly felt like we should slip on those little paper booties just to be here—we continued to explore, eyes wide and mouths catching flies. Following the main staircase, we crept up to the bedrooms; two on this floor each decorated in a modern yet romantic theme that somehow felt both contemporary and antique.

The battered antique features of a classic row house were balanced out with modern light fixtures in black and brass, and brightly patterned accent rugs and pillows. Not to mention the art. It was everywhere. Large oil paintings bursting with sweeping strokes and chunky paint to small charcoal drawings hinting at the beauty of the female line, to every style in between. Small figurines and oversized glass vases. It shouldn't work, these contradictions, but they did.

Each room had so much personality it was hard to believe so much creative inspiration could be from the same man I'd met a handful of times he'd been in Green Valley to help with the renovation of the Lodge. The same man I'd thought I had totally pegged. The same man I …

"I think Gretchen may be having a stroke," Kim said when we finally made our way back to the kitchen on the first floor. The kitchen was on the smaller side but with modern amenities including a hammered copper espresso machine.

I cleared my throat, feeling off-kilter. I didn't like how blown away I was by his home. I didn't like getting people wrong. Could I have really misread Vincent Debono? A stodgy workaholic with no sense of humor couldn't be capable of producing this beautiful home. Though he always did look impeccably stylish. His expensive yet classic accessories were always perfectly on point too. And his sharp jawline emphasized his finely manicured beard. Not that I paid that much attention to him. A lady just noticed these things.

"It's just this place," I said.

"My socks are knocked off too. I'd expected a sterile cement loft in Manhattan. But this is …" Roxy trailed off and we all just nodded dumbly in silent agreement.

My frustration grew inexplicably. It was bad enough that I'd been struggling with feeling certain unwelcome desires regarding Vincent lately. It was bad enough he'd crept into my thoughts more and more. Now I had to see how wrong I'd been about him. Gretchen LaRoe was never wrong. Okay, well, rarely.

"How is he not taken?" Suzie asked as she studied an unidentifiable kitchen utensil in confusion.

"Seems like a lot of house for one guy," I said.

Roxy raised an eyebrow at me. "He wasn't always alone. His wife passed away a few years ago."

"Aww, that's sad. And sweet," Kim said softly as she admired a painting close up, hands linked safely behind her back as though we were strolling through the Met.

Roxy's words settled in. I had known that he was married once and lost his wife to cancer. A tragedy that we both shared—the loss of a spouse too soon. Was that where the color and vibrancy came from? A feminine touch was all over this magazine worthy home.

"That explains it," Suzie said, sharing my thought process. "Ford's idea of decorating is cleaning until surfaces shine and everything is in its proper place. It was always Jack that brought the character to their house."

Jack and Skip had moved in together after their engagement and out of the home that Jack and Ford once shared, renting it to some of the young adults that were a part of Triple F. Earlier this year, Suzie and Ford moved into a home of their own off Bandit Lake when a rare opportunity presented itself thanks in part to a connection from Devlin, Kim's boyfriend.

"Same with Devlin." Kim sighed. "I love our house, obviously," she amended when we all shot her a disbelieving look. Devlin had one of the most beautiful homes on Bandit Lake. "But he hired a designer for that."

"Actually, Vincent transformed this place," Roxy said. "He moved here after his wife passed. It was a mess. He completely restored and refurnished it. I think it helped him heal. This is all him. It's pretty remarkable. No wonder Donner Lodge wanted him on board for their renovation."

Great. Now visions of Vincent stripping out of his suit to swing his massive sledgehammer danced through my brain.

That weird feeling of discomfort threatened to darken my mood. Vincent Debono was handsome and obviously put an effort into his appearance, which I appreciated. It was a sign of self-respect that I admired. That was more than I could say about ninety percent of the hillbillies in my area, but I'd never allowed myself to see him as anything other than Roxy's boss. Except that one time. He was so closed off. Countless times I drove him to and from the airport and he'd hardly spoke a word. Honestly, I had pictured him for Roxy for a hot minute before the whole Sanders explosion. Sanders swept into her life, and anybody could see she was a goner.

My unease was more than the misguided preconceived notions about him. Gathered, I was not an interior designer, my appreciation for art came in the form of vintage fashion, but there was whimsy to this place. A beauty that shouldn't have worked. Dark, industrial fixtures contrasted against loud-patterned, colorful wallpapers. Lush sofas made for long naps were nestled against classic exposed brick. Antique, weathered furniture showcased luxurious fabrics. I couldn't try to explain it to the girls, I couldn't really explain it to myself, but there was humor and taste in these walls that spoke to a person with depth. A person who had already surprised me once.

I hardly ever thought about the night of Jack and Skip's engagement. The night I'd let down my guard. Okay, maybe sometimes I thought about it. At night. Alone with my Battery Operated Friend—BOF.

"Gretchen, you're being awfully quiet. What's going on under all that red hair?" Roxy watched me closely.

Too much.

I must have been making a damn fool of myself with my googly eyes. My palms itched to go explore his bedroom. I needed to get a hold of myself and focus on the reason we were all here. I didn't want to be thinking about Vincent this much. I didn't want to be thinking at all. I just wanted a fun weekend away with my girls. I was happy and pleased as punch that Suzie, Kim, and now even Roxy were in the glowing beginning stages of True Love. Especially since it was thanks in part to my machinations, if I do say so myself. And I do. But lately … it was a lot, to be surrounded by so many happy couples that were deeply in love. It wasn't jealousy. I had love once and felt blessed for that. It was just that our dynamic would be changing. Lives merging, new families formed. Old bonds would be there, but different. It was what happened, it was the cyclical nature of life. And I was okay with it. I was just being sentimental in this moment as I thought about the future. A lonely future at least for me.

I wanted this weekend to party with my girls like we were still in our early twenties and not creeping toward our mid-thirties. But you know, with less Jethro Winston and scary bikers.

"Nothing," I said brightly, answering Roxy. "I'm just ready to get this party started!"

"We have it all weekend. Vincent is traveling until next week," Roxy explained as she reached for a note resting on the counter.

"We only have until Sunday before we have to go back to reality and I don't want to waste a minute! What's that?" I snatched the paper out of Roxy's hand and opened it.

Neat, all-caps handwriting explained the best places in nearby Williamsburg, the bougie neighborhood in Brooklyn Vincent's brownstone was located in. It was titled: TO SAVE YOU FROM THE TOURIST TRAPS.

"These look great! Oh karaoke," Suzie said over my shoulder.

Vincent had taken the time to write out several restaurants, clubs he could get us into—okay, big spender—and various nearby activities to try if we had time.

"Wow, he put so much detail into this," Kim said.

"Here he mentions places we can walk to in heels. Now there's a man that gets women," Roxy said.

"He probably does this for everyone who stays here. You said he rents it out most of the time?" I asked.

"He does, but the letter is specifically addressed to 'The ladies of the SWS,'" Roxy explained with snark as she pointed to the header.

"How thoughtful," Kim added.

It was thoughtful and all the places he'd listed were totally up my alley. I wished we had all week to try each and every one of them. Okay, so Vincent was alright. That creeping feeling started in my chest again. Time to shut that shit down and get moving.

"Come on, ladies. Enough lollygagging." I grabbed a bottle of top-shelf vodka from a gilded liquor cart nearby. "Let's get dressed. The night won't wait for us."

* * *

I WAS FLYING. Arms raised above my head, I bumped to music. Sweaty bodies all around. *This*. This was exactly what we needed. Me and my girls.

The music drowning out all that pesky thinking.

Earlier when we'd gotten ready, Suzie had come out of the spare room and said, "Gotta admit, I miss dressing like a ho sometimes."

She spun so we could *ohh* and *ahh* over her. Suzie wore an ivory long-sleeved satin dress with sharp padded shoulders and wrapped to emphasize her tiny waist. If it weren't for the plunging neckline that went past her belly button and a slit up to her hip, it would almost be considered modest. But the curse of being a woman is that nothing looks modest when you had a body others objectified.

"No shame in that!" Roxy wore tiny leather shorts that made her legs look miles long, an Iron Maiden crop top and chunky boots that laced up past her knees. Her hair was in a high pony but the added extensions made the straight hair reach far down her back.

"How are your boobs so perky? Is it just from the pole?" I asked Suzie.

I couldn't imagine going braless. I needed something that could support these generous fun bags for hours. I was envious of women who could walk around with tiny little breasts, wearing any top they wanted without incurring censure for dressing like a temptress. Alas, I was blessed with handfuls of curves. Ephram never had a problem with it. In fact, he was quite obsessed with all my lovely lady lumps.

"A combination of boob tape, carefully placed pasties, and let's be honest, I'm not working with the same real estate that you are." She raised her eyebrows pointedly to the leopard-print corset currently hefting my chest to gravity-defying heights. I paired it with leather pants that took some work to hop into. My red heels gave me enough height so that I wasn't the shortest anymore, but I was still far from being tall. I looked hot, obviously.

"Y'all look amazing," Kim said. She wore a black lace long-sleeved minidress with fluorescent pink pumps. Her dark waves flowed halfway down her back.

"We all do," I said, raising my glass to our upcoming night of madness.

"No ex left behind," we said in unison and clinked glasses.

Now, hours later, I was checked out in the best way possible. I couldn't keep track of all the strangers I'd spoken to. People that tried to dance up on our core four. Drunken bonds I'd made with other revelers as I waited at the bar for the next round.

Groups of men made sad attempts to break us up all night. With Kim's dark hair and soft skin, Suzie's electric gaze, and athletic body, and Roxy's fashion model stare and legs for days, the men lined up for miles. Hell, I was the least good looking in the group and I was damn sexy. Individually, these women were knockouts, together we were a force to be reckoned with.

"I feel like I'm in a Baz Luhrmann film!" Kim yelled over the thrumming electric music. The crowd hopped all around us as the beat dropped. She was high on the music and energy, and maybe tipsy? I'd offered her some shots but never pressured her. She'd declined, saying her stomach was upset but really, I knew she didn't like to feel out of control.

"This place is amazing," Suzie agreed before dancing with abandon.

Even Roxy seemed lighter, lost to the pulsing energy of people and music. Okay, fine. Vincent's recommendations for clubs were amazing. Not only that but he had in fact put us on lists, just in case, and we got right in. Not that we wouldn't have gotten in all on our own, but it was nice to skip the line. A nice bald and tatted man named J-Dawg let us into this club, singing the praises of Vincent. What else was there that I didn't know about this enigma of a man?

This was the third (fourth?) club we'd stopped at. It featured a large stage and flashing colored lights. Sexy people dressed up in wings and draped in pearls. Giant sparkly balls bounced through the crowd reflecting the flashing lights in every direction as partiers kept them in the air. On stage, a DJ mixed a blend of new music and our favorite club jams from our twenties. Everybody was beautiful. Everything felt good. This was what I needed.

What *we* needed.

I took mental snapshots throughout the night. Moments I could hold onto later. The way the lights blurred as I tossed my head back to get a full breath of air. The ladies' smiling faces spinning past as they danced. The uncontrollable laughter when Suzie swore loud enough for half the club to hear, then swore again to cover it. Then swore again as she apologized.

"You can take the stripper out of Green Valley … yada yada," she said through gasps for breath. We laughed until our abs hurt. These would be the memories I looked back on when I was old and telling stories at the retirement community's bingo night to whoever would listen.

I was completely free. In my element. Nothing to hold me down, no heaviness to my bones that more and more lately made it hard to get up in the morning.

"I love you," I called to Roxy as we danced to a spectacular remix of "Toxic" by Britney Spears.

"You're drunk," she said and bent down slightly to swing a sweaty arm around my shoulder.

"*You're* drunk." I think. It was hard to tell when Roxy was drunk. Her steamy gaze only got more—steamier. She wasn't the type to get maudlin or sloppy. Lucky ho.

Next to us, Suzie led Kim through some steps to the song.

Roxy nodded at me and blinked slowly. "Yep. But I love you too."

"Let's never fight again," I said feeling my throat tighten.

"Deal."

Our fight last summer had been one of the worst times of my life. There were a hundred times I picked up my phone to text or call her but my damn stubborn streak kept me from admitting I had made a mistake. The thing was, I knew more than most that relationships were the most important thing in life. I squeezed her so hard that her lithe, tall frame smooshed into my ample curves. Now that we'd talked through things everything was right in the universe again. Almost everything.

I had to keep drinking to avoid my maudlin stage. I was close to that now. My ears rang loudly in the breaks of music. My throat was raw from yelling drunken compliments at women in bathrooms.

"Time for more shots!" I yelled and pulled the girls closer.

"Noooo," they all groaned.

I frowned at them each in turn. "Come on!"

"Gretchen, it's getting late," Kim said.

She stifled a yawn with the back of her hand as if to prove the point. Suzie leaned her head on Roxy's shoulder.

Seriously? We were having the times of our lives and they were ready to tap out? If we stopped now, I'd have plenty of time to think.

I crossed my arms in a dramatic pout. "It's barely midnight." *I think.*

"It's after one," Suzie said.

"We were up early for the flight this morning," Kim said, then added, "Yesterday morning."

Roxy watched me closely, her brow furrowed. I didn't like her appraising gaze. "We've had a great time. We'll do more tomorrow. We need to regroup and rest." Her tone was firm. No room for negotiation. She'd been more confident with me since our reunion, saying exactly what she wanted instead of letting me always push forward. I didn't always like it, but dammit, I respected it.

"We aren't spring chickens anymore," Suzie added.

"I already feel hungover," Kim said with a frown.

"You didn't drink," Roxy said as she pulled out her phone.

"It's a sympathetic hangover," Kim said.

Roxy had the rideshare app open and I was ushered to the front of the club.

"No. I want to keep partying. I don't want to go home." I didn't care how whiny I sounded. "We can sleep when we're dead!" I called out. I tried to fight them as they dragged me along.

It was no use. Moments later a gray sedan pulled to a stop in front of us. The driver handed us water bottles as we all filed into her car. "Drink up," the older woman said.

I sat up front with her and let the others have the back. I knew how it was to drive people around and be treated like a personal servant.

I kept myself busy back in Green Valley because I couldn't stand being still. Not many people knew that I didn't need to work since my husband's death. Living in a small town, having money wasn't exactly something I advertised.

"Oh man, I miss wild nights with the girls," the driver said as we made our way back toward Vincent's house. She wore a black velour sweatsuit with gold piping. Her white hair teased to great heights looked almost blueish. I was surprised to see her driving this time of night.

In the drop-down mirror, I could see Kim already asleep on Roxy's shoulder. Roxy smiled at me. "We had a great time," Roxy said before a jaw-cracking yawn. Suzie looked dazedly out the window, city lights flashing across her face. My foot tapped impatiently with wired energy.

"I bet you see all sorts, driving this time of night," I said to the driver.

"Yeah, there have been some wild stories. More deep cleanings than I would prefer. There's a puke bag there if you think any of them need it." I bit back a smile and shook my head as she continued to chat in her deep, almost cliché New Yorker accent. "Most people are either quiet or nice enough. People always ask me why I drive when I could be home. But I like the conversation and I don't have anybody at home. I get lonely."

That familiar anxiety crept up in my chest, like I took a misstep and was still trying to find the right footing.

"Plus," she added, "I figure if I get murdered nobody will care. It's just me. Never did the husband and family thing."

She laughed but when I looked at her she blinked rapidly at the traffic ahead through her bejeweled purple glasses. She chatted happily about the previous pickup she had and about a rat she saw that she thought was a cat. And a hairless cat that ended up being a rat. She spoke without being prompted. I suspected this was typical for her. A vision of her shuffling around a tiny New York apartment talking to herself flashed in my brain. I wouldn't pity her. Just because she didn't live a traditional life didn't mean she regretted it. I was projecting my own new fears of loneliness onto her.

"You're probably happy though. That you chose an independent life. You probably have the best stories," I said during a lull in her chatting.

She cackled so loud Kim snorted awake before falling right back to sleep. "Oh yeah. I was in my prime during peak Studio 54 days. Now those parties, at least from what I remember, were the wildest. Nothing has ever compared to those nights. I saw Andy Warhol once," she said with pride. "But you know, those happy memories don't keep me warm at night."

The *thump, thump, thump* of my heart seemed to echo throughout the car.

It was strange being on "this side of the couch." So many people over my years of driving had opened up about things that they probably never would have otherwise. Maybe it was the dark car. Maybe it was facing forward, not having to make eye contact, and not feeling judged. Or maybe it was just as simple as every person needing somebody to talk to. I felt that strange pull now. I would never see this woman again and I wanted to know if she had regrets. It felt important.

"Would you have done anything differently?" I asked.

"Yeah, I would have married a billionaire when my tits looked like that ones'." She gestured her head back to Suzie.

I laughed and heard Suzie chuckle softly.

"In all seriousness, probably not. I lived spectacularly. Plus, I'm a lot to handle."

The number of times others had told me, men especially, that I was just a little too much, was enough to cause me to interject. "You're not too much. They just weren't enough."

She looked over at me and winked. "I knew I sensed a kindred spirit in you." She let out a long breath, a little of her exuberance softening into something more serious. "But now that I'm closer to knocking on heaven's gates—hopefully," she held up crossed arthritic fingers, "I do wish I had someone to pass all those fun stories down to. Someone I could have shared them with over the years."

"What about your girlfriends?" I asked around a tight throat.

She shrugged. "Yeah. Sure. We kept in contact for a while, but you know how it is when everybody starts moving in different directions. We disconnected over the years. I found the ones still alive on that Facebook but that's not for me. I want to live, not stare at a computer."

Without meaning to I met Roxy's gaze in the drop-down mirror, her RBF exaggerated with a frown. She gave a small shake as if to say that won't be us. We wouldn't be the friends that drifted apart. But how could she guarantee that?

I brought my focus to the brake lights ahead of us.

The driver went on, "I just wish there was somebody left to carry my memory on. Without a legacy, it'll be like I never existed."

This time I avoided Roxy's gaze, but I felt it searing the side of my face. If I looked at her, she would see through everything. The creeping doubt that had been settling deeper into my bones with every day that passed. The feeling that I wasn't as happy as I acted. The fact that just maybe I was a little lonely and tired.

"Oh look," the driver interjected enthusiastically, the headlights passing over a sidewalk, "that rat's carrying an entire chicken carcass. God, I love this city."

CHAPTER 2

VINCENT

"Have You Ever Seen The Rain" - The Lumineers

I was drenched with sweat, back aching and shoulders cramped from almost forty-eight hours of travel when I was finally buzzed through to the maternity ward. My heart raced and fear made my palms clammy.

Nicole greeted me in the hallway, outside Lauren's recovery room.

"I got here as fast as I could," I said.

"You're fine," she said calmly. She had been waiting for me through the double doors and after one look at me she frowned with concern before gently shoving my shoulder. "We told you that you didn't have to rush home. It's the middle of the night!"

Maybe if I hadn't gotten the text about the baby being breech and Lauren's emergency C-section, but the second I'd seen her message there was no other option. I had only been in LA for a few hours before heading straight back to the airport to fly home to NY.

"She's okay?" My voice shook as I asked.

The pity on Nicole's face, melted into an exhausted grin. "She's absolutely fine. The C-section was a bit scary, but Lauren's doing great."

"And the baby?" My jaw felt like it hadn't unclenched since I got her text.

"Perfectly healthy." My sister-in-law radiated joy as she whisper-yelled,

"I'm a grandma!" Her hands were thrown out to the side and her eyes were wide with enthusiasm. She shared Elaine's goofy personality. The whole Walsh side of my wife's family did.

My carry-on bag dropped to the ground as I sagged with relief. My phone died during my layover in Chicago. I'd been an absolute wreck rushing from airport gate to gate to make any possible flight to get home. I shifted my balloon bouquet to the other hand and pulled Nicole in.

"Thank God." I squeezed my sister-in-law to my side. "And you're okay, Grandma?"

I looked down at her. Up close there were bags under her eyes and she trembled slightly in my embrace. For all her typical New York sharpness she was still a momma watching her daughter go through something major. Her blond hair was long and straight, and it was hard to tell if it was bleached white or if age had made it that color. Lines like parenthesis around her mouth and a softness to the skin around her eyes were the only signs she was even old enough to be a grandmother. I couldn't wrap my mind around it. She was getting older. I was getting older. It was hard to look at her and not imagine what my wife would have looked like in another twelve years. How she might have looked now.

"I'm fine. Glad you could make it." She sniffed and playfully tried to shove me off her. "Sorry to freak you out."

I held her even tighter, hooking an arm around her neck as she swatted at me. I felt a thousand pounds lighter knowing everyone was okay.

"Gross. You're all sweaty," she said.

I finally released her with a ruffle of her hair. We bickered like brothers and sisters half our age. I was almost forty and Nicole was in her mid-fifties. She'd been twelve when Elaine was born. We'd always been close and when Elaine passed four years ago, Lauren, Nicole, and I grew even closer over our shared loss.

After she smoothed her hair, I met Nicole's gaze. "I would have come regardless. You know that."

Nicole sniffed and swiped her eyes even as she rolled them. "I can't stop leaking. I'm so proud of Lauren. She did good, right? She did so good."

"That she did. Can she have visitors yet?" I asked, hesitating.

"Let me peek in and make sure she's decent."

A second later Nicole motioned me in her daughter's room.

Lauren sat propped up with a tiny bundle on her chest. A monitor was attached to wires coming out of her arms. The second she saw me her lower lip trembled, but she grinned ear to ear. "Uncle Vinny! You made it." Her eyes were swollen and bloodshot, but she smiled with her whole face. The Walsh women all had that in common too. "I have someone I'd like you to meet."

I set down my gift and washed my hands before I stepped to the hospital bed. I gently rested my hand on my niece's shoulder and tilted my head to get a glimpse of the little one.

"How are you feeling?" I asked softly.

"Like a tiny person tried to parkour her way out of my body. But happy," Lauren said. "This is Lainey Grace Anderson."

She turned the bundle so I could see the squished little face of my new great-niece. "Lainey?"

Lauren nodded, her eyes welling. "L-A-I-N-E-Y. We named her for Aunty Elaine."

I swallowed down the hard lump in my throat. When I glanced to Nicole, she gave me a half smile, eyes welling again at the mention of her sister.

"It's a beautiful name," I said to my niece, my voice rough. I wasn't always great expressing myself, but she smiled at me, knowing how huge the gesture to me was.

She grabbed my hand and squeezed. "Here." She carefully handed me the baby. The bundle was impossibly light.

I moved to a chair to hold little Lainey, not breathing until I sat down. The whole world narrowed down to just the tiny sleeping form in my arms. This was it. This little being that meant so much to just a few people. This was what made the hard days bearable and the good days glorious.

"She's so wonderful," I whispered.

"Another girl," Nicole said. "The Walsh line can't stop producing females."

"And why should you? When the women of this family are perfect?" I said memorizing this tiny, beautiful person in my arms.

"Maww," they said in unison. I felt more than saw Nicole and Lauren share a look.

I was used to those looks. When Elaine and I got married, Lauren was ten years old. It was hard to believe that the same little girl was now a grown woman with a baby of her own. Elaine and I had been there for all her major milestones and often helped her single mom as she put herself through nursing school. Elaine's family was as much mine at this point, and I couldn't imagine being anywhere else. I was lucky that they still treated me like family. It was another unbreakable tie to the woman I would never stop loving.

I glanced around the room, belatedly remembering there was a dad crucial to the process too. "Where's Troy?"

"He went to get some food. I think he needed a break," Lauren explained, shifting in bed with a wince.

"*He* needed a break?" I teased.

"Apparently, it's fairly traumatizing to watch me scream in pain for almost twenty-four hours," Lauren explained.

"I guess," I said. I turned my focus back to baby Lainey. Sweet, sweet Lainey. I couldn't see either parent in the smooshed newborn features. I pushed up the tiny pink hat to see a full head of super soft black curls. "I see she got Troy's hair." I pulled the cap back down.

"And how," Lauren said. "If she ends up looking more like her dad after I did all that work, I'm gonna be pissed."

I laughed. "Nah. Too beautiful." I was afraid to move too much, so I sat in an awkward hunched position as Lainey slept with short fast pants, eyes moving rapidly under her lids. Her hands were in mittens, but I took one off to see the impossibly small appendages. How could anything ever be so small? It boggled the mind.

"Elaine would have loved you," I whispered to the baby.

I was overcome by emotion. Not just sadness. Of course, I wished more than anything that Elaine could see her great-niece, but more than that, I was hit by the overwhelming reality of how fast time was moving. Not just moving but passing me by. It was like I was standing still, and life was blurring around me like a time-lapse camera.

I glanced up to Lauren. She was a *mom*. How could that be? I was just taking her shopping for colored pencils and notebooks. Picking her up from the mall. Teaching her how to drive. Deep in my chest, in my bones, there was a longing that I had denied for so long. There was a time where I assumed Elaine and I would have a family of our own. It'd been years since I even let myself imagine a baby. Yet once the thought hit me, I couldn't stop the deluge. I pushed the feelings down. As I always did. But now it felt like a flashing sign from the universe: TIME IS FLYING.

The baby stretched and mewed a little sound that instantly had me standing. Especially when she started turning her head into my arm, mouth gaping. "I think she needs her mom."

Lauren sighed. "Ma, can you get the lactation specialist? I'm having trouble getting her to latch."

Nicole left with a nod.

"I'll leave you to it." I gave Lainey back and lowered to kiss my niece's forehead. "I'm so proud of you. She's amazing. Just like you."

Lauren smiled and leaned into me. "Thank you."

An image of the little girl who would play soccer in our yard and told us stories about the drama of her friends, overlaid the image of the grown woman in front of me. She favored her mother so much, who favored her sister so much. In the exaggerated shake of her head. In the high arch of her dark eyebrows. If I'd had children with Elaine would that child look like Lainey? So many Walsh idiosyncrasies passed from generation to generation.

There was no point to this line of thought. I had to carry on. I'd lost Elaine four years ago already. *Four years*. We'd been lucky for the time that we had, lucky to have a chance to say goodbye to each other. Lucky the pain was minimal, and the end came swift. Lucky as one can be in the face of complete and random tragedy.

Nicole met me outside the room. "No offense, but you look like shit."

"Well, that makes sense. I feel like it." I scrubbed a hand over my face. "I gotta get home. I have it rented out this weekend, but I need some fresh clothes before I go to a hotel."

"Are you kidding me? Just come to our place. Lauren will be discharged in a couple days. You can stay with us." Even as she said it, we both knew it wouldn't happen. I believed her invitation but having a brand-new baby in the house, the last thing the new parents needed to worry about was another family member crashing there.

I waved her off. "You guys have your hands full. Plus, I'll need to fly back out tomorrow."

What I really needed was to get some sleep. I hugged her goodbye and headed out to my car. I would just drop in. Nobody would even notice me. Plus, Gretchen—I mean the ladies— would probably be still out and about anyway.

I shook my head as I drove home. The only good thing about the stress of the last few days was that worry consumed my thoughts, pushing out inconvenient memories that plagued me. Ever since Gretchen LaRoe had chosen me as her distraction of the night a few months back, I couldn't stop thinking about her. If I was being completely honest with myself, I had even had thoughts of her before the kiss. But actually having her pliant curves melt into me and her soft hot mouth on mine, had taken my silly crush to the next level. Gretchen was vibrant and vivacious. People with so much personality pouring out of them were nice to be around. My attraction to her didn't have to be more complicated than that.

Thankfully I was needed in Green Valley less and less. No more hitting up Roxy to try and get a chance to hang out with Gretchen. No more using

Gretchen for rides to and from the Lodge, when my rental car was covered in my travel expenses.

No more thinking about Gretchen LaRoe. Of her soft curves and full lips and amazing …

The car behind me honked. I took a steadying breath and refocused on the road.

This *crush* was getting ridiculous. The only cure was to distance myself from her.

* * *

Gretchen

I WAS FINE. I really was.

When we got home, the girls video-chatted their guys as I paced the house trying not to hear their conversations through the walls. I was too wired to sleep. The energy of the city outside still buzzed through my blood making rest impossible. My brain was too loud.

Eventually, the calls ended, and the house went silent. If I had known the girls were gonna clock out, I would have considered going home with that gorgeous bartender from two clubs ago with full sleeve tattoos or the hottie and his friend. Now I was a little drunk and alone with my thoughts.

And that was a dangerous combination.

Most of the time, I accepted my choice to be single. I was lucky enough to experience True Love once, when some never got it at all. Better to have loved and lost and all that BS. But this time of night, when silence rang louder than the clubs in my ears and the empty gap in the sheets was chilly, I couldn't seem to take a deep enough breath.

"Ugh," I groaned out loud at my sad ramblings and got out of bed to pour myself a nightcap. Okay, I wasn't actually sure what a "nightcap" was, but it felt appropriate to have one in this environment. I grabbed my glass of wine and crept barefoot around the silent house, taking in details that I hadn't wanted to gawk at earlier.

I went to check on the girls sound asleep in the guest rooms. Suzie was curled in a tiny ball on one twin bed and Roxy lay on the other, long arms and legs sprawled like a starfish. Kim was in the room across the hall sleeping by herself for the exact reason greeting my ears. My Lord, did Kim always snore that loud? For a dainty little thing she sure sounded like a middle-aged trucker named Buzzsaw. Poor Devlin. His musician's ears must bleed at night.

I silently crept up to the top floor where the owner's suite was. Vincent's space and explicitly off-limits, according to Roxy. I mean, Vincent hadn't said anything about it in his note.

Ugh, Vincent.

He was like this irritation to me now. Being here. It was a mosquito bite on the knuckle, and I found myself gnawing at the spot for relief that wouldn't come. I just wanted to see his room. Just because I was curious, it wasn't a big deal. I wouldn't touch anything. I wouldn't even leave tracks in what I was sure would be deeply plush carpet.

Truth was, there was something I'd kept from the SWS. Even Roxy. Which I *knew* was totally hypocritical because I'd be the first to throw a hissy fit if anything was kept from me. But that night … that was just a blip on the radar. A mistake.

There may have been a little lapse of judgement back in Green Valley the night of Jack and Skip's engagement. I had a little too much champagne and was deep in the throes of an epic pity party. I couldn't stand being alone in that moment. Nobody could ever replace my love for Ephram, but sometimes a warm body was a nice distraction.

And so, when I ran into Vincent Debono, hovering around the outskirts of the party, standing there in his stupid perfectly cut designer suit, hands in pockets, casual grin on his face … well, I snapped. He was there and *damn* fine. Something about his button-upped stodginess made me want to rile him up. That didn't mean I wanted to date him or even talk to him. Couldn't a girl just want to suck face and call it a night?

I stopped mid-step on the stairs as heat burned up my chest and ears as the physical memories flooded to the surface. My heart hammered so hard I had to close my eyes and press a hand to my chest to keep the dizziness at bay.

His mouth had looked so kissable. His arms so strong. I just needed them wrapped around me. I just needed to be consumed until I was out of my head. So, I did what any hot-blooded woman would do; I attacked his face with mine. He wasn't exactly a passive party in the experience.

I took a deep breath in and out, recalling the strong hands that greedily roamed my curves. His lips, soft and sturdy seemed to ground me to earth as my body tried to float away.

"Whew," I whispered out loud to myself. It was a hell of a kiss.

But it was a mistake and we had moved past it. No point in dwelling. Not like I'd ever come across the guy again. His time with the Lodge was sporadic and unpredictable and it wasn't like I hung around there unless Roxy needed something. Though he did seem to need rides a lot. Regardless. He was easily avoidable.

So why was I thinking about this kiss as I crept into the unlocked—*see*, Roxy—owner's suite on the top floor?

"Well shit." I let out a breath and tossed out my arms.

It was perfect. Behind a low-seated California king covered in luxurious bedding was an exposed brick wall. Above the bed was a collage of lovely art in various frames and styles. Heaven's bells, the room smelled like freshly laundered linen, furniture polish, and designer cologne. The memory of him pressed hard and wanting against me flooded back so fast, the tips of my toes tingled.

There were things brewing in me that I couldn't explain to the SWS. Not even to Roxy. It wasn't that I wanted to keep secrets. It was just that I didn't fully understand it yet myself. I felt myself longing for things I never had before, even with Ephram. Security and family, stability and comfort. Not just longing. Obsessing. I blocked the desires as best I could, but then my mind would drift. I knew I didn't want to date. I've had my fair share of hookups over the years that worked out organically and ended effortlessly but sometimes, especially in these quiet moments, I wanted *more*. At some point the narrative of my brain went from "happily single" to "passively looking for a life partner." My brain did this sometimes. It would decide something and there was no stopping it. I'd always been like this. Act first, don't overthink it.

But how could I want something that no longer existed? I had my chance and lost it. I wanted the dream that played in my head. The life that Ephram and I would have had now. I imagined a small home in the mountains where our borderline feral children would run barefoot through the trees. But that fantasy only existed with Ephram. There was no question in my mind that I would never find the love I had with Ephram again. That heart-wrenching understanding was what kept these secret longings locked inside.

I gasped as I walked into Vincent's closet.

"Lady boner alert." It was too *good*. Clean, organized, floor-to-ceiling shelving, racks of color coordinated sweaters and shirts. Perfectly organized. Head shaking, mouth hanging open, I took it all in. (That's what she said.) A separate glass-enclosed area displayed his designer tuxedoes and most expensive jackets. I squeaked.

I stood to peek inside the sleek, black drawers. They slid open silently, smoothly, displaying cuff links, rolled socks, tucked boxer briefs, everything a man of his caliber could ever need. I'd noticed Vincent's style—yes, it was mostly suits—contained flare and variety in all the little details, just like his home. Not everyone would notice the whimsy in his emerald green tortoise-shell cuff links or the brightly patterned socks. It was the same way his house reflected a deep understanding of style in its clash of opposing themes. It was clear to anyone that Vincent had style but his penchant for subtly playing with textures and patterns was often overlooked.

I gently ran fingers over the sleeves of dozens of dress shirts arranged appealingly in the rainbow spectrum and sighed. I wanted to rub my face in his collection. Imagine him coming home to find a clown-like imprint in his nicest white shirt from my sweating, makeup-covered face.

I chuckled at the thought.

There was a sleek black vanity on the left. A few lotions and creams, beard oil, and combs lined the surface. The man was neat as a pin. Maybe I should move things around … just to mess with his head. Then I spotted something that stuck out from everything else. A simple framed picture. A young couple. A beautiful blond, head tilted up to smile at the man she loved. Vincent. It felt so real, that love, that I almost looked away lest I intrude on a moment too personal for my eyes.

I imagined her with sophisticated grace. They made a perfect set. She would charm everybody they met at parties while he stood silently on guard, in awe of the beautiful woman he called his. I had to admit that he'd aged well. He looked handsome in this photo, but now he had that salt-and-pepper, slightly weathered thing going for him. He'd matured, and boy, could he work it.

I turned my back to the vanity. That was what was missing from the exquisitely curated space of his home. No pictures, no details of a personal life. Maybe because he rented it out so often. Or maybe because … it hurt too much.

Pain seized my chest. I had done the same with Ephram. Every trace of him had been too painful to bear witness to and had been stripped from my life, save for one picture stored deep in folders on my computer. A drunken selfie, where he was kissing my cheek and I was smeary with drink and dewy with youth. I rarely allowed myself to open it and less and less often lately. The girl in the picture felt so far removed from the person I was today. Would Ephram even recognize the woman I was now? A far cry from the messy biker chick that only had eyes for him. That former version of myself didn't even feel real when I looked at that picture and more than anything else, that was the most painful. We were supposed to grow old and change together.

I dug my nails into my palms as my nose tickled.

I thought of the rideshare driver's words. Were people erased to time if nobody remembered them? I squeezed my eyes shut and pushed the thoughts away. I understood the need to hide the pain of loss, but Vincent didn't hide his wife away. She was here to greet him, smiling with her whole body at the man she loved. Greeting him every morning as he got dressed.

Sudden emotion tightened my throat. That level of love … To have it and lose it. Those who haven't experienced loss like that just can't understand it.

I understood.

I groaned, needing to shake myself from this mood. I moved back to the shelves of dress shoes, some expensive brands I recognized, others probably too fancy for me to even know about. Most of my shopping was scavenging through musty depths of thrift shops and vintage dealers.

This closet. It was a real work of art.

"Jesus, I'm drooling," I said to the room.

"Glad you approve," a man rumbled in response.

I screamed and acted without thought. I grabbed the nearest thing and threw it in the direction of the voice.

CHAPTER 3

VINCENT

"Human Behavior" - The Decemberists

I pulled my underwear off my face—clean, thankfully—as Gretchen LaRoe fell into a ball on the floor. Her shout quickly melted into cackles of laughter. She laughed with her whole body.

This was probably the last way I ever expected an already strange and stressful day to end. Days? I'd lost track of time. But coming home to find Gretchen LaRoe salivating over my suits was up there with scenarios I would have never imagined. Not that I came up with too many scenes involving Gretchen and clothing …

"Jumping firecrackers, you about scared the Holy Ghost right out of me," she gasped out between breaths.

I hadn't even meant to be discovered, knowing I wasn't supposed to be here. I had planned to get in and get back out before they noticed. "My most sincere apologies," I said leaning against the door frame, a little shaken at her presence.

Not because I was upset to find her here, but because I had just been thinking about her. Like I had manifested her into my closet. Also, *what* was she doing in my closet?

I cleared my throat and shifted on my feet. I waited patiently as Gretchen gathered her wits. She wore nothing but a corset and tight pants that were close to bursting as she shifted to her hands and knees. My palms itched with the memory of what those curves felt like as I explored her mouth with my tongue. Her full breasts were seconds from pouring out. Since I'd found her creeping around my closet, I enjoyed the view of the little snooper a bit longer.

Eventually, the cackles stopped, and she held out a hand, gesturing me over to come help her up. She felt no shame for getting caught looking through my belongings. And maybe if it had been anyone else, I would have been more disturbed. As it was Gretchen LaRoe, I was mildly amused. I refolded my briefs and tucked them back into their designated spot before extending a hand to help her up. She was warm and soft under my palm. Her mascara was blurred and there was a gleam to her skin that spoke of a night out. That and the smell of booze wafting off her.

"Better?" I asked. Our hands remained clasped a moment too long. She flicked a gaze to them before I released her.

"Much." She wiped wisps of curled hair off her forehead with the back of her arm.

I scratched my beard, my eyes felt sandy with lack of sleep.

"You scared me." She not so gently shoved my shoulder. The action caused her to fall into me a little. Instinctually, I wrapped an arm around her waist and steadied her. She blinked up at me before pulling away. "What in the Sam Hill are you doing here?"

I folded my arms and tilted my head at her. "What am I doing here? In my closet? In *my* home?"

She crossed her arms, pushing up her breasts. I didn't even pretend to not look at them. I was too tired to have manners, and once again she was the one who was in my closet. "You know what I mean," she said with her typical bluster, but a hint of a blush rose to her cheeks.

I sighed. "My niece went into labor. I had to cut my trip short."

Her arms dropped, glare melting away. "Is she okay?"

I rubbed my eyes. "She is. The baby was breech and after hours of pushing they needed to do an emergency C-section."

My voice shook with emotion. It had been such a horrible and stressful twenty-four hours.

I hadn't noticed Gretchen move until her hand landed gently on my shoulder. It would be so easy to lean into her.

"And the baby?" Gretchen's voice was tight too. The silly defiance I'd seen in her only moments ago melted into genuine concern.

"She's fine. Seven pounds. Four ounces. They're both fine, thank God.

Perfect." I rubbed a hand over my eyes. I still didn't have a plan of where to go now. "I just came home to change then I'll get a hotel or something."

"Don't be a fool," Gretchen said. "You're not going anywhere. I've drunk my weight in tequila tonight but even I can see you're dead on your feet. You're staying here."

"But your visit. I didn't mean to impose on the SWS."

"We'll survive," she said and led me to the ottoman in the middle of the closet. She put pressure on my shoulders until I relinquished and slumped to sit. Before I knew it, I'd been stripped of my business coat and tie. She knelt before me and briskly shucked off my shoes. In the back of my mind, this action felt deeply personal, but I was too exhausted to make anything of it. Having shared the events with her about Lauren seemed to cause the tension to instantly melt out of me, but not in a relaxing way. It seemed to release the last bit of strength that had been holding me together, allowing the weariness to sink deep.

It was surreal to come home and be taken care of like this. Like I had a partner again. *I miss this.*

Gretchen sat up, still kneeling in front of me. She patted my knees. "Get changed. And go to sleep."

"Girls' trip," I mumbled as I watched her pop up to stand, breasts jiggling. Suddenly I wasn't feeling as tired. Restlessness stirred me. We were here. We were alone …

She rolled her eyes. "I'll tell the girls in the morning. You just get some sleep. We're planning to be out all weekend anyway."

"I honestly didn't expect you to be home yet." I unbuttoned my dress shirt.

She watched my fingers as they worked the buttons, swallowed, and then busied herself searching my dresser, opening and closing drawers.

"One to the left," I said.

She reached back, passing me a set of cotton pajamas. "You know how couples are." Even with her back to me, I could see the wince in her shoulders. So, she knew about Elaine.

I opened my mouth to say it was okay, but she quickly added, "But I don't remember being this lame when I was married."

In the mirror of the vanity, she flicked a gaze to gauge my reaction to her news.

"You were married?" I asked softly.

"Yeah. He … passed away also."

I had so many questions. I had no idea. Gretchen struck me as one of those people who chose to be perpetually single. The cool aunt that always had great taste in music but never a stable relationship. We had both misjudged each other.

I spoke without overthinking. "Listen. I'm too keyed up to go to sleep. You want to have a nightcap?"

She snorted softly at something I didn't understand, before she nodded. "You change and I'll meet you on the veranda," she said over her smooth shoulder in a grandiose accent.

"I assume you mean the roof, since I don't have a veranda," I called at her retreating form.

She cackled, sashaying out of the room.

I let out a long slow breath. I looked to Elaine and shook my head with a smile.

"She's a character. You would've liked her."

* * *

GRETCHEN HAD CHANGED TOO when I made my way back out. She stood at the drink cart in the most absurd piece of clothing I'd ever seen.

"Tell me you didn't pack that."

She twirled around at the sound of my voice. The great sheer robe she wore, spun out with drama. It was light pink but was lined with black fur. Underneath, short shorts and a thin-strapped shirt were barely visible under all the rippling fur and fabric.

"Of course, I did. Don't worry it's faux fur." She smoothed her hand down the length of the collar. "I'm glad I did too. This is the exact mood for pouring nightcaps before we go out on the veranda." She dropped her voice to a sultry growl.

"Now I'm positive you don't know what that is."

She waved me off and spun again with flourish, the ridiculous robe flew all around brushing against my shins. The fresh scent of something floral met my nose as she handed me a few fingers of amber liquid. She'd washed her face and I was taken aback. Gretchen LaRoe without makeup. She looked … younger. Softer, somehow. Still breathtaking, but that was Gretchen LaRoe—a scene stealer.

"How did that even fit in your suitcase?" I asked and she shrugged. "It's a weekend trip. Tell me you didn't check a bag."

"I didn't check a bag," she said. "I checked two." She stuck out her tongue and fluttered her lashes at me over her shoulder.

"Of course you did." I took a sip and let it ease me. Gretchen always dressed in extravagant outfits. The first time I ever saw her she was wearing a pinup cowgirl outfit and her clothes had only gotten more eccentric from there. I remember thinking how much confidence it took to be able to wear such loud outfits and yet look at people like they were the ones out of place.

"But look. My shoes," she said playfully, using one hand to lift the hem and point a toe at me. On her dainty feet sat tiny pink slippers with a fuzzy pink ball on top. My eyes traveled up over the shape of her legs. She had such delicious curves. There was so much there to … grip.

"Very cute," I said dryly, turning away to let out a slow breath. "Let's go to the roof."

I grabbed a light blanket on the way. Though it was still summer, night had cooled the city and she was half naked.

As soon as we were outside, she stopped to take in the view. "Oh, come on," she said tossing out her arms.

I chuckled at her fake annoyance. At least I hoped it was fake. "You don't like it?"

Even in the dark, I could feel her roll her eyes. "It's all so hideous," she said dryly. "The furniture. The design. The view. I'm disgusted."

Her reaction made me proud.

I had taken care with the rooftop, as it was one of the biggest draws to this place. It faced the East River and you could clearly see the lights of Manhattan in the distance. The area was decorated with comfy chairs and white fairy lights. I had to travel so much for work that I wasn't home a lot. I often thought a family should live here, but I assuaged my guilt by renting it out while I was gone. The exclusive homeshare site more than made up for the investment.

But I knew that wasn't why Gretchen LaRoe was annoyed. She had thought she had me pegged the moment we met. And every moment since. I liked surprising her.

She rubbed her arms and I led her to the loveseat that I hung from a wooden beam on sturdy chains so it could swing. She let me wrap her up in one half of the blanket as she continued to grumble. "You know, I can't tell if you're suddenly super hot, or if your house is just messing with my mind," she said.

"I've always been super hot," I teased with a grin. "You were just too snobby to notice," I shot back. If she was trying to shock me with her direct nature, two could play at that game. I was a New Yorker after all. I squeezed into the space next to her, also covering myself with the soft blanket.

I felt her gape at me. When I turned, her eyes narrowed into a glare. "I am not a snob. I'm from Green Valley, Tennessee."

"Yeah, and the second you met me, you thought you knew everything about me." I held up my glass. It took her a minute before she swallowed her pride and clinked hers to it.

"Fine. You're right. I judged you."

I waited until she took a drink before asking, "Is that why you wanted to make out so badly that night? To try and ruffle me?"

Just as I hoped, she coughed on her drink. I didn't have to specify. We both knew the night in question. It was the elephant in the room she thought I would ignore.

"I can be blunt too, Miss LaRoe," I said in an exaggerated Southern drawl.

To my utter surprise, she threw her head back and laughed. That laugh traveled through me, delighting me. A direct hit of serotonin my brain would absolutely get addicted to.

She leaned back in the loveseat and used her slipper to push us gently back and forth.

"Oh God, that accent was terrible." She shook her head before saying, "Ah. That night." She let out a long sigh. "I guess if we're doing the whole honesty thing, I was just lonely. Love was in the air. It makes me horny."

The electricity of her confession shot straight to my dick. We'd been so close to more than kissing that night. But here now, with her body pressed to mine, the heat of her luxurious shape warming my hip and thigh, it was easy to imagine having gone further.

But even then, I had sensed something was wrong with her. She seemed too eager to get out of her own head. In the moment I was disappointed, it was probably for the best that things hadn't gone even further. Despite her outward confidence, Gretchen was a woman in pain.

"See, I can surprise you. You've gone quiet." She took a sip of her cocktail, looking at me coyly over the glass.

I leaned closer. "You don't have to talk about your husband if you don't want to, but I know when I'm being redirected."

Her eyelashes blinked rapidly and her mouth shut slowly. "I'm not usually so transparent," she said with a hint of hurt in her tone.

And maybe with others she wasn't, but I recognized her need to change the subject. We could do flirtation, if that was what she wanted. It was safe enough.

"I'm on to you. You gave me a lot of rides," I said.

She coughed again, wiping her mouth with the back of her hand.

"Back and forth. To the airport?" I prompted, fighting a smile. I hardly spoke on those drives, content to listen to her soothing updates and small-town gossip.

She narrowed her eyes at me. "Nothing gets past you." She studied me a moment, her gaze flicking to my mouth before she broke the connection to tilt her in thought. "I guess that's true. I didn't realize I was such a Chatty Cathy. But I'm not exactly surprised." She shrugged and brushed it off.

"Plus, people like us, we sense our own," I added softly.

"People like us?"

"Those who have lost love."

She stiffened next to me. I didn't want her to retreat into bravado, but I also wanted her to know that this was a safe place to share.

"I never talk about Elaine, my wife. It makes people uncomfortable." In reality, I didn't talk much at all. After Elaine, I just didn't really feel like being around people. And I wasn't exactly extroverted before that. Working as much as I did, I understood why Gretchen had preconceived notions about me.

She nodded. "Same with Ephram. It's been so long since I've talked about him, I worry …"

I waited for her mouth to catch up to where her mind had wandered. "Do you think a person stops existing if there's nobody to remember them? If their stories aren't shared?"

I sat back and thought. If I stopped thinking of Elaine every day, would that detract from the love we shared? Would it cause her memory to fade away? "Maybe. That's a big fear, isn't it? Being forgotten." I swirled my drink, watching the ice. "You can talk about him if you want."

"Not tonight." She shook her head. "I've been thinking about things a lot lately. Choices I've made. That maybe I'm lonelier than I thought."

I made a sound of understanding.

"I couldn't sleep tonight," she said. "I was all in my own head because of something our driver said about leaving a legacy behind."

These worries had been stirred in me too while holding baby Lainey. An intangible anxiety about time moving too fast.

I asked, "Is that why you were snooping? Restlessness?"

"Guilty." She held up a hand like she'd been caught, before wrapping herself back up. "I always thought I'd be content to be single after losing Ephram. But lately …"

I nodded in understanding. There was nobody else for me. Elaine was my only true love. But knowing that, didn't make the solitude any easier.

"How long has it been?" I asked.

"Almost seven years." She leaned back and whispered, "Seven years," under her breath like she could hardly believe that. I understood the shock. Time moved so fast even for those with broken hearts.

"I can't tell the girls about this," she said. "They'd try to fix me up, bless their hearts. And I don't want to do the dating thing. It sounds terrifying and exhausting."

"I'd rather have annual colonoscopies," I said.

She snorted. "You *are* funny, aren't you?"

"I don't know how to respond to that."

She laughed again. "Next time, I'll keep my compliments to myself."

"If it was a compliment, you shouldn't have sounded so surprised," I said with a smirk.

"Fair point. You're one of those sneaky types. Dry humor." She shook her head. "Boy, did I read you all wrong."

"You're not the first."

"You just come off as sort of …" She pursed her lips, as if contemplating the best way to insult someone without meaning to.

"A square," I helped. She nodded with a wince. "Yeah, I know. Elaine told me that all the time."

I should be offended, but honestly, at this point in my life, I was used to being misread. I let my work and time speak for themselves and anybody that still didn't like me wasn't my problem. There was some freedom in being almost forty. And there was satisfaction in proving people wrong. Especially her.

I put my arm around her shoulders. She looked at it and then at me. "What are you doing?"

I shrugged and studied her face, from her smooth pale skin and round brown eyes, to her incredibly full lips and pointy little chin.

What was I doing?

"Just snuggling." I sounded so coolly indifferent, as though this was something I did all the time. Needless to say, it wasn't. What was it about this woman that brought out so many sides to me?

"Just?" She sighed and leaned into me.

"I'll keep my hands where you can see them." I settled deeper next to her.

I swore I heard her mumble about that being a shame. Then we were quiet. There was an ease with her that I experienced with very few people. I didn't want to overthink. Not tonight.

"I don't know if I'm allowed to admit this, but this is one of the things I miss the most," I said softly, tucking her head under my chin. She smelled sweet of floral shampoo and a hint of sweat.

"Snuggling?" she asked.

"Holding and being held. Touching for no reason."

She was quiet so long doubt crept in. Had I been too forward? Then I heard a soft sniffle. "Yeah. Me too," she said tightly, pressing herself even closer, wrapping her arms around my waist.

"I do miss the regular sex too," I added, to bring her smile back.

She snorted and shouldered me without force.

"And not just regular sex," I added. "Freaky married-people sex." She started to giggle. "When you know somebody so well, have been doing it so long, anything goes." She laughed harder and nodded with a sniff. I continued, "You could walk into a room holding a can of whip cream, a pineapple, and handcuffs, and your partner would just stand up and say, 'let's do this.'"

She lost it then. She folded forward to laugh so hard she went silent. Nothing like the healing strength of laughter after you've been crying. I smiled softly watching her.

"Oh my God, it's true," she finally said and sat up wiping away a tear. She dropped her head to my shoulder. "Thank you."

I closed my eyes and let myself sway with her, let myself enjoy her nearness.

"I'm just tired," she said eventually. "Not for me. For everyone else. For the world. I've seen all my friends date. I've set up countless people. I've learned all the atrocities of online dating. I don't want any of that."

"Agreed."

"But sometimes I miss being married. You know? I miss the ease of it."

"Yes," I said, my throat went tight again.

"I miss all the little things. The glances across the room. The stupid inside jokes that wouldn't make sense to anybody else and aren't really even that funny."

"The built-in excuse to get out of a social event," I added.

"The comfort of knowing, no matter what your day was like, you come home to a listening set of ears."

I hummed in agreement. Sadness gripped my chest, only slightly dulled by time.

Gretchen suddenly sat up, her familiar energy returning. "I want to make a dating service for modern-day marriages of convenience. When you're sick of the bullshit of dating. You just want to be married. You find someone completely compatible, and you just commit."

I smiled, assuming she was joking. "It's not very romantic," I said.

She looked at me closely. "But we know that's not what marriage is all about, not really." She continued, passion gathering. I liked her like this. Inspired and scheming.

"Ephram and I didn't have too long together but I *knew*. I knew already that as the initial flame of lust burned lower after we were married and the day-to-day monotony took over, that I would still choose him. I would make it work. We *would* make it work."

She wasn't joking at all. I nodded thoughtfully. There was more to marriage than just what people talk about. There were layers upon layers. Life changes, tragedy and joy, and everything in between. But above all the choosing. The commitment. The everyday growing and changing together. Emotion swelled in my chest, but I couldn't understand why.

I swallowed down conflicting thoughts and focused on the here and now. "So, a dating service, huh?"

"Yeah, an 'I'm too old for this shit' marriage app. TOFTS. You match with a person. Sign some paperwork that says you're on the same page commitment-wise, yada yada. And pow. You're married."

"You know, part of me thinks it's so cynical and the other part of me wants to be the first customer," I said.

"*I* want to be the first customer." She laughed then seemed to think about it. I fought a frown at the thought of her marrying some stranger. She turned toward me more excited. "Okay. I'm not saying this for pity or anything, but I know, in my heart of hearts, that I'll never love again. Ephram was it for me. And I know that was a gift." Tears welled in her big brown eyes.

I grabbed her hand. "I understand. I feel the same exact way." I took a steadying breath. "Elaine was it for me. But I can't exactly start a relationship like that. 'Sorry I will forever be in love with my wife, but I'd still like to make babies with you.'"

She threw her head back and laughed. *Ding, ding* went that serotonin hit.

"But you could with TOFTS!" She sat up and started looking around. "I'm gonna be rich. Rich, I tell you!" She patted my pockets and looked around the outdoor space. "Do you have a phone or notepad? I'm serious about this. I'll start with myself. I'll be the prototype. I'm going to make a list of everything I could possibly want in a partner—"

As she spoke and looked around panic grew in my chest. We'd been having a moment. All these months of wanting to get to know her and I finally had a quiet moment of sharing. I felt her slipping away. It was too soon. It wasn't long enough.

"Gretchen, stop," I snapped.

She froze mid-sentence and turned toward me slowly.

I was inexplicably angry and … protective. She was too good for random men on the internet. Some app couldn't capture the light and beauty of her. A four-line bio would never be able to capture her effervescent and magnetic personality.

She blinked up at me, her cheeks pink but not angry, she almost looked like she was surprised?

My reaction surprised us both. I hadn't felt like this before, this fierce protectiveness. That was a young man's emotion. I was past all that. I cleared my throat, calming myself.

"Just be here right now. Can't this wait?" I clarified, gentling my voice.

Her raised eyebrow lowered slowly. "Yes, sir," she said holding my gaze.

I swallowed. Hearing her say those words, joking or not, caused my heart to race. Did she remember that she said that right before she kissed me?

She watched my mouth. A flush spread up her neck.

"Gretchen—"

She spoke at the same time, breaking our eye contact. "Sometimes I decide something and then zoom, I'm off to the races. But you're right, it can wait. Let's just keep this moment as it is." She rested her head against my chest with a long humming sigh.

I understood the underlying message. Tonight wasn't for a messy hookup. Despite my body's frustration with me, my heart and mind understood that Gretchen scared easy for all her bluster. If we crossed a line tonight, I wouldn't get another chance with her. And I did want a chance with her, didn't I? That was perhaps the most alarming part of all this. I was conflicted. I desired her. I found her presence soothing and natural. I always had. But it was confusing and not at all what I was used to or had been used to with Elaine. On the other hand, I'd been alone a long time.

I would wait until the time was right. I could do that.

It was such a familiar feeling to hold someone. It shouldn't be. It should be too intimate, we hardly knew each other, but maybe our broken hearts needed this safe space. Maybe we could just take these minutes and not overthink it. It felt good. So good.

We sat for so long in silence. It wasn't until the bruised light of predawn crept over the city that the soft sounds of sleep from Gretchen shook me from my thoughts.

I leaned back and closed my eyes to let myself enjoy the moment. Just a little while longer couldn't hurt.

CHAPTER 4

VINCENT

"Love, Reign O'er Me" - Pearl Jam

By the time I woke up the next afternoon the women of the SWS were already out of the house. I did my best to push Gretchen out of my mind but the scent of her lingered sweet in the air. It clouded my mind, causing me to want things I had no right wanting. Like her.

I had to return to LA for the next two weeks. I had commitments. Nothing had changed. So what if I understood more than ever that time was fleeting? So what if Gretchen was occupying more and more of my mental space? So what if I was tired of being alone? None of that changed anything. But maybe I could try and see her just one more time …

I called Nicole to let her know my schedule and see how they were doing. She demanded I stop by and bring food before I left again. Who was I to argue against getting to see baby Lainey again?

I picked up some deli sandwiches, chips, and sides, and made my way over.

Nicole met me in the waiting area and took the food before even greeting me.

"Oh God, this smells amazing." She looked tired but grateful.

"Hi. Nice to see you. You're welcome," I kept my voice quiet even though Lauren and the baby were through the doors. "Are they sleeping?"

She frowned apologetically at my hopeful expression. "The baby is, so Troy and Lauren are trying to catch up too."

"No worries. They need the rest. Have you slept?" I asked.

She tilted her head side to side. "A little."

"Nicole," I said with worry.

"Yeah, yeah. I know. I'm just helping them get situated and then I'll take care of myself."

We moved to some chairs and balanced the food on our laps.

"Like you're one to talk," she added, scooping pasta salad.

"I slept," I defended. After I stayed up until sunrise to talk to Gretchen.

"I'm not talking about sleep." She shook her head with a sigh. "You know exactly what I'm talking about, Vinny."

"Let's not have this conversation again."

This was the same talk we'd had a dozen times over the years. After Elaine passed, it wasn't even a question if I'd stay in Nicole and Lauren's life. There was never any weirdness between us. We all leaned on each other for strength and to keep the cherished memories of Elaine alive. Lauren was older now so I didn't need to help out as much anymore but we all still lived in Brooklyn, still shared Sunday dinners when it worked with our schedules. Spending that much time together, I knew what Nicole was going to say next before she even opened her mouth.

"You could date again. Hell, you could fall in love again. Plenty of people do," she said.

"I'm sure they do," I said. *But they weren't married to Elaine.*

"I saw how you looked at Lainey. You made such a good father figure to Lauren."

"Wow, we jumped straight to babies." But she wasn't wrong. Holding Lainey had shifted something in me. That didn't mean I was able to talk about it. "Lauren was such a good kid growing up. You did everything. Elaine and I just babysat from time to time."

"It was more than that and you know it. You were the male role model she needed," she said.

"And then you were both there when we needed you. When I needed you." I swallowed. "It's what family does."

"Damn straight." She sat with a sigh. "You never think about having babies?"

"Of course I do. At least, I did. But when we found out about Elaine, knowing we couldn't, it never mattered. Being with her and the time we had, that's what mattered."

She nodded sadly before biting into a cold roast beef sandwich. "I understand."

"Now … it feels too late."

"It's different for men. And it's not like you're in your eighties."

I scoffed. Was it too late? Lately, I'd been reexamining so many stories I told myself. Thoughts like, I'd always be alone. That I was too old to be a father. That I *wanted* to be alone.

"I'd be the oldest dad at the park, they'd think I was a grandpa," I finally said.

She rolled her eyes. "Please. You're gonna need a better excuse if that's what you're going with. Plus—and I mean this in a non-gross way—you keep yourself in way better shape than men half your age."

I shook my head dismissively. I had too much free time and ever since that kiss with Gretchen, a new well of sexual frustration. Details I would definitely not be sharing.

"Elaine told me often that she wished for you to be a father. Especially at the end. You know she wanted you to have a life after her," Nicole said around a mouthful.

I focused on opening a bag of chips. I knew. "She told me too. Made me swear to it. Joked about spending all those years making me a better man and not wanting it to go to waste."

Nicole laughed. "Of course she did. But she was right. You two were a hot mess in the beginning. I'm not saying she did all the work, but you've come a long way from those dramatic fights when you first got together."

"What?" I gaped at her. "It was never like that."

She snorted. "Okay."

"It wasn't. Elaine and I, we were always easy." At least, that's how it seemed to me now.

"Wow. You have selective memory," she said. When I frowned at her, she went on. "In the beginning, you two were all passion and fights. Normal beginning of relationship stuff as you found your footing."

I shook my head, blinking as I searched memories of our college days. I guess we did break up and get back together a few times. Elaine could be obstinate, and I was insecure until we learned how to better communicate.

"I guess I just remember how things were at the end," I said.

She nodded, taking another bite.

Elaine and I were young and had never been in anything so serious. Things got serious so fast for us. Thinking about Elaine, made my incredibly strong reaction to Gretchen even more confusing. I sighed long and low again. The beginnings were always so messy. I was too old for all that, despite what Nicole said. But wouldn't it be great if there was a way to skip the awkwardness of dating and just settle in with someone you clearly hit it off with, without all the complications? The long conversation with Gretchen last night rose to my thoughts yet again.

"Actually, I …" Could I talk to Nicole about Gretchen? Would it be weird?

When I didn't continue, she perked up. "Wait, what were you going to say?" She'd known me way too long to hide anything from her. "Oh my God, have you met someone? Who?" She leaned forward studying my face as though a name might be written there.

I scratched the back of my neck, unable to meet her eyes. "It's nothing yet. Don't get excited. We're just friends. Or maybe not even that. I don't know. I'm just having surprising feelings in regards to her."

"Like what?" she asked, clearly trying to play it cool but eager to know more.

I struggled to put my interactions with Gretchen into words. "I'm feeling protective. Jealous thinking about other men not appreciating her."

"Wow. Those are some pretty big feelings for 'just friends.'"

"It's just some weird midlife crisis. I'm reverting. I'm too old for all that."

Nicole rolled her eyes. "Please. Age has nothing to do with it."

"Elaine and I were never … chaotic." My eyes widened. "Not that Gretchen and I are even a thing. I'm just saying—"

She snorted. "Gretchen, huh? Isn't that the chick from Tennessee you mentioned a few times?"

I grumbled something unintelligible, mentally kicking myself for revealing so much to Nicole. She'd never let it go if she thought I was harboring a crush.

"Interesting," she said before shoving a mouthful of potato salad in her mouth. "I'm just saying, you shouldn't use Elaine as a measuring stick. That's a good way for nobody to ever live up to her." She wiped her mouth. "Maybe love just feels different with different people and you need to be open and accepting to it however it shows up."

"Whoa, whoa." I held up my hands, heart racing with panic. "I never said the L word."

Nicole rolled her eyes at me. "Fine. Pretend I said like or even crush. Whatever. I'm just saying don't expect it to be exactly like it was last time. It can't be."

That was a good point. Gretchen and Elaine were totally different people, why would I expect anything about my feelings to be the same? Whatever those feelings were.

"You should follow your gut and see what happens with this woman. She must be special if you've let yourself even think about her."

I frowned at the ground. She was special. And she consumed my thoughts but I was terrified to admit that.

"And you should," she added quickly. "It's more than time." She kicked my foot until I looked at her. "Just think about it."

That was the problem. I had been thinking about it. I hadn't stopped thinking about it. I couldn't imagine Gretchen with anybody else and it was startling. If she wanted to try her little experiment, let it be with me. Nobody else. The thought was so aggressive, and so sure. I couldn't ignore it. I needed to change the subject.

"What about you? It's been years since I've seen you date," I said. "Not that you need a man," I teased.

"Damn straight."

"But are you happy?" I asked gently.

Nicole was always in scrubs and rushing around helping others. She worked hard as the head nurse in the pediatrics unit. I wanted to see her thriving, as much as she wanted that for me.

"Meh. That ship has sailed," she said.

I narrowed my eyes at her. "I see how it is. You can dish it but can't take it."

"Yeah, yeah. Change the subject why don't you. I'm just saying. If you were curious enough about this woman to bring her up with me, you should at least explore what that means."

I did think about it. I thought about it all the way to LA. I thought about it while trying to focus on another hotel renovation.

I especially thought about it when Gretchen texted me with her partner wish list.

"I'm totally doing this!" she had written. I stared at the phone, hardly able to read the list my hand was clenching so hard. "Must be open to having children. Must like to travel. Must take off his shoes when he comes in the house …"

I thought about it even as I changed my flight destination from New York to Tennessee.

CHAPTER 5

GRETCHEN

"No Surprises" by Roman GianArthur feat. Janelle Monáe

I hefted the picnic basket and blanket onto my arm before making my way to the iron gates. It was a beautiful day at the Green Valley cemetery. Summer was coming to an end and the wind shook the leaves with the warning of the upcoming season change. Already the sun was setting through the foliage of the massive old trees. It was different from New York and beautiful in its own way. Not that I was even thinking of that trip to Brooklyn, or the amazing brownstone, or the long conversation with Vincent Debono. Or the way my body melted into his and my libido went wild under his gaze. Or the way his deep gravelly voice made me want to do whatever he commanded.

Nope. Nary a thought about him had entered my mind since I saw him two weeks ago.

Today I was here to talk to Ephram about my new venture. I knew he'd support me. He always did. Great thing about one-sided conversations, that. I'd texted Vincent about my marriage app but he didn't even respond, the stinker. He seemed interested in my idea that night and then he totally ghosted me. Honestly, it was probably for the best. The app idea was sort of dead in the water. I was still interested in the idea of an easy marriage for me but turns out having an idea but absolutely no coding skills, does not an app make. Not like I wanted his input. Not that I even cared what he thought…

I stopped in my tracks. *No*. Bad, Gretchen. We weren't thinking of Vincent or his kiss or his cuddles or his surprise humor. Or his beautiful, beautiful home. I was here to start moving forward.

Ephram always loved my style so I liked to keep it fresh for our visits. I'd switched up my wardrobe as the summer melted into fall. I was moving on from the retro pinup looks of the fifties to a more boho/rocker seventies esthetic. I parted my hair down the middle, long and straight. I found this great pair of authentic bellbottoms from a thrift shop in Nashville and a colorfully striped turtleneck sweater. Topping off the look, was a jaunty beret I'd found in a hip store I dragged the girls to in Brooklyn on our trip. I needed way more time in that glorious city. We'd barely scratched the surface of one borough. Maybe Vincent knew of more fun vintage shops? Probably that was how he'd found all those vintage art pieces for his house.

Ugh, no. Bad, brain, no. We were here for Ephram.

I frowned before I shook out my tresses, straightened my shoulders, and kept moving forward.

On my way to Ephram's grave, I passed Everett Monroe standing head bowed at a grave. His granddaddy had just passed away. I wondered who owned that empty storefront across from Stripped now? He nodded his head respectfully as I passed, and I smiled with a little wave of my fingers. Now there was a sweet man. He needed a good girl. Immediately match-making mode clicked on. What about that quiet gal from the library? No, she's too shy. The two of them would never get a conversation out. He needed someone with a little fire.

At Ephram's grave, I laid out the blanket and pulled out the lunch I packed while catching him up on the latest Green Valley gossip.

"I saw Jackson James at the Piggly Wiggly. Well, I saw him and then I hid. His dad is still weird about the whole gun thing. But guess who I didn't see? Zora Leffersbee. Supposedly they're still engaged." I chomped on a grape. "Something is up there, I'm telling you. Betcha five bucks by the end of the year, they call it off."

I ripped off a hunk of bread, ankles crossed as I chatted happily. "I've got all the SWS gals taken care of, at least for now. Who knows when another of Jet's exes might pop out of the woodwork. Like you always said, Ephram, 'Love is just shit unless you treat it like manure and spread it all around.' So that's just what I'm doing. I'm making you proud and I'm bringing love to the world. I can do that at least."

After I spoke his words out loud, I recognized a shift in me. Was I living as he would really have wanted me to? Was I living as I wanted myself to? If I was being honest, of course not. I needed more than just focusing on everybody else.

I sighed, leaning back on my elbows to let the sun warm me. Through my giant shades I watched the leaves dance in the sparkling light.

"This is getting silly, isn't it?" I paused as if my late husband might respond. "Coming here and talking to myself." I sat up. "I'm tired of talking to myself, Ephram." He would always be in my heart, but he wasn't here. "That's actually something I wanted to talk to you about." I was suddenly nervous, which was foolish, all things considered. But I wanted a sign. I wanted to know he was okay with me moving forward. "I've been thinking of making some sort of app or dating service. I don't really have it figured out yet, but I know I want to help people. Like you always said. I think I can."

This time his voice in my head didn't respond. Only the breeze shaking the leaves replied. Maybe he was calling my bluff. Maybe he knew that the app was only a thin excuse.

"Okay, fine. I want to find someone for myself. I don't want to be alone anymore."

If it weren't for that damn conversation with Vincent. If it weren't for how nice it just felt to be held. He understood how it felt to walk around like a zombie, existing even though half of yourself had already passed on. There had to be a happy medium. There had to be a way to hold Ephram in my heart and still allow my body to have the things it needed.

Things it *craved.*

Touch. Intimacy. Conversation. Babies. Family.

I couldn't believe all the longings I'd had since my conversation with Vincent. It was like he'd shaken every dormant desire loose like fruit falling from a tree. If he could still want more from life all while knowing he'd only ever love his wife, then maybe that didn't make me a bad person for wanting the same. Ephram wouldn't want me to live this half life. Ephram wanted everything for me.

"I'm tired of pretending that this life is all I want. Maybe I've painted the independent woman picture, and that won't change, let's be honest. But I could still be Gretchen LaRoe and have someone to talk to." I winced. "You know, that's alive. No offense."

A strong breeze blew back my hair, so I closed my eyes and leaned into the caress.

"It's time, Ephram." I stood, feeling more resolved than ever.

* * *

I PACKED up the picnic and made my way back to the car. After I loaded the basket in the trunk, I pulled out my phone and made a rash decision. I called Vincent.

I had planned on leaving a voicemail. I was scripting it out in my mind when he answered almost right away. Like a psychopath.

"Hello?" a deep voice rumbled in my ear.

I pulled the phone back to check the screen. Had I dialed the wrong number? This was what I got for making a phone call instead of texting.

But nope, it said his name.

"Hello? Gretchen?" he asked.

"Uh, hey. Yup, it's me." I shifted foot to foot, rolling my eyes at myself.

"Weirdest thing. I was just thinking of you." Goosebumps spread over my arms. His phone voice was too much. It was even more rich and sexy than in real life. *New kink unlocked.*

"Really?" I squeaked and then let out a breath.

"Is everything okay?" he asked.

I really couldn't get over how sexy he sounded. And why was I reacting like this?

"Is this Vincent?"

His soft chuckle hit me. "You called me, remember?"

"Are you sure this isn't a phone sex line?" The words tumbled out of me. I was unaccountably nervous. Why had I called him? What was even happening right now? "Because your phone voice …" I made an unintelligible garbled sound.

"Well, thank you. I'll have to add that to my résumé." I could hear the smile in his voice.

"My God. Can you just tell me a story or something?"

"Gretchen."

"Maybe read from a phone book? Honestly, I'm not picky."

"Gretchen, why are you stalling?"

I bit my lip with a curse. How could this man read me so damn well, even through a phone?

"I was just wondering if—" I said.

I stilled just as I went to close the trunk. The overwhelming sense that I wasn't alone had me reaching for the bat tucked in the compartment with the spare tire. I discreetly glanced to find that Everett Monroe was gone. There was nobody else around. I'd been visiting this cemetery for years and this was the first time I felt like I wasn't alone. The presence I felt was of the living sort.

"Gretchen?"

I shushed him. I went to hang up but if I was about to be attacked maybe it would be better to have a witness on the line.

A car door slammed. Footsteps approached.

The chances that the Wraiths might want revenge for my little incident with the gun were slim, but never none.

I gripped the baseball bat as the footsteps grew louder.

When a hand landed on my shoulder, I spun around swinging with intent.

Vincent Debono had just enough time to jump out of the way before I possibly broke his ribs.

"Jumping Mary and Joseph." I slumped back against the trunk, hand to my chest. My heart slammed against my palm. "Never, ever sneak up on a scorned woman. Never. That's twice now. The first time with your underthings. The second time I had a bat. You don't want to think about the third time."

Vincent hit a button on his phone, ending our call before tucking it into a pocket in his suit coat. "I thought you heard me."

"I did not." I straightened off the car and threw the bat into the trunk. I grabbed my phone and put it away too.

"Sorry." He did not look in anyway sorry. He looked like someone who just got complimented for having a phone sex operator voice.

I fixed my hair and looked him up and down. He looked delicious in snug gray trousers that emphasized strong thighs with a softer gray plaid pattern. He wore a simple white button up with no tie today but the shirt was crisp and I knew just how it felt to run my hand over it. His muscles seemed to be stretching the buttons to max capacity. Had he always been so fit?

I realized I was staring but couldn't feel too bad because his own gaze moved up and down me. He always did that. Like he didn't have to hide his obvious interest. But was it interest in my style or the curves that caused those lingering stares?

"I like this new look," he said.

I put my hands on my hips, cocking one to the side. "Thanks. I felt like mixing it up."

His white shirt was slightly opened at the collar. His hair was slicked back. He'd been growing it out more. His beard a little too, though it was still relatively short and tidy. But longer than when I first met him. Maybe all these visits to Green Valley were rubbing off on him.

"What're you even doing here?" I asked. If this was some sort of prank from the universe or Ephram, I didn't get it.

"I came to see you." He stuck his hands in his pockets and stood with his feet wide. It really emphasized just how nice those pants were tailored to him. "I dropped by Stripped and Suzie said you come here on Wednesdays."

I nodded, feeling unaccountably nervous at the sight of him. I had been talking out loud to Ephram and kept the thoughts of Vincent to myself, but had I somehow conjured him? My family always claimed we were from a long line of witchy women. Something about us attracted dangerous men. I suspected it was just my great rack.

"So, speak your mind, Vincent. You came all the way here." I hadn't even known he was in town. Not that I knew his schedule. Roxy just happened to mention that his visits would now be fewer and far more between as the Lodge renovations finally got under way.

His dark eyebrows scrunched and he rubbed the back of his neck. Okay, now he had to be pulling those angles just to show off his body. Or maybe the fact that we almost hooked up again was still burned into my brain. I wanted to give into my lust that night in New York. I was mostly glad I didn't. Mostly. Yet my teeth were on edge with the need to bite those biceps.

When I looked up at him, he caught me staring again. Busted. He licked his lips and stepped forward so there were only a few steps between us.

Yep, the heat was most definitely still there. "Why were you calling, Gretchen?"

I shrugged and looked around. "I honestly cannot remember." As he took a step closer, my eyes must've gone cartoonishly wide. "Uhm, whatcha doin'?"

"I saw your list," he said. His dark brows pinched into a frown.

"Okay?"

"I had a few notes."

"How nice of you." I crossed my arms and raised an eyebrow. If he flew all the way down here just to mansplain my own list of requirements to me—

"Stop that." He stepped forward even more. I swore the command rippled through me.

God, I liked it when he used that voice on me. It went against all my feminist instincts but when he ordered me around, I wanted to obey. I would do whatever he said when he used that voice on me.

"Let me explain," he said, softer this time.

"You have about five seconds before I get the bat back out."

His mouth pulled into a smirk. He uncrossed his arms to place his hands on my shoulders. His thumb brushed along my jaw and a chill traveled down my spine.

"I'm flexible on children. But there should be a clause for foster and adoption," he said.

My brain stuttered to a stop before they could fully process his meaning. What *was* his meaning exactly? My jaw must have dropped to the ground. This wasn't … he wasn't suggesting …

"And no shoes in the house. Ever. That's nonnegotiable. I'll buy you house slippers if you need them." His hand around my neck tugged gently on my hair as his other hand wrapped around my waist and brought me closer. The action caused my head to tilt back so I could look at him.

My heart was in my throat. "Vincent—"

I couldn't think. He was all around me. His classy scent infiltrated my brain. I blinked slowly at him as he licked his full bottom lip.

Hooo boy.

"Our financials can be discussed with a lawyer. But I'm fine with a prenup." His fingers gripped my waist, they'd found an inch of exposed skin and were now caressing me there. "Whatever you want," he growled.

Okay, my jaw officially swung in the wind. I closed my mouth and swallowed. I couldn't think clearly with my hormones screaming, *Just shut up and do whatever it takes to get his pants off!*

His thumb brushed my bottom lip. Was he shaking?

"I'm sorry, Vincent, what exactly are you trying to tell me?"

Then he took a deep breath and stepped back. He reached into his pants pocket and pulled out a velvet box. Oh, okay, so that's what I felt.

Wait. Why was Vincent pulling out a box? Why was Vincent opening a box? Why was there a gorgeous but giant emerald sparkling in front of me?

"Gretchen," he said and I reluctantly brought my attention back to his face, "Will you marry me?"

CHAPTER 6

GRETCHEN

"With A Little Help From My Friends" - *Joe Cocker*

The timing couldn't be more perfect. Roxy told me we needed to hold an emergency SWS meeting to discuss something. Mama didn't raise no fool. I'd bet my life savings that I was the subject of this emergency meeting. It'd been almost two years since Ford and Suzie got together and with every successful coupling of the other girls, the knowing glances grew. They kept insisting that I was next. I kept insisting I was fine being single.

And that was true. Until it wasn't. People were allowed to change their minds with new information. Humans were complicated, feeling beings.

So here we were, tailgating at the Race Track at the Canyon. The SWS thinking they were about to drop some truth bomb on me, all the while, I was waiting patiently with a little bomb of my own. None of us were particularly thrilled to be at the racetrack, truth be known. There was always the off chance of running into a Winston, but it was something to do, and it beat taking a literal hike. Sanders was really rubbing off on Roxy. Wasn't sure I cared for that aspect of their flourishing relationship.

The Race Track at the Canyon was little more than an oval dirt road outside Green Valley where all types came to enjoy the pumping testosterone of revving engines and close calls. We were there for the racks of ribs and coleslaw. We balanced plates on our knees and ate as gracefully as anybody sucking BBQ meat off a bone could. Thankfully, there wasn't a Winston in sight on that chilly fall day. Just a cooler full of beer and my girls.

The drivers were all setting up or whatever they did as we huddled in the back of Skip's truck. He and Jack had business with Triple F—formerly known as Ford's Fosters—and said we could borrow his truck to tailgate. Kim offered to be DD as always and so far the Sunday was progressing nicely.

Even if they were obviously bracing themselves to share news with me.

After cleaning off with a wet wipe, I jumped up to grab a round of drinks for us all.

"Okay, gals. You can spill it. What's this all about?" I said to the rest of the core four.

Suzie, Kim, and Roxy sat hip to hip on the folded-out trailer bed and exchanged a knowing look. I stood in front of them in my short brown corduroy jumper worn over a billowy cream silk blouse paired with high brown suede boots. An outfit like this must be observed by as many as possible.

"Okay, so you know how Ford was sort of a dick when I first met him but now we're happy as pigs in—" Suzie self-corrected, "now we're so happy?"

"I do. Congrats and you're welcome," I said with a little curtsy.

Suzie rolled her eyes at me. Their engagement the previous new year had thrilled us all, and over the summer they moved into a new house. And on New Year's Eve we get to watch them say their vows. I wasn't one to say I told you so, but I also absolutely was. I was the first person to fold Suzie into our little group and she fit in better than any of us could have imagined.

"Thank you," Suzie said with a pinch of sarcasm. "The girls have noticed, since our trip last week, and actually for a little while now, that you've been more distant. Like physically here, but you seem far away in your mind."

I remained perfectly still. I wasn't tracking exactly on how these things were linked but I didn't like that they had been aware of what I thought I was hiding so well. I hadn't allowed myself to be completely truthful with the girls, for fear of making them feel like they needed to contain their joy somehow.

"We were just thinking," Kim started when I didn't say anything in defense. Best let them get it all out. They clearly had a plan. "Well, see we were talking. About you and how we're all so thankful for you." She played with the ends of her long hair. "Well, okay. So, you know how happy Devlin and I are?" She chewed her lip as she shook her head, frowning. "That is not what I meant to say. Well, sort of. Because you helped us get our lives together."

"Same with Sanders and I," Roxy cut in. "You were coming from a good place when you set up our reunion. Even if I hated it at the time."

I especially didn't comment on that. That reunion had caused our big fight. Again, I waited to see where this was going.

I tilted my head patiently.

"We've been worried about you," Suzie said.

"Yes. And we want you to be happy." My eyebrows shot up. Obviously, they wanted me happy but I was curious as to this lead up. Kim blew out a breath between puffed cheeks. "I'm so not good at taking the lead." She threw out her hands in frustration.

"We want to line up some dates with several eligible bachelors," Suzie said, jumping in to relieve Kim.

"Or bachelorettes," Roxy added, and I winked at her.

"No Winstons," Kim said quickly.

"Obviously not," I said. "The only single one left is Roscoe anyway. And he's a baby."

"Those Monroe boys are cute," Roxy said.

"What about the Buchanans?" Kim asked.

"Aren't they cursed?" Roxy said and Kim's eyebrows went up with her shoulder shrug.

I waited patiently.

I knew all of this of course. I had a whole encyclopedia of all the people in Green Valley in my brain. None of those people were viable options but I wouldn't spoil their fun.

"You're being uncharacteristically quiet," Roxy said.

"I'm just listening," I said with a smile. "I can tell y'all put a lot of thought into this."

"Well. That's it. We just want to start setting you up on dates," Roxy said, her full lips pouting slightly.

"We think that once you get back into the swing of things, it might start to feel right," Suzie said.

"There's no harm in trying," Kim added.

I held up my drink and waited for them to mirror me.

"To the SWS, the best damn women I've ever known." I brought my own beer to mouth, waiting until their drinks were to their lips before saying, "But you don't need to worry about me being alone. I'm having a baby!"

I took a big sip, smiling as each one of them choked on their drinks. Am I the drama? Maybe I am.

"Holy duck!" Suzie said as she coughed.

"What?" Kim paled visibly.

"Gretchen!" Roxy wiped a bit of dribble falling from her mouth. "You did that on purpose."

I shrugged innocently and took another long drink. I felt great. Lighter. Even though I knew a long conversation was ahead of me.

Far behind us, an engine roared to life as I waited for the deluge of questions.

"When did this happen?" Suzie asked.

"Are you okay?" Kim asked.

"Who's the father?" Roxy stared so closely at me, a prickle of anxiety made me look away.

Kim gasped and grabbed my beer from me.

"Technically, I'm not pregnant yet." I grabbed the beer back with a frown.

"Jesus, Gretchen," Roxy swore.

"That's not really something to tease us about," Kim said with a furrow between her brow.

"I know," I said and sobered my features. "I'm not joking though. I've decided to make my own little family."

Three sets of eyes blinked back at me. A roar went up from the crowd around us. Suddenly the deluge of noise felt like too much. The people hollering. The tires kicking up dirt. The engines so loud it felt like my chest was rattling. Maybe this hadn't been the best place to have this conversation. I hadn't meant to make it a joke. I was entirely serious. I did however wish I would have recorded their reactions.

"I don't understand," Roxy said. "Some crucial details seem to be missing."

"Let's go where we can talk." Kim rubbed at her temples. "These fumes are making me dizzy. That or this conversation."

Suzie pointed to the trees. "Over there."

We collected a bag of beers and water and walked to a picnic table that gave us enough distance from the noise to talk and be heard. Once they were all settled again, still hip to hip, I paced in front of them. Suddenly, it was like I was delivering a TED Talk to a bunch of eager eyes.

I let out a breath. "Vincent Debono and I have decided to start a family."

Kim was so still I wasn't sure she was still here, mentally. Suzie took a long drink of her beer, eyes wide. She drank and drank until the beer was gone.

"Oh, and first we're getting married." Suzie coughed again and this time I got a taste of the ire that had earned her the nickname Short Fuze. "I didn't do that on purpose this time," I said, wincing.

Roxy continued to shake her head. "Vincent? *My* Vincent?"

An alarming fierceness cut through me. "Well, he's hardly *yours*." I smoothed my hair. "If anything, he's mine now."

Roxy fussed with her bangs. She let out a long groan of frustration and some mumbling that sounded like swearing and my name.

"Isn't he like fifty?" Roxy asked.

I gaped, appalled. "He's not even forty-five. Not that it matters. He's aging like fine wine." It wasn't that Roxy had insulted him, but it was her tone that raised my hackles to defend my man—*err*, Vincent.

"It's how he carries himself, I guess." Roxy frowned. "He just seems so—"

"He's often misunderstood by people." It was me. I was people. I lifted my chin.

"I get it." Suzie nodded as she seemed to think about it.

"He definitely has something about him," Kim agreed. "He's so well put together and very handsome."

"Vincent Debono?" Roxy repeated.

Kim put a hand on her shoulder. "You had Sanders goggles on while you worked together, otherwise this wouldn't be so shocking."

"I guess," Roxy said not sounding convinced.

"Trust me when I say sexual compatibility will not be an issue," I said.

Their eyes widened even more and I cursed my accidental innuendo. I had just been trying to show that Vincent was a huge catch, but I let too much slip. I was shocked to feel a blush burn up my neck.

"Have you slept together?" Suzie gasped.

"No," I said quickly. Then I winced as I added, "But we may have made out the night of Skip and Jack's engagement party."

Kim sucked in her lips to hide a smile. Roxy looked away, mouth slightly open as though just now putting pieces together.

"He did bring you up a few times, now that I think about it. And he was always asking for rides. Which I thought was weird because he could have easily rented a car on the Lodge's dime," Roxy explained.

The confession caused something that felt an awful lot like giddiness inside me. Just how long had Vincent been noticing me?

I needed a distraction. I didn't want to share how hot our makeout session had been or how my body always took notice of him. I especially wouldn't share that I found myself dressing extra nice when he was in town. It was my business anyway.

I jutted out my hand. "See. Engagement ring."

"I thought that was costume jewelry," Suzie said.

"Is it real?" Roxy asked.

I nodded.

"What is happening right now?" Kim asked in a high-pitched voice. "Is it the exhaust fumes? Am I high?"

"If you are, then I am too." Suzie shot a worried look to Roxy.

"Okay look. It's not all dramatic as all that. I'm sorry I messed with you, but I promise this is a good thing. This is exactly what y'all were just talking about. If anything, you should be ecstatic!"

Roxy snapped her head back to me.

I smiled but none of the SWS smiled back. Okay maybe I had not presented this whole decision the right way, I wanted their support, but I also wasn't one to change my mind after a choice had been made. If anything, their surprise caused me to dig my heels in deeper. They would see in time that Vincent and I were good for each other.

"Start talking. What in the hell happened since we went to NYC?" Roxy demanded.

I explained my conversation with Vincent that night on the roof. How nice it had been to find someone who had experienced similar trials in life. Then I told them about the rise and fall of my million-dollar app idea. But how ultimately it made me understand that I wanted to find my own partnership.

"Vincent and I have a connection that's hard to explain. I mean, in some ways it's the wound that binds us. But in this case a little … deeper? Heavier? So when he showed up earlier this week and proposed, it felt like a big sign. I said yes." I ended with a little shrug. "Plus we're ridiculously compatible."

The girls sat in silence while they absorbed my words.

"I still don't understand. When did all this start for you?" Roxy asked, looking more befuddled than the others. "Why not just start with dating?"

"I don't want to date. It's bad out there. I know my options. I've seen the ups and downs. I want to skip the drama," I said simply.

"*You* want to skip the drama?" Roxy asked flatly.

I did not appreciate that tone.

I shot her a glare before explaining how my brain had been telling me for some time that I needed a change. How when I talked to Ephram, I realized I couldn't go on as I was. I put it all out there.

"Look. I know it seems sudden. Or rash, but I promise it's not." I bent and picked up a stick, twirling it through my fingers. "Vincent and I spent the last two days talking. We're on exactly the same page about everything. It's a good thing!" I looked to them each excitedly, hoping to spread some of the joy I had been feeling earlier. "Y'all were right. I've been a little lonely. And Vincent gets it. He and I ..."

How did I explain the connection I felt with him? The aching pit in each other's souls that linked us? The fact that we were safe to comfort each other without worrying about the pesky complications of becoming overly emotional. Or in love. *Blah.*

"We want this. We're happy with this decision," I finished. "We came to the same conclusion, rationally, after a lot of talking. We want to be married. We want the partnership and support. We want to try and start a family too."

"You of all of us know the sanctity of marriage," Suzie said. With her upcoming nuptials, I had worried that she might think this was some ploy to steal her thunder. I had to trust that she knew me better than that. "It's not just a fun thing to try."

Her words stung but only because I knew she was blindsided. "I do understand. Both of us do. That's why we're doing it like this. We're taking away the years of misunderstanding each other. We're going in on equal footing. On a strong foundation of communication and a contract with exactly what our expectations are. We aren't joking about this. We want to make it a real marriage. A commitment to staying together."

The girls stared back, but seemed to relax. Maybe just a little.

Roxy was still staring at her Converse. Suzie and Kim shared a look. "Seriously, y'all, I'm not trying to make light of the situation or of marriage." I looked to Suzie. "We aren't planning a big wedding, just a simple ceremony at the courthouse before Halloween." To the others I said, "We didn't just drunkenly decide to do this after a few too many shots. We talked about everything. We're getting a contract drawn up. We're exactly on the same page. We spent all weekend talking about our plans."

It had been so easy to decide on everything over the past couple days. Every decision from where we would live, to who would drive on road trips was decided simply and efficiently.

They didn't seem as relieved as I hoped. My good news was falling flat. I threw the stick into the trees.

"What about a baby?" Kim asked. "Shouldn't babies be a product of love ... not just a checked box?"

"This is a form of love," I explained, starting to feel defensive. "We want a baby and it's coming into this world with a guaranteed family. Plus ... I told him that I was never on birth control with Ephram and that I may not be able to conceive. He understood. We have options."

"So the whole point of this isn't to have a baby?" Roxy asked.

"It's part of it. We have decided that we'll try for a year and then if it doesn't work we'll look into adoption. There are many babies who need a family. We *will* love that baby." My voice cracked, the seriousness of the situation finally seemed to hit them all at once.

"But, what about love? Real love? You preached about the importance of it to all of us," Kim said.

A shout of cheers roared behind us. I waited until the crowd settled before continuing. I needed to act confident and sure as I do in all things or they would interpret it as indecision or regret. Even if deep in my brain existed some anxieties, ultimately this was the smart and safe choice to make.

"I know. And I still believe in love. Of course I do. I had it. You all have it. It's a wonderful miracle that you all met your partners." I played with the big brown button on my romper. "It's not going to happen again for Vincent or me. At least not in the way that it was with our first marriages. We understand that. But, you know, I think we'll grow to love each other. In a way." I wouldn't. He wouldn't. But they needed to have hope. "A love built on mutual respect and communication is still a stronger foundation than many marriages."

"That's true," Suzie said.

My shoulders sagged in relief to know that one of them was starting to get it.

"I guess," Suzie continued, "we're just worried you're throwing in the towel a little too soon."

I nodded happily. "That's the opposite of what I'm doing. These years since Ephram was killed, I'd been living as if he was it for me. That my ship had sailed and I was bound to be alone. But in talking with Vincent, I'm understanding that that's not really what I want. This is me making a choice and finally moving forward. I *want* to move forward. This is how."

"It seems you've really decided," Roxy said. Her face was inscrutable.

"You know we support you. You've been there for all of us at our worst. No ex left behind," Kim said somberly.

The girls all shared one more tenuous look. I couldn't help but feel like my news still wasn't well received. That the women of the SWS were all disappointed in me. They would come around. They would see that this was the right choice for Vincent and I.

"I'm happy, y'all," I said holding each one of their gazes. "Happier than I have been in a long time. Hopeful."

It was Kim who smiled first, holding up her water bottle. "Then let's toast. To a different sort of love."

"Marriages come in all shapes and sizes," Suzie added.

“If you’re truly happy,” Roxy said, holding my stare. Not allowing me to look away for even a second. “If this is what you really want, you know we have your back.”

I nodded seriously, not breaking our eye contact. “This will work out. You’ll see.”

I plastered on a huge smile and winked. This was going to be fine. We were being rational. And yet for the first time since deciding, the smallest feeling of foreboding curled inside me.

CHAPTER 7

GRETCHEN

"The Way You Look Tonight" by Harry Connick, Jr.

I was late for my wedding.

In my defense, my hair wouldn't cooperate for the first time ever. My makeup kept smearing from sweat. Why was I even sweaty? And then Kim struggled to find parking at the Blount County courthouse which was surprisingly packed for the middle of a Monday, this October 21st.

By the time we scurried up the courthouse steps, we were twenty minutes later than we'd planned.

The other three walked briskly up to the counter as I stayed a little behind to steady myself and double check my outfit. I'd found a pristine 1950s pale blue a-line dress, knee-length with simple lines and a tightly cinched waist. Big buttons lined the front and an elegant matching cape with chocolate brown lining paired perfectly with the vintage pillbox hat that sat tilted on my updo. Fragile lace acted as my veil, extending from the edge of the hat laying across my forehead and left eye. That took for-freaking-ever to get just right too.

Suzie, Kim, and Roxy looked good standing all in a row with their coordinated outfits. I'd mentioned what I planned to wear in passing but honestly didn't think they'd make the effort. A small part of me worried they wouldn't come at all. At that moment, I couldn't have been more thankful for their presence.

Suzie was in a blue and white maxi dress with a pattern that reminded me of fine china. Kim's conservative knee-length was a deeper shade of blue with a white geometric shape across the hip. Roxy looked business chic in an electric blue suit and matching sneakers since she had to go to work right after.

We almost looked like a real wedding party. Imagine that.

"Weddings are in the other building," a bored-looking clerk told the SWS.

"Oh, for cluck's sake," Suzie muttered.

"We can't be late," I mumbled as I was quickly ushered back out. Normally, I was the one to take charge but today I was content to be led around, focusing only on calming my breaths.

The picturesque historical building of the courthouse was two-story, yellow-colored brick with a large portico and four columns rising to a wide pediment. It was where I had envisioned my simple second wedding. Now we were being ushered to a squat ugly brown brick building. I tried not to take it as a metaphor.

I focused on my footing. These peep-toe wedges were dangerous as we cut through the grass between the buildings.

"It'll be fine," Kim reassured. "You look beautiful and there is plenty of time."

I nodded and fought the urge to wipe my palms on my skirt.

As soon as we made it through security—not exactly romantic— I found Vincent pacing in the main lobby. He glanced at his watch before sensing our presence.

He looked up and his gaze immediately found mine. He swallowed and took a step toward me. I took one forward and stumbled on absolutely nothing. He was there in a flash to steady me. I was not some nervous blushing bride. I was Gretchen LaRoe and I made this day happen. I tried to rally myself.

"We'll go ahead and find the guys," Roxy said.

"They're down the hall," Vincent offered as she and the others walked away.

His focus never strayed as he examined every inch of me.

I barely registered what they said. Vincent wore another gorgeous suit, this one dark blue with a crisp white button-up, that managed to match elegantly with my simple gown. His beard was trimmed short and his glasses were gone. I swallowed at the sight of him. Lord, he smelled amazing.

A new wave of nerves caused my head to spin. I felt out of my body and dizzy.

"You look breathtaking," he said.

"I'm sorry I'm late. We went to the wrong building. It wouldn't kill them to put up a few signs in this place. I'd lived here my whole damn life and I couldn't even figure out where the heck to go." I tugged at the cape to let in some air under.

The hallway was boring and musty-smelling. In the distance, phones rang and someone shouted. The energy of this place screamed parking tickets and civil disputes. The low ceiling hummed with bad fluorescent lighting. Nothing about this place was romantic. Not that it mattered, this was basically a business deal after all.

"Gretchen?"

I couldn't believe how my heart raced. There was no way I had been this anxious when I married Ephram. There had been no doubts. Like everything in my life, I barreled full steam ahead. So why was I nervous now? It made no sense. I had no doubts here either. If anything, I should be less nervous because there were no risks. But it did all seem to be happening really fast. Typically, that was my favorite way for things to happen.

"Gretchen," he said again.

My gaze frantically searched for the right room. Where had the girls gone? "Maybe we need to get going. We can't even be a minute late. The women who helped us fill out the paperwork and set up the time slot told us we would miss our chance." And she had freaked me out. They did a wedding every hour and there was no margin for error. A bead of sweat trickled down my back and a flush grew across my cleavage. I needed to chill, or I'd be all splotchy for photos. Photos we would look at the rest of our life because we were getting married.

We were getting *married.*

"Hey. Look at me," Vincent snapped.

I jerked back into focus when Vincent grabbed my sweaty hands. His were warm and firm. He leaned closer until I met his dark eyes, narrowed in focus.

"Breathe," he demanded.

I blinked at him in surprise before I whispered, "Yes, sir."

His eyes darkened as I took a slow deep breath in and out. His gaze flicked to where my cleavage rose and fell.

"You look absolutely breathtaking," he repeated.

This time I smiled at him. "Thank you. You look perfect too. I mean, you match perfect. What are the chances?"

I fanned myself as one half of his mouth lifted into a grin.

"Speaking of." He bent to pick up a small bouquet of flowers from a bench behind him.

"How did you …"

I examined the light and dark blues of the hydrangeas, mixed with white dahlias and tea-roses, and pops of rich-green eucalyptus sprigs. The man truly had a sense of style, but how could he have known how perfect this would be?

"I didn't even think about flowers," I said frowning. I noticed then the matching corsage pinned to his lapel.

"I've got you," he said simply and confidently. And he did.

He tugged me toward the room where the girls were waiting just near the door. I grinned up at them feeling my shoulders relax and my breaths come easier.

I shrugged out of my cape and handed it to a waiting Roxy. Just before I stepped inside, she grabbed my hand and tugged me to where Suzie and Kim also waited, smiles on their faces. Vincent clasped his hands and grinned at his shoes, waiting patiently.

"One last thing." Roxy handed me a blue metal thing that may have been a clip.

I studied it in my shaking hand, confused. "Um?"

"It's one of Sanders' carabiners. You can *borrow* it," she explained with emphasis.

Understanding dawned. Hiding the trembling of my lip, I looked for a place to put it.

"Here. Just clip it to your flowers." She reached to help me.

I pulled the front of my dress out and stuck it down in between my boobs, then shivered at the unexpected cold.

"Or that works." She chuckled.

A wave of unexpected emotion swelled in me. I pulled her close and squeezed her tight. This day suddenly felt more important than just filing paperwork and a few words exchanged in front of a judge.

"Thank you," I said with a shaking voice.

"Borrowed and blue," Kim said, grabbing my hand. "Two birds, one stone."

"Your dress is old," Suzie said. "Vincent's flowers are new."

They coordinated to make this happen. Each of them smiled back as I looked between them.

"You're good to go," Roxy said.

I swallowed down a lump and nodded. "You guys didn't have to do this. It's just a—"

But I couldn't finish the thought. This wasn't *just* anything. It was a marriage. It was a smart choice and it made sense, but it was still a big commitment. Just because our hearts weren't involved, didn't make it any less momentous.

"It's important," Roxy said firmly holding my gaze. "We're here for you. No matter what."

It felt like an apology for her initial reaction to my news. She had my back. These women always would. I let out a shaking breath and smiled.

"We're giving him the benefit of the doubt," Suzie said.

"After all, he's obviously not an idiot if he's marrying you," Roxy said.

"That's what I'm saying," I teased.

"But that doesn't mean I don't have more questions." Suzie crossed her arms and shot a look to him. His dark eyebrows shot up and he glanced behind himself before waving.

"We'll be spending more time with him. That's a promise," Kim said trying to look intimidating and succeeding not at all.

"Fair enough," I said.

When I glanced up again, Vincent was watching me closely. Maybe I should be a little worried for him, but I had a feeling he'd surprise them just as he had me.

"No ex left behind," Suzie whispered as she hugged me one last time. The other two women did the same before going to meet their partners.

I squared my shoulders and lifted my chin. I was Gretchen LaRoe and I had a plan. Vincent's hand slid into mine as he appeared at my side.

"Ready?" he asked.

I looked up at him and nodded.

Hand in hand, we stepped into the room.

Things were a blur after that, but one moment stood out.

"A marriage is not just a ceremony but a serious commitment to each other built on mutual respect and trust," the tiny judge said. She looked closely at each of us in turn.

Though still facing forward, Vincent's hand found mine and squeezed. We were on the same page. We were doing the right thing. A feeling of peace settled over me.

"Go ahead and kiss the bride," she said a few short minutes later.

We turned to each other. Vincent had a soft smile on his face and if I wasn't hallucinating, were his eyes gleaming?

I jumped at him and wrapped my arms around his neck to give him a peck on the lips.

The SWS and their men clapped behind us.

As I sunk back down to pull away, Vincent tugged me closer to him, making my escape impossible. His head tilted and he lengthened the kiss. He had the decency to keep his tongue in his mouth—dammit—but the heat was there.

Eventually, he loosened his grip and I slowly leaned back, staring up at him in surprise.

He cocked an eyebrow, and I narrowed my eyes. Sneaky, sexy man. His gaze roamed over my face, and I wished more than anything to know what he'd been thinking in that moment.

But maybe it was better that I didn't know. He had to leave right after this to catch a flight back to New York and the heat in his eyes made promises for things we didn't have time for.

Outside, after a picture on the stairs of the historical building, Vincent grabbed my hands pulling me away from the others.

"I wish I didn't have to leave already. Maybe we should have picked a day where I could have stayed longer," he said.

"It's okay. There's nothing but time. Husband," I added.

His brow furrowed with emotion so fast I couldn't read it. Had I freaked him out?

He seemed right on the verge of saying something when his phone pinged a reminder.

He ran a hand over his face. "I have to go."

"I'll see you in a few short days," I said.

"Short for you maybe," he mumbled as he looked me up and down again.

A tiny trickle of nerves had me glance away. Our chemistry was one of the things that felt so simple between us. It shouldn't feel any different now. We were married but other than that, nothing had changed.

The plan was still in place.

CHAPTER 8

VINCENT

"Careless Whisper" by Seether

Halloween weekend had me back in Green Valley. It'd been a little over a week since we were married. We were *married.*

I'd been so nervous waiting for Gretchen at the courthouse that day. I'd paced thinking about my first wedding, an elaborate affair. How'd I'd waited for Elaine at the end of a massive cathedral complete with stained glass and Neo-gothic architecture. A far cry from the dingy city building in rural Tennessee. I'd thought of how beautiful Elaine had been in her massive gown walking toward the alter of All Saints Catholic Church. We'd been babies then, it felt like looking back. But what I surprisingly hadn't felt was guilt. I thought that I might but if anything, I imagined Elaine looking down at me, shaking her head with humor.

"You've done it now," she'd say.

Then I'd been thinking of Gretchen. I was so sure she'd come to her senses, realize she was way too good for this arrangement, and not show up. But then she was there, looking beautiful and flushed. She rambled nervously and all at once, any nerves washed away. I stepped up and took the lead and it felt so natural.

I took her hand and walked her to the judge. Roxy and her partner Sanders were there, as well Suzie and her fiancé, Ford. Kim and Devlin came too but that guy freaked me out, so I didn't really chat with him. I didn't have anybody to ask and that was fine. It would have been too hard for any of the Walshes to come out last minute. We made our vows and just like that, I was married again. I never thought it could happen. But Gretchen had made me feel so many things I never thought I would. The whole day felt surprisingly right. Until I had to leave. That felt very wrong.

Now I was back in Green Valley and still hadn't even seen her. She had to run around all day and said she'd come get me before the Halloween party. I didn't want to think she was ignoring me but a small part of me stung at her absence. I didn't want to make any assumptions about what might happen tonight, but I also couldn't stop thinking about her.

The schedule was simple. I still had a home in New York and Gretchen still had hers in Green Valley. We would accommodate each other's life into our own with as little disruption as possible. Every month I would fly in, near to her ovulation as possible, and we would …

"You know when I said follow your gut and reach out to Gretchen. I didn't think you'd go this far." Nicole said dryly.

"I'm not one to half-ass anything," I said.

Nicole wanted to check in by video chat and was still in scrubs from her last shift. I think she wanted to see my face and make sure I hadn't had some sort of mental breakdown. We had hardly spoken since the wedding, because of our conflicting work schedules.

I'd let them know beforehand, of course. I laid it out as clearly as possible; Gretchen and I were two highly compatible people who were deciding to commit to a life together and if possible, start a family. They had remained cautiously supportive, though understandably shocked.

"Apparently. So how was the wedding?" she asked shaking her head. "I still can't believe you did it. All these years not even a date and then, pow. Marriage!"

It was rushed. But any time worry creeped in, I imagined Gretchen marrying someone else and there went all my doubt. I would make this work.

"It was nice. Simple. She doesn't really have a relationship with her parents, so it was just her closest friends and their partners. It was nice," I repeated.

I kept to myself the swelling of emotion as I said my vows. As I promised to be there for her through thick and thin, too grow old with her.

"Okay. Nice. Good." She squinted closer to the screen. "Are you're sure about this? I mean, it's a little late now. But you're okay? You want this?"

I smiled. "It was the right decision."

She gave me a flat look, my typical brevity in details annoyed her.

"And did you mention your minor crush on her?" Nicole asked and I fought a wince.

I had hoped that she'd forgotten about that. "Gretchen is … she needs time."

"What are you afraid of?" Nicole asked.

I was afraid that Gretchen would not want to go through with the marriage. If she thought I did this just to get laid or something equally ridiculous, she'd have called the whole thing off. I needed time to show her that I was serious about the commitment to her. My attraction to her was minor and could be controlled. Well, maybe not minor but definitely controllable.

"It's better that we go into this as friends with a mutual understanding," I settled on.

Nicole nodded, scrutinizing me.

"In time, things will happen naturally," I said.

Seeing she wasn't getting any more out of me about *feelings*, she moved on.

"I'm sorry we couldn't be there," Nicole said genuinely.

I was no longer legally bound to my … to Elaine's family. I hoped our relationship would remain just as strong.

"No, no. Don't be. Plus, it's a little weird, right?" I scratched the back of my neck.

"Not at all. If it weren't for the baby and work, we would've been there. We're always going to be family," Nicole said.

I let out a long breath, not realizing how much I needed confirmation that my connection to the women I've known so long would remain.

"Thank you," I said through a tight throat.

She shook her head again, disbelieving. "Are we going to meet this woman? She must be something to be up for this."

"We're super compatible. Even though she's totally different than me. It works." Everything had been so simple. So effortless. The prenup and the stipulations for trying to get pregnant. It was all so amiable and amicable. "And yeah, of course you will meet her."

"You're there now? In this Green Valley? Sounds like the place to be," she asked.

"Yep, I'm staying at Gretchen's when I'm here. And she'll stay with me when she comes to the city," I explained.

"I would assume so. Being married and all."

"It's actually really beautiful here." There was something about Green Valley and the Smoky Mountains. I'd admit when I first started working here last year, it seemed very … small town. There was a magic that seeped into your bones. It was less anonymous than New York, that was for sure, and that was nice in its own way. People always said hi and asked how you were, seeming to actually mean it. "You and the girls should come visit. Troy too, I guess," I teased.

"We will, as soon as Lauren and Lainey are up for a trip. You know we'll be there." Nicole smiled and the bags under her eyes looked heavy with exhaustion.

I smiled back.

"Okay," Nicole said, "I'm not sure what the etiquette is on asking about this … but I figure we're way past that." There's that New York directness. I braced myself. "You're trying for a baby already? That's why you flew in?"

"Yeah." I tried to keep my face as neutral as possible. We hadn't actually tried yet. We hadn't touched since the wedding. I couldn't think about it without a trickle of excited tension. But I suspected, that if we put too much pressure on ourselves, it would never work. But the thoughts were always there, lurking at the back of my mind. I needed to make sure Gretchen was fully ready. And I would enjoy getting her there.

"The good old-fashioned way? P in V?" she asked.

I chuckled at the same time Lauren yelled "MOM!" from off camera. "You can't ask Uncle Vinny about his sex life. Don't be gross."

"Please. You of all people should have no qualms with modesty after what I saw during your labor."

"Jesus, Mom."

Nicole rolled her eyes at her daughter and brought her focus back to me.

I flushed and cleared my throat. "Uh yeah, the good old-fashioned way."

"Wow. You could have a baby within the next year. Crazy to think about," Nicole said.

A small thrill raced down my back. I could be a dad by the next holiday season.

Lauren popped onto camera, baby Lainey in her arms. She also looked tired, but her face had a rosy youthful glow. "Lainey and the baby could be best friends!"

She held my great-niece up to the camera, sound asleep but wearing a little ladybug costume.

"Cutest ladybug ever," I said.

I smiled, my heart hammered at the sudden imagery of two fat toddlers wobbling around and giggling. One with dark curls like her dad and that Walsh smile and one that looked like …? What would our baby look like? Would the baby have the pale skin and fair hair from her mixed Scandinavian and Irish heritage? Stronger brows from my Italian side, maybe? New excitement grew in me. I pushed the thoughts away. I didn't want to get my hopes up too soon.

"Hey, what's with the getup?" Lauren asked, leaning closer to the screen.

"We're headed to a Halloween party later," I explained.

"You're wearing a costume?" Nicole said with a jaw-cracking yawn. "How can you tell?"

The only thing visible from their view was my white collared shirt and suspenders. I picked up an orange-tipped shotgun and cocked my fedora forward. "Can you guess now?"

"A mobster?" Nicole tilted her head.

"A used car salesman?" Lauren asked.

"It'll make more sense when I'm with Gretchen," I explained. "It's more of a set."

"Wow. Couple costumes. You're moving fast," Lauren said.

Mother looked at daughter in disbelief. "Yeah, marriage was one thing but couple's costumes, oh my gawd." Nicole's voice went up at the end as her hands flew dramatically to her cheeks.

"So, what're you going as?" Lauren asked, ignoring her mother.

I stood up and moved back so they could see the whole costume, flinging a coat over my shoulder with flair as I held a bag with a money sign on it. Both just shrugged. "Bonnie and Clyde?" I said, tossing the fake gun and money bag to the side and sitting back down.

They both said "Ahh" in unison.

Gretchen has a flare for vintage fashion, so I didn't have to buy much," I explained.

She'd left the costume pieces out for me when I arrived at her apartment earlier in the day. I took the time to check out the retro glam living space. It suited her perfectly. Teal cabinets with black and white checkered flooring, a sparkling Formica kitchen table with bright red metal chairs. Around the apartment were little flares of her quirky style in the retro ceramic figures with rosy cheeks and big eyes, or the bright oranges and yellows of the patterned curtains. Daisies and peace signs, lava lamps, and hanging beads. I found myself smiling with every new detail discovered. It was so Gretchen, a little over-the-top and balancing the age of tacky. It was perfect.

"She looks very pretty in the pictures you've sent. Very different from

Aunt Elaine." That comparison felt unnecessary and caused my heart to skip a beat, but Lauren went on. "Is Gretchen smart? Funny? Charming?"

I nodded along. "Yeah. All those things. She's … a character."

"What about a history of heart disease? Diabetes?" Nicole asked, straight to business.

"All clear. Same on my side too. But she is concerned about her ability to conceive. She was married before."

As I spoke, I realized there were no signs of her first husband in the apartment. I found myself curious about the sort of man he was.

Mirrored eyebrows shot up on both the women. I scratched the back of my neck. "That's another reason why it's such a perfect arrangement. She's been widowed as well. We're on the same page."

"Both of you are still in love with your partners, you mean?" Lauren asked softly.

Direct hit. Emotion had me clearing my throat. That was what we had based our marriage on, Gretchen was clear that she would never love again. And yet I found a stirring of jealousy over the man who would always have her heart. I didn't care to examine anymore of these young man emotions that she stirred up in me.

"We just understand that lightning doesn't strike twice." I sighed. "I wish you two wouldn't do that mom-daughter look thing."

They broke their silent exchange to focus back on the screen. It was the same look Elaine had given me many times over the years; highly skeptical but waiting for me to figure it out on my own.

"It seems like you've thought of everything," Nicole said on a yawn.

"I totally can't see any possible way this might go wrong," Lauren said dryly. "Ouch." She flinched where her mom elbowed her.

I was about to respond when there was a knock on the door. I glanced at the clock; Gretchen wasn't supposed to be home for another hour. She was helping Roxy and the others get ready for the Halloween party.

"I better get that. You two get some rest. We'll talk soon. Love you," I said.

They said their goodbyes and love yous.

It took me a minute to register what, or rather, who I was looking at when I answered the door.

"Suzie?" I asked.

She shook her head and held up a badge hanging around her neck. "Leeloo Dallas. Multi-pass," she said in a clipped voice before winking.

"You look great," I said laughing.

Suzie's dark bob was replaced with a bright orange wig, textured and dirty with little twists. Her white crop top and gold pants were connected by a long piece of orange rubber that acted like a full body thong.

"Thanks. You don't look too bad yourself." She gave me a quick once over. "Ready?"

I looked behind me and then at my watch. "For what?"

"It's your lucky day."

"Okay." I had a feeling that whatever was about to happen would make me feel anything but lucky.

"Consider this a wedding present. You get a VIP lesson from yours truly." She held out her hands.

I swallowed. "Um."

"You, me, and the pole, baby. Let's go!" She grabbed one of my suspenders and pulled. There were no options. Nowhere to run.

CHAPTER 9

VINCENT

"Ride" by Misterwives

This did not feel right. I had not been warned about a dance lesson.

"I don't think this is a good idea." I examined the gleaming pole in front of me.

Windows lined the front of the small dance studio. Giant open windows that faced Main Street where just about anybody could walk by and look inside.

"It's a great idea, sugar. Now I can get to know you and you get access to the best pole dance instructor east of the Mississippi."

"Suzie. This is … I am not really fit enough for …" I tried to think of excuses as Suzie played music on the surround speakers. Louder I said, "We're all dressed up for the costume party. We don't want to ruin anything."

She winked at me. "No worries, doll. This'll just be some basics."

Her attempt to be polite and "get to know me" felt borderline aggressive. Like a test.

My eyes narrowed as I held her gaze.

Her eyes narrowed as they held mine.

We were at a standoff.

"Gretchen wants this," Suzie said.

"Gretchen wants me to learn how to pole dance?" I asked flatly.

"She wants us to be friends, this is how I make friends."

I didn't buy it at all. I mean, maybe Gretchen wanted us to be friends, but this idea was all Suzie's. Gretchen's friend smiled brightly under my speculative gaze. She was being protective. I got it.

I thought of Gretchen the night on my roof, the sadness in both our souls. The doubtful looks of Lauren and Nicole. The people in our lives didn't understand the decision Gretchen and I had come to. As always, it appeared I was going to have to prove my worth through my actions.

I would show the SWS that I was serious about Gretchen and our future life together.

I shrugged out of the double-breasted suit jacket and set it on a couch in the corner of the room, near an exit. I thumbed my suspenders and rolled my head side to side. "Alright. Let's do this."

"Thatta boy! You can use this mat." She pulled over a blue rectangle from the wall and dropped it under the pole she just finished wiping down. "I had to rush to get ready after my last class and haven't had time to clean the others yet. Just don't tell Jack. He's a bit of a clean freak and won't love that we're using it."

"Uh … I can just wipe one down," I suggested, thinking of as many ways to kill time as possible.

It wasn't that I had anything against pole dancing. I was firmly in support of it as a sport or general exercise. But that did not mean it was something I had ever considered participating in. I also respected bungee jumpers, but that did not mean that I was about to throw myself off a cliff in solidarity.

"Now, come on, don't be chicken. Come closer, I don't bite," she said.

"I somehow doubt that," I grumbled.

"What?"

"Nothing."

She raised an eyebrow at me. Suzie was an incredibly beautiful woman. Even with the pretend smudges of dirt on her cheeks and the hokey wig, she exuded an effortless sort of beautiful that likely left most people breathless.

"This is called the fireman. Literally anybody can try it," she explained.

"I still think you're setting the bar too high," I grumbled.

"Right-handed?" she asked.

"Left actually."

"Really? So is Gretchen." She took my left arm and lifted it. "Grab as high as you can. Get up on your tiptoes. There ya go."

"I didn't know she was left-handed," I said. Would our children be left-handed? The thought came so unexpectedly that my palms started to sweat.

Suzie frowned so quickly I almost didn't catch it. "I'm thinking there's lots you don't know about each other." She pulled on my shoulders. "Stand up straighter, shoulders back."

The pole was slick and hard to grasp. "It's thicker than I expected. I can't seem to get a good grip."

"That's what she said," Suzie whispered.

"What?"

"Nothing. Baseball grip. What're ya even doing?" She adjusted the fingers on my hand.

"You act like I know anything at all. Assume that I know nothing."

"Okay, Jon Snow. Now take three steps around."

"Wait, I'm starting?" I asked. "I don't even know what I'm doing."

"You're fine. You're stronger than I expected. That's good. You look like you actually have some upper body strength."

"*Actually*? Thank you for sounding surprised."

The smallest flash of a smile lit her features before she went to a nearby pole. "Just do this. One, two, three." With three quick steps, she spun around the pole with an effortless flourish that I knew, without a doubt, would not happen if I tried to duplicate it.

But I could do this. I *would* do this for Gretchen.

I took one, two, three steps. My left knee smashed against the pole and I winced. "Shit."

"Try again."

And so I did. I tried again and again. My left palm burned, and the muscles of my underarm were smarting. After countless tries, I managed to hook my leg around the pole like she had. *Success*! But the celebration came too soon. A second later my balls smashed into the pole. I gasped and fell forward, hands on knees, gasping in short breaths.

"Ouch," Suzie said, but not with a ton of feeling.

I stood up with a scowl. The pain made me angry. "You know, I'm not going to hurt her. She wants this as much as me. You should trust your friend."

Suzie's face remained impassive. "I trust her. I don't know you."

"Just ask me. I'm an open book." I threw out a hand, the other cupped my poor battered body.

Her shoulders dropped. "You know, Gretchen was born and raised here in Green Valley. She never went to college. She barely graduated high school because of …" She shook her head.

"Okay," I said, not understanding where this was coming from. Gretchen had already mentioned those details when we talked about our educations.

"I bet you have a degree or two."

I nodded. "A double master's in business and design."

Suzie's frown grew. "I saw your house. Where you're from. You probably go to swanky parties and have bougie friends."

I shrugged. "From time to time. I don't think my friends are …"

"And you're gonna take Gretch as your wife? You'll take her to these parties with her on your arm? Gretchen doesn't have a filter, you know. And she loves to stand out. Her outfits and hair. It's part of who she is. She's not gonna change into some Housewife of Williamsburg just to please you." Suzie frowned, foot tapping.

Is that what this was about? She thought I would be embarrassed by Gretchen? "Of course not. I mean, of course I don't want her to change," I clarified.

"It's awfully convenient how you said she could stay here. Like you don't want people knowing about her."

"I didn't want her life to be disrupted." Is that what they saw with our arrangement? We both had lives, we thought it would be easier to only visit when she was ovulating or special occasions.

Suzie pursed her lips.

"Listen," I went on. "I'm not ashamed of Gretchen. What's to be ashamed of? She's funny and gorgeous and full of life. If anything, I'm afraid she'll be embarrassed to be seen with me. I know I come off as a corporate stick-in-the-mud. And I'll admit since I lost my wife, I've been a little more, uh, withheld from society." Suzie nodded in kind understanding. "I don't have a super active social life, but of course I want her to be a part of what I do have. Gretchen is a light in every room she walks into. I'm just happy to be by her side and feel some of her glow." I spoke without filter, there was no holding back. Suzie's arms relaxed to her sides as I spoke. "If anybody's getting the short end of the stick here, it's Gretchen."

Suzie smiled wide. "Damn straight. And don't you forget it." She stepped forward, her eyes gleaming with emotion. I flinched before realizing she was just putting a hand on my shoulder. "Gretchen is the most loyal person you will ever meet. If she chooses you to be a part of her life, she will do anything for you. It's a damn gift to know her."

I swallowed. Then nodded once, message received. "Okay."

She sighed. "Come on. We can stop."

"No, no. I'm determined now. If Gretchen wants to see me ride a pole, then

I can do that."

Suzie sucked in her lips. "There's so much there, I'm not even gonna touch."

"Yeah, yeah." I shook my head with a smile. "Come on. Teach me the fireman thing."

After several more painful minutes, I managed to swing myself around the pole.

"There ya go! Good," Suzie yelled from the sideline.

In a rush of newfound confidence, I pushed hard against the pole and swung out too far. Suzie had just enough time to duck under my flying leg. Dizzy and turned around, I stumbled off the pole and lilted dangerously to the right, straight for the front window. Suzie sprang into action, shouting louder than necessary. I gasped as her strongly muscled body tackled me, and a shoulder shoved into my gut. She managed to save me from crashing into the glass by shoving me so that I fell into a stack of mats instead.

We lay there in a mismatched heap, panting in silence. Then, a second later the stack of mats crashed down on top of us.

Once everything was settled, I started to move out from under the heap.

When I shifted, Suzie yelped.

Using one arm to shove off the pile, and the other to make sure no more would fall, I saw Suzie start to wiggle then still. "Shit. I mean shoot. This stupid wig."

"Stuck?" I asked. Of course, she was. This was all going brilliantly.

"On your, uh, pants."

"Can you take it off?" I cringed. "The wig, I mean."

"I used glue," she whined. "It would take a long time to fix."

Suzie was half bent, her bright orange hair snared in the bottom latch of my suspender.

"Damn, okay. Let's try and get out," I said.

We shuffled in tandem out from under the pile, her crawling backward on hands and knees, and me waddling on my knees.

"How did it even get stuck there?" I asked.

"Lord knows."

Back on the mat, I bent to help her. "Okay you just … okay, yeah, and I'll …"

"There."

Suzie's head snapped up just as I bent down to help her. It was the crack heard 'round the world.

"Oh cluck." She stood up, her wig a mess. Her eyes widened as liquid warmth came gushing out of my nose.

"Oh, no the mat!" she yelled.

"My nose!" I cupped my hands to my nose, looking around for something I could use to stop the bleeding.

Suzie grabbed a rag from behind a small desk near the front door. I reached for it, but she just dropped to the ground.

She scrubbed madly. "You bleed like a stuck pig!" she accused.

"I'm terribly sorry." My voice came out muffled and congested from me pinching my nose closed.

Suzie was on hands and knees, scrubbing the blue mat. "Jack won't be happy about this blood. *Ohhh.*" She groaned in distress. "No, no, no." I threw my head back, moaning in pain. I held tight to my bleeding nose, afraid to move and do anymore damage.

A door slammed and I froze. *Now what?*

I understood the reality of our situation, of course, but just stumbling into such a scene, whoever entered might put together an entirely different story. Suzie below me. On her hands and knees. Moving rapidly. Bits of her bright orange wig sticking out somewhere above my crotch area. Blood on the ground. My head back as I moaned.

It could not have looked good.

I turned my head to see Ford enter the studio. I watched as his eyes took in the madness in front of him then traveled back to me. I'd never seen a person, so calm in demeanor one second, manage to turn into a beast before my very eyes.

Suzie's head shot up. "Hey, baby—"

She glanced to her fiancé currently staring daggers at me. Her own analysis of the situation happened in a flash.

"Wait, wait. Hang on, baby, it's not what it looks like," Suzie said, arms lifting in supplication as her tone grew more panicked. "Ford, just wait!"

But it was too late. The very, very angry man came right at me.

Ford grabbed my costume gun as he went and raised it to my face. "Yippie-ki-yay, mother clucker!"

* * *

Gretchen

I REACHED for the back door of my building when an unexpected wave of something—nerves maybe? Anticipation?—crashed over me. I had kept myself busy all morning; running around checking on tenants, picking up more gossip, and finally spending the afternoon helping the girls get their costumes on. Keeping my hands occupied so my mind couldn't wander. But now I was home. Vincent would be upstairs. Waiting? We were supposed to go to the party at the community center, but would he expect something else first? I mean, that was the whole reason he was here. I was ovulating according to the app I was using to track my periods. But surely, he wouldn't want to just jump right in? But then again, maybe he would? The heat in his eyes on our wedding and in New York was a memory that often popped up.

So, maybe I was being a bit of a chicken when I insisted that Jack and Skip ride over with me so that we could all carpool to the Green Valley Community Center. I'd like to think that I was being efficient. It wasn't that I didn't want to make our marriage official in the biblical sense, I definitely did. I wasn't sure what my sudden shyness was about. I needed some time to think about it.

We were just entering the back entrance to the building when a loud crash came from Suzie's downstairs studio, Stripped. I stopped abruptly causing Jack and Skip to stumble into my back. The three of us froze, exchanging looks.

"What was that?" Jack asked me before shooting a worried glance to Skip.

Skip's shoulders bunched and his face contorted into a frown.

"There shouldn't be anyone down there," I whispered.

Silently, we crept to the door that would let us in the back way to the studio.

Ear pressed to the door, I listened closely.

I heard two muffled male voices and Suzie calling out in worry.

"Suzie!" I whisper-yelled. Grabbing the emergency bat I kept next to the stairs—just for this sort of situation—I moved into action.

But before I could run to my friend's rescue, Skip threw an arm around my waist, holding me back as Jack gave me an incredulous look.

"Men first," Jack whispered.

I rolled my eyes and muttered, "Sexist."

Skip's grip on me tightened before he set me down firmly behind them.

The guys bust through the door, fists raised and ready for action. My heart hammered but the thrill of a rumble had me ready to go.

Jack and Skip stopped as suddenly as they started. It was hard to see exactly what was happening as I tried to peek through their blocking forms. But even if I could see, absolutely nothing about the scene in front of me made any sense.

Ford, dressed in black cargo pants, an orange tank top, and heavy black boots was holding a (hopefully) toy gun at a man's head, his face contorted with rage. "Yippie-ki-yay mother clucker," Ford said ominously.

Suzie was on her knees, arms up and out wide, eyes huge in alarm. There was blood on the ground and pouring out of the man's nose.

It was Vincent!

Was Ford about to pummel Vincent? *My* Vincent? Aw, hell no!

I dropped the bat and ran forward, throwing myself into the mix. All at once everybody started yelling.

"Ford!" Suzie screamed as her fiancé launched himself at Vincent.

I yelled, "Watch out!" as I dove at Vincent who ducked to cover his head.

"My favorite mat!" Jack lamented from where he and Skip remained just inside the doorway.

Ford came to a halt before me standing in front of Vincent, who was now curled up in a ball.

"What in the sam hill is going on?" I yelled.

Ford kept the fake gun aimed at Vincent. "I have to kill this man."

Suzie got up and put a gentle hand on her fiancé's arm. "Aww, my sweet man. But it's not like that."

"What is it like?" I asked, my voice was edged in incredulity. My mind raced, trying to make sense of anything. Why were the three of them down here anyway? And why the hell was Ford so worked up?

"I was trying to … well, I was just trying to give Vincent a bit of a hard time and then my hair got stuck in his thingy." She gestured to his pants with the gun she had now secured from Ford.

"His what?" Ford ground out.

"Ugh, the mats went crashing and we got all tangled up," she tried.

Behind me, Vincent slowly moved to stand. "Can someone please hand me a tissue?"

As Suzie finally placated her man by explaining what had clearly been a misunderstanding of epic proportions, I found a roll of paper towels and guided Vincent to sit on the couch in the corner. I forced myself to calm down. I don't know what I thought could have happened, but I had a very strong reaction to the sight of Vincent in pain. As Suzie went on, and I understood the series of hijinks that led to his nosebleed, I felt giddy laughter bubbling up in me as the worry melted away.

"Are you okay?" I asked, searching his face.

He shrugged. "Yeah." A small smile tugged at his lips. "You're trying so hard not to laugh right now," he accused.

"No … I'm totally"—cough-laugh—"sorry that this happened." I forced myself to breathe normally and stop smiling.

His smile grew as our eyes held each other's.

I clear my throat. "Ford really is a good guy."

"Yes. I especially liked when he launched himself at me and threatened me with a gun."

"Fake gun." Damn my smile was back. He made me smile a lot, this man. "He's protective of Suzie. She's had a rough time and his past isn't exactly a picnic either. Sometimes he reacts a little, uh, strongly."

He glanced to where Suzie was nurturing Ford with hushed murmurs of comfort. His gaze came back to move over my face, taking in the makeup and wig and hat. "Well, I guess I can't blame him for that."

There was a softness to his tone that made my toes curl.

"Why were you even down here?" I asked.

"I was waiting for you upstairs." He swallowed and something about the brief hesitation spoke to the tension I felt about this evening. Had he sensed it in me? "And then Suzie brought me down for a 'lesson.'" He used one hand to mime air quotes on the last word.

I frowned. "Aww, I'm sorry." That wasn't like Suzie. "I'll talk to her."

He checked the tissue held to his nose to see if he was still bleeding. "Don't be hard on her. She was just protecting you."

"Protecting me?" I glanced pointedly to the discarded bat.

"I'm sensing a protective theme in your group of friends," he said. "She wanted to know my intentions," he said with a cocked smile.

My heart inexplicably did a little flippy-doo in my chest. "Oh, and what did you say to her?"

"Just the truth. That I wanted the same things you wanted," he said as he lifted a hand to my beret. I'd styled myself to match Faye Dunaway's look in the film *Bonnie and Clyde*. The answer was true but for some reason that same flippy-doo, floppy-*flopped* in my chest.

"That's true."

He tugged the blond wig I wore. "And that I wasn't near good enough for you."

"Oh. Well." I swallowed. "Oh." I repeated, clueless as to how to respond to that.

Slight purple bruising was darkening under his eyes and there was a gash on his nose.

When I returned my focus to his eyes, he was watching me closely in return. "She was worried I would want you to change."

"Why mess with perfection?" I said lightly, even though I felt shaky with post-drama nerves.

It never even occurred to me, but I could see where Suzie came from: Vincent was a very highfalutin Yankee and I was from the sticks. Maybe I *should* be worried about that.

His thumb brushed over my cheek. How was he so damn free with his touch? I would have never thought when we first met that he'd be so damn touchy-feely. "My sentiments exactly."

I coughed, a flush burning up my cheeks. "Hardly perfect. Plus, it's too late," I said.

His brow furrowed.

"I've already changed. I'm blond now," I said with a wink and stood up.

I had to break the tension between us. My reaction to seeing him bleeding, caught me by surprise. I still felt my adrenaline pumping. Our arrangement was simple. No sense in mucking it up with thoughts and feelings.

"I still have some questions," I said loudly for everyone to hear as I approached the others in the group. They were much more settled now. Jack and Skip were laughing quietly side by side. Suzie was still soothing Ford in hushed whispers. He at least didn't seem to be seeing red anymore.

I felt Vincent come to stand behind me. I fought not to gasp as he slid his hand around my waist. I mean, sure we were married and all that, but he was really leaning into the role.

I flicked a glance to Suzie who also noticed the gesture. She raised an eyebrow at me before saying, "I'm sure you do."

"One." I looked to Ford. "How could you, even for a second think, that Suzie was doing … whatever it is you thought you saw."

Ford flushed and frowned. "I don't know. I wasn't really thinking." He used the toy gun to scratch his hair. "I'm sorry," he said to Suzie before turning back to me. "My mind blacked out. I heard her saying 'no, no.' I saw a man above her and blood. I went to a dark place."

I thought of Suzie the night Ford rescued her from the G-Spot, the horror of it. He had transformed from stuffy professor to wild animal when she'd been hurt.

There was nothing I could say that could take all that back.

"Oh my sweet, scary man." Suzie nuzzled into his neck.

"Okay but my second question is this," I said. "Did I actually hear Ford threaten Vincent with "Yippie-ki-yay, mother clucker?"

Vincent's hand on my waist tightened as he laughed softly.

"It's Bruce Willis," Ford defended.

Jack groaned.

Skip covered his mouth as his shoulders shook with silent laughter.

"What?" Ford asked looking at each of us. "I'm Bruce Willis."

"Oh sweetie," Suzie said gently.

My ab muscles were getting a workout from trying hard not to laugh. "Bruce Willis as Korben Dallas," I said.

"Okay, so?"

Jack looked to the ceiling. "Come on, man. We watched *Die Hard*. Last Christmas. Suzie and I made you."

"Exactly." Something seemed to click in Ford's mind. "That's not this movie?" He gestured to his and Suzie's costumes.

"No," a chorus called out at once.

Ford frowned, looking more like the grumpy professor I first met. "We all know my pop culture knowledge is lacking."

Vincent whispered behind me, his warm breath sending chills down my spine. "He knows it's not mother clucker too, right?"

I turned to respond. His mouth was right there, a breath away from mine. I watched as he licked his lips. His eyebrow half-cocked, lowered as he watched me studying him.

"That's because of Suzie. She doesn't swear," I explained. "It's a whole thing."

He nodded, still confused.

Trying to get my bearings, I said loudly, "Also the context doesn't really work."

"Okay, okay. I get it. I'm the worst at movie references. This is going to be a thing now, isn't it?" Ford frowned.

Suzie nodded and patted his cheek.

"No," Jack said smiling. "I'm sure none of us will ever bring this up again."

Just then, Roxy and Sanders came into the studio followed by Devlin and Kim.

"Hey, I thought we were meeting upstairs—" Kim stopped, looking around.

"What did we miss?" Sanders asked, in his affable Australian accent, already smiling.

"Ford can see dead people," Vincent said.

And we all laughed. Laughed like any group of long-time friends would. Except this time I had an arm around me too, I wasn't watching from the outside, involved but alone. It felt pretty damn good.

And the second I realized it, I was hit with a wave of guilt.

CHAPTER 10

VINCENT

"I Put A Spell On You" by Annie Lennox

I'd done enough epic Halloweens in New York to appreciate a small-town gathering at the Green Valley Community Center. I wouldn't miss crowded bars that smell like stale beer, drunk woo girls screaming in my ears, or lines twenty people deep for a bathroom that was no better than a Porta-Potty.

"I can't wait to try this infamous coleslaw," I said with a grin as Gretchen tried to gather our group in front of the community center like some preschool pageant director.

She frowned at me. "I can't tell if you're being sarcastic." Then she turned to the other couples, making last minute adjustments to their costumes. "If y'all don't get your acts together, there won't be any food left by the time we get in," Gretchen yelled.

"Yes, ma'am," Sanders said with a cheeky smile.

She shot him a look and he hid behind Roxy.

"Okay, Suzie and Ford. You first." She scooted them together in front of a bale of hay stacked with pumpkins. Suzie stood with her arms hanging down at her sides, a slightly dazed look on her face while Ford squinted and held up his gun.

"Those abs tho," Kim said about Suzie's figure.

"Right?" Gretchen said, "I don't think Leeloo's knockers were anywhere close to that size in the movie."

The girls all laughed, and the guys smiled at the ground. Ford preened and pulled Suzie closer.

"Smile and say, 'Happy Trails,'" Jack called.

"That wasn't the same movie," Skip whispered to his fiancé.

"Not like he knows."

"I can't hear what you're saying," Ford said keeping his serious action-hero face, "but I'm sure I'm being made fun of." The middle finger facing his best friend went up.

Kim and Devlin were up next. I hadn't talked much to those two, there was something a little scary about the big guy. The black bandana he had covering half his face didn't help. His eye contact was a little too intrusive when it found me. He was dressed in an all-black cowboy outfit that looked straight out of a spaghetti western. Kim was an old-timey sheriff—I think. She wore a fringed leather vest over a checkered shirt, a gold star, and a cowboy hat. One handcuff was around Devlin's wrist and she held the other end.

"Kinky," I whispered in Gretchen's ear, making her jump. I'd been doing that to her all night. If I was being totally honest with myself it was partly because I liked the way it caused tiny little goosebumps to break out over her neck and hardened her nipples. She really had fantastic breasts. How did she ever get anything done with those things? If it were me, I would just touch myself all the time. Also, I enjoyed the freedom of touching someone again without having to overthink it.

I asked, "Who are they supposed to be?"

Gretchen stood ramrod straight and cleared her throat. "A bandit and a sheriff." She flicked a glance up and licked her lips when she found me so close again. There was a satisfaction to ruffling the unruffable Gretchen LaRoe. "That's my outfit." She pointed to Kim.

"You know, I guessed that." I rubbed some tension from her shoulders as she held up her phone to take more pictures. "Even the handcuffs?"

She swallowed. "You sure are a touchy-feely person, aren't ya?" she asked with forced lightness.

"Not usually," I said quietly.

I touched her without thinking. I touched her because it felt like the most natural thing to do. I touched her because I couldn't stop myself.

I gently pushed down on her shoulders until some of the tension melted out of them. My thumb traced up the back of her neck as she leaned subtly into my fingers. There was a part of me that wondered at my actions. Who was this man that couldn't keep his hands to himself? I had never been like that with anyone since Elaine. Never wanted to. But there was so much to Gretchen that called to be caressed and squeezed and explored. Maybe if I got her accustomed to my nearness, it would be easier later … less pressure. Or so I told myself.

"You're playing with fire, mister. Two can play that game." She sent me a coy look over her shoulder before yelling, "Okay, now Roxy and Sanders." She gestured the next couple over.

Roxy made an absolutely perfect Morticia Addams. Her long, slim frame seemed to go for days in the black dress that clung tightly before flaring out into tendrils at the bottom. Her eye makeup was as dark as her long straight hair that looked like it had been dyed to darken it.

Even Sanders made a decent Gomez. Though he looked nothing like the character, he more than fit him in personality. His normally blond hair was sprayed black and slicked back and someone had drawn exaggerated eyebrows and an absurd little mustache on his face. He dramatically kissed up Roxy's arms, whispering dramatic proclamations of love and adoration. I'd spent enough time around the couple to know that this was no act. This was just Sanders. Roxy looked down at him with the slightest coy smile.

"Too perfect," Suzie said. Kim agreed.

"Next!" Gretchen called.

Skip and Jack looked perfectly dressed as Finn and Poe from the newest *Star Wars* film. They threw their arms around each other and smiled at the phone.

"Cheese," they said in unison.

Jack pulled in Skip and kissed him on the cheek, drawing a deep blush from Skip. I was reminded of the night of their engagement, and I pulled Gretchen even closer, kissing her neck once. Fighting the overwhelming urge to bite her. Maybe later.

Later.

"I'm going to make you pay for that. Roxy is looking," Gretchen whispered through clenched teeth.

"So? I had to see her and Sanders moon over each other for weeks. Do you know how many times I walked in on those two about to go at it?"

Gretchen laughed. "They thought they were so subtle." She glanced at the people in various costumes streaming into the community center around us. "Too many people are showing up. I'm gonna have to trip Scotia Simmons if I wanna get any coleslaw."

"Not so fast," Kim called.

"Don't forget about you and Vinny," Suzie said, cocking her hip and putting her hand there with attitude.

Gretchen's slightly taken aback expression told me she *had* forgotten about us. "Vincent," Gretchen corrected.

In her mind, we still weren't an "us," which was understandable. It would be weird to expect no adjustment time whatsoever. And yet, there was a little part of me that bruised at the oversight.

"Vinny is fine," I said, passing Gretchen's phone to Suzie. "That's what my family calls me."

"See." Suzie gave a pointed look to Gretchen. As the two women passed, Suzie whispered, "We're all a big family now, after all."

They shared a look. A look I couldn't quite understand. Women. All these years on earth, always surrounded by them, and they still felt like such a mystery.

"I haven't worn a couple costume in years," I said as Gretchen and I wordlessly stood back-to-back, holding up our toy sawed-off shotguns and bags of money.

"Same," Gretchen said quietly. "I'm usually the one taking the pictures from the side by myself."

Her voice remained neutral but the words caused me to turn toward her. I slid an arm around her waist, bending her backward so that she had to hold on to her beret to keep it from falling off. Our faces were inches apart. "You're not alone anymore."

Her eyelashes fluttered, her mouth parting slightly. She looked like she wanted to be kissed. "Neither are you," she whispered.

The artificial sound of a shutter closing interrupted the moment and she straightened.

"Damn, you two make a great Bonnie and Clyde," Suzie said.

I turned to the camera again but kept an arm around her. "I hope my nose didn't ruin the pictures," I said as we walked to the entrance of the building.

She glanced up at me from under my arm. "I like it. Makes you look dangerous. Adds to our whole vibe."

"Dangerous," I repeated squinting off into the distance.

As we crossed the threshold into the center, Gretchen took a deep breath in and out before saying, "Time for Green Valley to meet Gretchen LaRoe's new man."

* * *

Gretchen

Between leaving Stripped and heading to the community center, my mood shifted. It didn't make any sense. Parties were my jam. People in costumes, good food, and being the center of gossip, these were all the things I love in life, so what was my deal?

When our big group entered one of the jam session rooms, it should have felt good to have so many eyes drift to me. Normally, I preened, lifted my chin, and soaked it up.

But tonight was different. I looked and felt different. And Vincent was here, holding me, touching me like it was nothing. I wasn't used to being uncomfortable in my own skin but suddenly, it was like I'd forgotten how to walk and gossip at the same time.

I just needed to figure out my deal, but he was always at my side. My very own little lamb, everywhere that I went, Vincent was sure to go. And so what? Wasn't that the point? Wasn't that what I wanted? What *we* wanted?

I just needed space to think. I couldn't smile and listen while his hand caressed my hip. I couldn't tell funny stories when his breath tickled my ear. How was a girl to work a party?

Sanders pointed to a scar on his tricep and talked about a rock-climbing trip gone wrong. Vincent shared a story about a time he broke two fingers on his right hand also rock climbing.

"Ouch, that must have sucked," Sanders said, hand around his Morticia's waist.

"It could have been worse, I'm left-handed," Vincent explained.

I glared at the side of his head. He was left-handed too? He broke fingers? He rock climbed?

I zoned out, my heart hammering in my chest. Ford, Sanders, and Skip were making plans to check out a local place with Vincent. I was happy the guys seemed to be hitting it off, and yet … and yet.

Thump, thump, thump. My heart rang through my ears. And Vincent was still touching me. His thumb had found its way between the band of my wool skirt and sweater. Brushing back and forth. Turning me on.

Dammit.

I stepped away, worrying my lip as I tried to find somewhere to breathe.

Right on cue, Vincent showed up at my side. "This is really fun," he said, trying to get me to dance. "Good music. Let's go back to the room with that one hairy guy and the pretty redhead. They were really good."

I stopped and looked at him. I stuck out my chin. "I don't want to."

His dark brows furrowed. People were looking. Were they comparing him to Ephram? Not that this side of Green Valley knew much about what went down with the Wraiths, but still. That wasn't the point. The point was I didn't want to go listen to Billy and Claire. Okay, maybe I did. They really were good. But I didn't want him to tell me where to go and what to do.

"What do you want to do?" He crossed his arms over his chest.

This wig was too tight. I used a nail to scratch a particularly annoying itch near my temple. "I don't know. I just need some space or something."

"Space?"

I looked up to find Scotia Simmons watching me closely. I stepped back without thinking. He glanced to where I'd been looking. I regretted it when a flash of hurt crossed his features.

"Gretchen?"

"Everybody is looking at us."

"I thought you anticipated that. I thought you *wanted* that. For the people here to know me better. As more than the grumpy man at the Lodge."

"What will they think?" I snapped.

"Since when do you give a shit what people think?" he snapped back.

He was right. Since when did I care? I couldn't explain what I was feeling. Tonight was supposed to be fun but I was freaking out like it was my first high school dance.

My sweater was too hot. I pulled at the collar to try and get some air. This damn place was too hot.

"Come here." He dragged me into a corridor. He tried a couple doors until he found a small room sometimes used as a classroom. Long tables were pushed up against a wall with a whiteboard hanging on it. At least it was dark and cooler in here.

"Now what's going on?" he asked.

I stood in the middle of the room, fanning my face. He stood a few feet away, giving me space. But dammit, now I wanted him to hug me. No. I didn't. I wanted him to stay over there.

Since when did I not know exactly what I wanted? My heart and brain warred with each other and I didn't know who to listen to.

"I've gotten used to being on my own. Doing everything on my own terms," I said.

"Okay," he said. "So go where you want. I thought you wanted to be together."

"Don't boss me around."

He went to pinch the area between his eyes, then winced when he bumped the cut. He sighed and said, "Is that really what you thought I was doing?"

I was all caught up in my stubbornness now. "I don't like you … just touching me. Like I'm yours."

He stepped forward, his face hardening. "You are mine," he said. His voice was so low and steady, I had to fight back a shudder. That voice.

My jaw dropped. That was so, so not okay. His words nor my naughty reaction to it. So what did it mean that heat sizzled through me?

"I'm not your property. This isn't the eighteen hundreds or whatever," I said oh, so eloquently.

"You want to walk around here acting like you're still single? Well, too bad. We *are* married."

My heart hammered in my chest. He prowled forward until I was forced back against the wall.

"You're free to freak out about this marriage. But don't project your regret onto me, Gretchen. I don't deserve that."

"What?" I stood up on tiptoes to get in his face. "I'm doing no such thing."

"You committed to me. You said we were on the same page."

"We are."

"So then what's this really about? You don't want to be seen with me? Are you embarrassed?"

"Embarrassed of the hot rich guy? Hardly."

His eyes narrowed, color rising up his neck. "Then what's going on? You've been weird since we got here. I'm not letting you shift focus. You've got something to say, you say it. The whole point of this—" He gestured between our chests. His knuckles brushed my cleavage and left a trail of heat with the contact. "Is that we aren't playing games. If something is bothering us, we say it. We aren't doing the dramatics."

I swallowed. My chest heaved. I crossed my arms, and his gaze studied my cleavage for a flash. Heat was there but he cleared it away just as fast. He groaned and ran his hands roughly through his hair. "Sometimes you make me feel like I'm a teenager again."

It did not sound like a compliment the way he said it. Only the tiniest part of me took joy in seeing him ruffled.

"I'm too old to be acting jealous—" He smoothed his hair back in place and took a deep breath in and out before turning back to me. "Do you regret marrying me?" he asked, his tone softened.

I couldn't figure out what my deal was. Was I freaking out about the wrong things? Was it about people seeing us? About being touched? Or was it about something entirely different and my brain was just choosing the nearest thing to latch on to? It's hard to know what was real or imagined when it was all the same mind lying to you. But I did know one thing for sure.

"I don't regret marrying you," I whispered, staring at the buttons of his vest.

So why was I shaking? What was I afraid of …

"I have a theory," he said removing any of the remaining space between us.

"Of course you do. You know me so damn well." I tried to sound like my old self. I mostly sounded petulant.

He tilted back the fedora on his head and lowered his forehead to mine. "I think you're nervous about tonight. Or what you think might happen tonight."

Heat instantly flushed up my collar and cheeks. "Am not." Well, that was a blatant lie. Why did I say it like that? Why was I acting like a teenager?

"Well, I am." He nudged until I made eye contact again. My panting chest brushed against his with every inhale. "Nervous. It's been a long time since I've been worried about impressing somebody. A long time since … I had to woo somebody. Maybe I'm going about this all wrong."

What the *actual* hell? Was he just the King of Open and Honest Conversations? What did he think this was? A freaking … marriage?

The air sagged out of me like a bouncy house with a hole. My hands rested on the wall behind me, and I looked up at him. "You don't have to woo me. We skipped all that, remember?" I smiled up at him, softening.

"You deserve to be wooed." He moved an arm above my head and leaned over me. "I want to make it so fun for you."

Something like a squeak followed by a moan came out of me. "I'm sure we'll have a very nice time." I sucked my lips. *A very nice time? Smooth, LaRoe.* "I guess I am a little nervous too." As I spoke, understanding settled in. The real reason I was starting to feel so frustrated. "I didn't even know you were left-handed until ten minutes ago. This is all sort of surreal, you know?"

He nodded. "I get it. I'm totally out of my element here. You've known these people your whole life. They know you better than anybody."

I frowned in thought. "Actually, everybody here has known me my whole life, so I'd argue they know me the least. They have no idea who I am now." I scratched under the wig. "They hold on to one image or memory of me formed a lifetime ago. You probably know the most current version of myself better than anybody."

His face softened with a smile. He nodded like he understood. Which was good, because I hardly comprehended what I was trying to say. Just that, looking around this room, it reminded me how alone I felt. How few people actually knew me.

"I'm either Jethro's ex, or the girl who gives rides, or the loud redhead, or whatever. Or the widow of that kid that used to ride with the Wraiths. You know?"

"We have so much to learn about each other." His hands went back to my shoulders. "Is this okay?"

"It's okay." And Daisy's donuts were just alright. I collapsed against his chest.

His entire front was pressed against me. It was better than okay, it was alright, alright, alright as Matthew McConaughey would say. The scent of him. The heat of him. The solidness of his thighs, his torso, his arms …

He wrapped his arms around me, tucking my head under his chin. It reminded me of the night on his roof. How natural it felt. I remembered now, that this was what we had. An ease. An intangible connection. I remembered.

"Maybe, even though we're doing this a bit out of order, we can still take some things slow." His voice was deep and grumbly against my ear. "Get to know each other without jumping right to the sex."

God, even hearing him say the word sent a thrill of nerves through me.

When had I become such a prude? Obviously, I was attracted to him. I was all but panting with him this close. I wasn't nervous exactly, but it just didn't feel right yet. It felt too planned. I couldn't say that though, because that was the whole point of our arrangement. We had a solid plan. And yet, I needed something more, but I couldn't put my finger on it.

"Take things slow," I repeated.

He nodded, tilting my head back to thumb my lower lip. He really liked to do that. I really liked that he liked to do that. It sent pulses of heat through me. Same with the heated glazed-over look he got when he stared at my breasts. He never stopped glancing at them. In his defense, they looked amazing under this sweater. I wore a pushup bra and the tiny peek of cleavage was fire.

"That'll be good." I cleared my throat.

"There are plenty of other things we can do to learn what we like and don't like," he said, his hands smoothing over my back.

"This is true." Did my voice sound higher than normal?

We stayed like that for a while. Just holding each other. Eventually, reluctantly, I broke the hug when my stomach growled. "Alright. Let's get out there."

"Do you want some space?" he asked, his head tilted patiently. "I understand if you do."

"No." I grabbed his hand and threaded our fingers together. "I just want some damn coleslaw."

CHAPTER 11

VINCENT

"Addicted To Love" by Florence + The Machine

The ground tilted as Gretchen helped me out to her car.

"There was something in that moonshine," I slurred.

"Yeah, moonshine." She led me as best she could, her arm tight around my waist. "It's meant to knock you on your ass. I can't believe you drank it."

"How was I supposed to know?"

She laughed. "Well, the fact that you got it from the back of some guy's truck and not in the community center was probably a red flag."

We walked for hours on ground that wouldn't stay flat, I would've sworn it. I wouldn't complain though because she'd just say it was all our fault that we arrived so late. Ten years later, we reached her car in the very back of the parking lot, almost hidden by the surrounding forest.

"I'm trynna fit in around here." I slumped against the car as she released me.

She blew the strands of blond wig out of her face and fanned herself. Her cheeks were rosy with exertion. It suited her. "You did great tonight." She smiled at me like I was a sad, helpless puppy.

She looked beautiful. I missed her red hair but really any look was a knockout on her. How many times had I looked at her across a room and thought how captivating she was? I couldn't keep track anymore.

"What's the moony look for?" she asked.

"Come closer," I whispered.

She huffed and rolled her eyes but did as I commanded. I brought her to me by her wrists, until there was no more space between us. I tilted my hat back to inhale her neck. "You smell so good," I moaned.

"You smell like a future hangover," she teased.

I pulled back and frowned at her.

"Fine." She flicked the brim of my hat. "You still smell good. You always do. It's that cologne you use." She tilted her head, exposing her neck to me again. I didn't hesitate at the invitation and traced my lips up and down her tender skin.

"No cologne. Just my natural manliness."

"So modest." She relaxed against me but there was a slight edge to her voice. Something held her back. I felt her desire so strong sometimes, and other times …

"Feel so good." My hands roamed her curves, squeezing and groping.

"Is this you taking it slow, Vincent?"

I had said that, hadn't I? Stupid integrity. Stupid past self. I groaned and stilled my hands. But then I remembered that right now I wasn't Vincent.

"Who's Vincent?" I took off my hat and set it on the roof of the car. She watched me with a raised eyebrow and arms crossed. "I'm Clyde and you're my Bonnie," I said, watching as her face shifted.

She went from flippant and amused to intrigued and serious in a flash. "Is that right?" she asked breathlessly. Her pupils darkened as her mouth parted, revealing the tip of her tongue as it toyed with her teeth.

"There are no rules for bank robbers." I turned us so that her back pressed against the car and lifted her thigh until her skirt was shoved up and tight across her full hips. The slit up the side revealed the end of a dark stocking attached to a garter belt. I groaned at the sight. When she got into character, she really committed.

"How very dangerous of us." She arched her back, eyes heavy as she looked me up and down. She tugged on the suspenders under my jacket, bringing me back to her.

"Especially out here in the open," I said. "Any cop could wander by and find us."

Color rose to her chest. "So naughty. Come 'ere, Clyde."

If she wanted to get into character too, I was here for that. There was a deep part of me that longed for fun and games in the bedroom. I never had an opportunity to be commanding and adventurous until I met Gretchen LaRoe but suddenly it was clear that I wasn't the only person looking for a little bit of escapism. I was up for anything.

One arm held my weight as I leaned over her, the other hand roamed the leg held up around my hip. My fingertips traced the line of her tights on the back of her knee, she gasped softly. I followed the silky material until I reached the clasp.

"So smooth. So soft." I leaned in and kissed up her neck.

Her breaths came quicker. I kissed up until I reached her chin. I hesitated a breath away from her mouth. It was the smallest tension in her body that told me she was lost in her head again. I wasn't too buzzed to notice that. She needed to let her body do the thinking.

"Kiss me," I demanded, using the voice she couldn't resist.

"Yes, sir," she whispered, and it shot straight to my cock.

Her lids fluttered closed, as her mouth fell open. I had just a moment to study her soft features before my mouth was on hers again.

We both let out a long groan. She was soft and hot and tasted amazing. It was better than the first time. Even hotter. I wanted this beautiful woman so bad. I had that rushing, out of control feeling again. I should pull back. I should give her space. She had asked me for space.

She untucked my shirt and rubbed her hand up my stomach and chest.

Fuck space.

I wanted our bodies to be so intertwined that she couldn't remember what it was like to not have me in her. She's mine.

Our bodies rocked against each other as our mouths continued to clash. I couldn't get enough of her. My hand released her leg as it moved up higher. I protected her whole body with mine, distantly aware that we were still outside in a parking lot. I forgot the thought as soon as I reached the satin of her underwear. The fabric was soaked. I teased her, sliding my finger in and out. I used the wetness to gently caress up and down her. Tested. Listened. Seeing where her breath hitched. When she groaned. I would learn every inch of this sweet woman. I slid my finger back to her core and dipped it back in, deeper, hooking my finger. My thumb teased her clit. So swollen. So hot. Gretchen began to gasp hot little breaths, hands searching for purchase as I ratcheted her up higher and higher … until …

"Fuck." She threw her head back with a groan and I could feel her pulsating on my fingers. I kissed her softly as her body softened again. I removed myself from her, discreetly wiped my hand on my handkerchief, then held her as she shuddered with occasional aftershocks.

I was overwhelmed by want for her. I couldn't think. I needed more. I needed to sink inside her. So soft. So good. I'd never wanted anything so bad. I rested my forehead against her neck to collect myself. I listened to her heartbeat pound against my ear for a couple minutes.

A throat cleared behind us. I stiffened. Gretchen instantly straightened and put herself in order. Hopefully the dark parking lot hid what we just did.

"Whatcha doin'?" Roxy asked sweetly.

Gretchen moved to stand in front of me, thankfully hiding the erection that was taking its sweet time going down. Roxy and Sanders stood with Jack and Skip, all sharing equally amused looks.

"We're leaving." Gretchen crossed her arms and lifted her chin.

"I thought y'all left a while ago," Roxy said. "Isn't that why we had to drive the guys home?"

"We're goin'. Just getting the drunken sailor here into the car," Gretchen said.

I waved at the group from behind Gretchen. Roxy bit back a smile and I heard a few stifled laughs.

"Goodnight y'all," she said and helped me into the passenger seat.

"Goodnight," they all sing-songed back.

She stuck her tongue out at the others as she walked around to the passenger side. I loved watching her walk.

At some point on the drive home, I was lulled to sleep by the passing trees and gently rocking car. I vaguely remembered her dragging me upstairs and complaining about my weight.

"You liked my muscles before," I said, half asleep.

"Only when you're in control of them," she grumbled, helping me to change and get into bed.

Sometime later I woke up with a pounding headache and a racing heart to find Gretchen asleep at my side. She'd been cuddling up next to me and that must have been what woke me. I lifted my arm and she nestled under it in her sleep like it was the most natural thing in the world. Long missing comfort seeped into my bones as I let my body slip back into sleep.

I woke up again a few hours later. A glance at the clock on the nightstand said it was barely three a.m. Gretchen was still on my chest, sleeping soundly, one leg thrown over mine. My hand was cupping her ass. I had half an erection pressing against my underwear.

I closed my eyes as thoughts of the evening berated me. I shouldn't have drunk that questionable stuff. Never trust a man with a gold tooth and a mischievous glint to his eyes. I shouldn't have kissed her and lost control like that. I took a steadying breath to stop my racing heart from waking her up. I couldn't believe how out of control I was with her. I couldn't remember ever wanting anybody this bad. With Elaine, our love had been so innocent at first. Afterwards, it was amazing and tender.

I stopped that train of thought. Not while I held Gretchen in my arms.

Gretchen brought out a darker side to me. I should be afraid of it, but all I wanted to do was explore it. She made me want things I never wanted before. Which could be dangerous. She wanted this to be easy. Simple. I wouldn't go scaring her off with my passion for her. Our marriage might have occurred for convenience but there was nothing convenient about how badly I desired her.

My hand was still on the silk fabric of her sleep shorts. I'd been massaging her ass without realizing—I couldn't help myself. I tried to put some space between us but she moaned in her sleep softly, pulling herself closer to me. She squeezed my thigh between her own, grinding against me once. I could feel the heat from her on my upper thigh. Her hand brushed across the hair of my chest, her thumb brushing my nipple. I grew rock hard. God, she felt so good. So hot and wet …

"Gretchen?" I whispered softly.

Her breathing didn't change. How did my pounding heart not wake her? I swallowed and let a slow breath out. I needed to get myself under control. I wouldn't ruin what we had. Last night had been amazing but I promised myself I would be taking things slow.

Her hand squeezed my bicep in her sleep, and she moaned again.

Lord, help me.

CHAPTER 12

GRETCHEN

"Beggin'" by Måneskin

Whoever dared call me before eight a.m. would pay with their life.

I groaned and checked my phone. A missed video call from Vincent. Which wasn't unusual. We talked regularly since he left last. It had been one looooong week since our freaky fun in the parking lot.

"Well, I'm awake now," I groaned to the room.

I lived my life by the calendar now. Every morning I woke up to a cold bed before checking to see how many days until I saw Vincent again.

Married almost two months. Days spent in bed with Vincent? Shockingly few.

When the SWS asked about the status of our more intimate relations, I had nothing to report since Roxy found us halfway to home base on Halloween. He'd been a perfect gentleman for the rest of his quick trip while still showering me with his constant physical affection. They at least, seemed to be happy about that. I got the impression, despite their support, they still felt like this whole marriage thing had been rushed.

I was less thrilled. I'd gotten a tease of what was hidden under all those dress slacks and needed to see the real deal up close and personal. Plus, I had to admit I missed *him*. I'd grown used to those easy touches and his dry humor. And did I mention the massive bulge? Okay, just checking.

I reached across the bed and caressed the cold pillow. I sighed and debated bringing out my vibrator. Would that be cheating? Not cheating, obviously … but maybe if I built up things more it would be easier the next time he was in town. Twenty more days. Twelve hours. But who was counting? He was taking things slow for me, but I didn't even think that's what I wanted anymore. No doubt he was taking care of himself in New York. I bet every morning he had morning wood like he had when he woke up spooning me …

"Ugh," I groaned.

I didn't want to be thinking about stuff like this. I didn't want to imagine what Vincent and his cock were doing this very minute. And yet here I was.

Our marriage was supposed to be easy. And it was easy—when he was next to me. But when he went away, it felt like starting over despite our constant communication. When had his presence become so damn reassuring? Necessary even?

We talked every day since the Halloween visit. Texting throughout the day, discussing everything from the mundane to plan making. I even video-chatted regularly, which I hated to do because the only thing worse than shitty lighting, was having to sit still. But it worked with him. Probably didn't hurt that he sounded like he should be narrating sexy books on the phone. Sometimes he would listen while he worked out and I drove people around, making comments in my ear.

"Okay, this is fun," he said once after hearing a couple fighting during one of my rides.

"Told you," I'd mumbled back.

Other times, I would listen to his struggles with people he worked with. Or issues Lauren and Troy were having with sleep and the baby. We had become good friends. Friends was good. It would suck to learn that he used the wrong form of your/you're in texts or hated RuPaul's Drag Race. Some things were unforgivable. But the more I learned about him, the complex and compatible he became. I knew that his go-to feel good music was Hall & Oats—and obviously made fun of him for it—but when he worked out, he only listened to death metal. I knew how he liked to unwind on his phone at the end of the day by playing sudoku. The nerd. I knew that he couldn't get into bed without brushing his teeth first.

I talked about my love of vintage fashion. Clothes were one of the worst things for the environment. I would rather have a higher quality article of clothing I could wear a long time. I talked about some of my tenants and the dramas of Green Valley. I shared my favorite playlists, consisting mostly of covers. "There are few things I love more than one favorite band covering a different artist I love."

Then he said, "There's just something in your bones that loves giving previously loved things a second life."

We went a bit silent after that.

He even called me once when I went to visit Ephram. I didn't talk to my first husband anymore. Just sitting near his grave was enough. Vincent told me that he wanted to go talk to him sometime when he was in town, and I had smiled liking that idea very much.

Things were going well with Vincent.

It's easy to fit with someone you never see, a voice in the back of my mind warned.

No more making excuses or delays, we needed to get down to business. The plan to go slow was good in theory, but in reality all it had done was make me build up my expectations for when we finally did the deed. It was just sex, for crying out loud!

Full disclosure, I was pretty horny. Maybe it was because I was more aware than ever of my ovulation cycle or maybe they put something in the prenatal vitamins I choked down. Or maybe it was how easily he made me come apart with just a few delicate strokes of his finger. God, it had felt so good and had been shockingly easy. I couldn't even make myself come that fast.

Or maybe because the first thing I thought about when waking up was Vincent making himself come. ARGH. Now I was imagining his O-face; head thrown back, neck straining, eyes squeezed tight. I bet he was loud in bed. If his freedom with his touch was any indication, the man didn't hold back.

I mean … what he wouldn't know wouldn't hurt him, right? We hadn't explicitly said we couldn't touch ourselves. Other people, obviously a no-no, but ourselves? Surely, he was experiencing the same frustrations.

I surreptitiously glanced around the empty apartment bedroom. I reached into the bedside table and grabbed out BOP—Battery Operated Pal—I preferred to keep my toy genderless. Like a Pavlovian instinct, the sound of the vibrating instantly had me squirming in the sheets. I closed my eyes and leaned back against the pillows and cozied up to BOP.

Wait, that vibrating wasn't my toy, it was my phone. I growled and checked the caller ID. Vincent was video calling me again. I looked around panicked, feeling like I had been caught red-handed. Or rather one-handed? Struggling to shut off BOP, I answered the call with the slide of my thumb.

"Hey!" I said with far too much pep. I cleared my throat and smiled. *Tone it down, LaRoe.* I relaxed against my headboard. To my surprise, he was still in bed too, half popped up on a stack of pillows, shirtless. One muscled arm was slung lazily over his messy bedhead revealing a hairy armpit that should not be doing things for me but *damn.* His firm shoulders and pecs were also on display. Not. Helping. The. Situation. I thought he'd be getting ready for work already, not lounging around seductively like some lothario.

Jesus, I needed to get laid.

"What's up?" I asked with a squeak.

Cool as a cucumber, that's me.

"Sorry, I just—" His arm dropped, and he moved the phone closer to his face. "What are you doing?"

I saw my eyes widen in the tiny picture of me in the corner of the screen. My cheeks were flushed, and my hair was a mess. "Me? What? Nothing." I blew a strand of hair out of my face. "I just woke up."

"Gretchen LaRoe, have I caught you in the act?" He smiled like the fox that got the hen. More like the cock that caught the hen masturbating.

I smoothed my features and shifted in bed, trying to gather my dignity. "I have no idea what you're talking about."

Just then BOP, *freaking* BOP, decided to go off. The traitor. The sound was as loud as a shotgun in the silence. "That's just my phone." I struggled with my phone as I tried to turn off the vibrator off camera.

When I picked up the phone again, Vincent had put his glasses on and his mischievous grin was replaced with something much darker.

"Gretchen," he all but growled. "What are you doing to me?"

It made my insides clench. *What am I doing to* him? That hair. Those glasses. I bet he was all warm and smelled like sleep. I bet I could just cuddle right up to his hard heat and rub myself all over him. "I'm doing nothing … that's the problem," I added the last part cheekily under my breath.

"Were you touching yourself?" he asked before his tongue came out to lick his bottom lip.

Damn him and his bluntness.

"We never said we couldn't," I defended.

"I'm not mad." He pushed up his glasses and rubbed the bridge of his healed nose. "I'm fucking jealous."

"Oh."

I couldn't see his hand, but his shoulder flexed as his arm moved up and down. "I woke up rock hard thinking of you on Halloween. In that costume."

I grinned. "You did?"

"Only every day since I saw you in it." He turned the phone to show his hand in his briefs stroking something very hard indeed.

I let out a breath. "Oh wow."

"You have a thing for blondes, huh?" I asked before internally wincing at the comment. Way to bring up the past.

"I have a thing for you. And those outfits you wear."

My cheeks burned but more than anything I thrilled at the blatant desire in his words. It was dirty and shameless. Was that why he called? Did he need to get off? Were we doing this? Like everything else the next steps came so naturally. And God, I needed this.

"Which outfits do you like best?" I asked.

The sound of the vibrator humming back to life was obvious, and he sat up straighter, getting more comfortable, not commenting. "All of them. But the night of Jack and Skip's engagement you wore this little black number."

"Oh yeah," I said. I moved the tip of my toy to the edge of my panties. "A classic LBD."

"Yeah." He huffed a short breath. "It clings to your body perfectly. Your hips, your ass, your breasts." He closed and leaned his head back and his shoulder flexed, moving up and down. "God, those breasts. If you only knew what I thought about."

"What did you want to do to me? When you saw me in it?" I asked, amazed at my boldness.

It should be weird, but as always with us, it felt like a natural progression.

"Before or after you attacked me with kisses?"

I shrugged, sucking in my lips, and teased myself a little more. I could feel the cotton of my underwear growing more damp. "Both?"

"I thought of the heated glances you sent my way a few times," he said. "You always looked at me like you were sizing me up. And I liked it."

"I was."

"I thought about showing you that I couldn't be pushed around. Manipulated."

"I had you all wrong. I really like your glasses," I said. Apropos of nothing.

He grinned the cockiest grin I'd seen on him yet. And there had been a few. "I know. You always seemed pissed off when I wore them. I purposely wore them if I knew I'd be seeing you. I like getting under your skin."

"You're there," I confessed. He was. More and more he invaded my thoughts. "Those fucking glasses. You're like a sexy secret agent. I want you to push me against a wall and frisk me."

"I'll gladly oblige. I'll tie you up and make you beg for freedom."

"My safe word is 'cattywampus,'" I joked because I was getting too hot, too fast.

"Noted." He smiled despite himself, despite the incredible dirtiness of our confessions.

We were silent for a moment, imagining all the things. The only sounds came from BOP, flesh on flesh, and our fast breaths.

"You have me tied up?" I prompted. I needed more.

He shook his head. "You got me all off track. First, we're back at the Lodge. Which is despicable of me, because I work there."

"Naughty, naughty," I said, squirming when I accidentally grazed my most sensitive part. "Can't even control yourself."

His nostrils flared. "You push my buttons. You were mouthy. Always running that pretty mouth of yours. I knew just what to do with it."

He knew exactly what I needed to hear. It would only work here, in this safe space, my kink of being bossed around.

I licked my lips.

"God, you're so fucking sexy, Gretchen."

I flicked a look to what he saw. I was a sex kitten. Red hair wild around me, mouth parted, chest panting, flushed with need.

"More," I moaned though I was embarrassingly close to the edge. The toy was too much. I was too sensitive already. I tossed it aside, opting for my fingers, pretending they were his. A cheap knockoff of the real thing. I teased myself slowly, trying to stretch this out.

"I imagine taking you to my office and locking the door," he said.

Heat spread, I was on fire. My fingers moving so fast, heels looking for purchase in the sheets.

"I come up behind you. I have better access to everything that way. I suck at your neck inhaling your hypnotic scent. I rub my hands all over you. I tug your top down and I finally play with those gorgeous tits. I pull your dress up so I can squeeze your ass and grind my hard cock against it. I love that I can touch every inch of you."

A wanton moan escaped me. Man, could he dirty talk! He went quiet as he collected himself, jaw clenched and nostrils flared. Then he said, "I pull you into my lap as I sit back on my chair. I spread your legs over my knees so you're spread to the room."

"Jesus," I gasp.

"I find you soaking. You're always so wet for me." It's true. My fingers were drenched. "I brace you against my chest, holding you in place. I kiss your mouth hard so you can't talk back. And I fuck you with my fingers."

I groan and call out as I come. "Holy shit." I lay there panting as I came back to my body. Distantly he grunted and hissed in a breath.

"Sorry," I said.

"There's nothing you could possibly be sorry for," he said. He was panting too and it made me feel proud though I hadn't done any of the work. Color was high on his bearded cheeks and his eyes were almost closed.

"You didn't get to finish your story," I said.

"Trust me. I finished."

We held each other's gaze and he smiled in a soft way that made my heart flutter. *Freaking orgasms, man.*

"I can't believe we did that," I said, getting situated as he did the same on the other side of the phone.

"I can't believe we didn't do that sooner." He sighed back into the pillows. "Would've saved me from a lot of cold showers."

I laughed and suddenly missed him with an ache in my chest. But that was normal. For our completely weird and not normal marriage. It didn't mean anything more. I missed people all the time. No big deal. No reason to worry. We were just getting more comfortable with each other. Which would make having sex easier. No big deal.

"So, tell me about your plans for the day," he said, and I smiled.

We so totally had this.

CHAPTER 13

GRETCHEN

"Friday I'm In Love" by Yo La Tengo

I was a mess.

Vincent was coming back to Green Valley tonight. I was jittery with nerves as I fluttered around the apartment, getting ready. I hadn't seen him in person since Halloween. We hadn't brought up our video phone sex though we had done it twice again since then. Why break tradition after all? This morning he had a super early flight in and I had to get ready for Friendsgiving.

I had pies to make.

And by make, I mean purchase from Donner Bakery.

It was the last day the SWS would see each other before we all split up for the Thanksgiving holiday. Ford and Jack were taking Suzie and Skip to meet up with their parents Carol and Joe in Washington. Roxy and Sanders were enthusiastically invited to join them since they didn't really have any other family.

"I doubt my parents know it's even Thanksgiving," Roxy had said.

Kim and Devlin were going to Devlin's folk's house with his whole family, and Kim's parents were joining them too. And I … I was going to go finally meet Vincent's family in New York. Elaine's family really. We leave first thing tomorrow morning. It was fine. I wasn't even nervous. What's not to love? I had nothing to prove. No shoes to fill. Nobody expected that.

So why was my stomach hurting?

A few hours later, he walked out the arrivals door and my heart jumped. Of course, he dressed up to travel. He looked so gorgeous, in his sharp suit and dark shades. He probably got pictures taken of him paparazzi-style because he just looked like a *Someone*.

He kissed my cheek after dropping off his carry-on in the back seat. "Honey, I'm home," he said low and grumbly.

I snorted but a weird tightness had me swallowing.

"I'm supposed to be ovulating on Thanksgiving," I said before pulling out of the pick-up lanes.

"My flight was fine, thanks for asking." I felt him studying my profile.

I swallowed. "It's not like we can just sneak off to a guest room while they pass around the potatoes."

"A little turbulence but not bad."

"I guess we could sneak out to the car." I glanced in the rearview mirror.

Vincent coughed then said, "Gretchen."

I hadn't looked at him since he got in the car. See. It was weird. Every time he left and came back, no matter how much we talked, it was still weird.

"Maybe we should just stay here," I said with finality.

"Gretchen, pull over into that cell phone waiting area."

I grumbled in defiance.

"Do it."

Reluctantly, I pulled into an almost empty waiting area.

"Look at me," he said.

Why was this so hard? I was supposed to be making a life with this man. Just look at him.

"Gretchen!" He half laughed, half yelled. He grabbed my face and turned me to him so my cheeks were smooshed between his palms.

"Wha?" I asked through pursed lips.

"It's just me. It's just you and me." He loosened his hold and his thumb moved over my bottom lip.

I collapsed onto his shoulder across the center console, letting out a long breath. Inhaling deeply for the first time since Halloween. Why was it so hard to breathe when he wasn't around?

"Sorry," I said into his shoulder. He smelled like flying. But also like him. I nuzzled into his neck. "I'm weird."

"You are not. This situation is just unorthodox." I loved how his chest rumbled when he talked. It was so damn comforting.

I nodded against him. He lifted my chin and kissed me. Just like that. It took me a second to even respond I was so taken aback. But then I was fully committed. We kissed deeply and fondly. Everything realigned with my soul and the anxiety melted out of me. The kiss gently tapered off. I leaned back and closed my eyes to take a second.

He gripped my hand and squeezed. I turned on the headrest to examine him. His mouth opened to speak as his gaze searched my face like I was one of his sudoku puzzles. He closed his mouth and cleared his throat before turning back to face forward.

"As far as ovulating goes. Let's take things one step at a time." His fingers tapped a pattern on his knee, and it occurred to me for the first time, I was ashamed to admit, that he might be anxious about today for his own reasons. "First we only have to worry about getting to Devlin's house. And ensuring he doesn't kill me and hide me in his basement."

"He wouldn't do that." I put the car in drive and headed out of the parking lot. "It's his studio down there. He wouldn't want to ruin the acoustics."

"I feel very comforted." Vincent put his hand on my shoulder and rubbed. Always touching. "What's with all the boxes back there?" he asked after glancing into the back seat.

"They're pies. We're in charge of pies," I said with a sharp nod.

He turned around again to count the boxes. "There's at least ten."

"I wanted to make sure our bases were covered."

"I thought it was just the SWS. Or did they invite more people?"

"Ten of us total. One pie per person. Shit, you're right. I should have gotten more. What if more than two people want chocolate mousse?"

"I've never seen you so tense." He turned back around in the seat. "You're freaking me out a little."

"I'm not tense. I feel better now with you here." I shot him a quick smile that he matched. "You've just never had a Jennifer Winston pie."

* * *

"THIS IS AMAZING—" We pulled up to Devlin's house, Vincent stared up through the windshield, craning to get a better look in the setting sun. "Look at this house. Who built this?"

"No clue." I shrugged. Just then Kim came running out the front door. "Oh no."

"Is that Kim? Is she okay?" Vincent asked.

I had just been reaching for the gun in my glove compartment, when I remembered that Vincent maybe shouldn't know about that. That would be a story for another time. We may not need it anyway. Plus, Kim looked more distraught than terrified. I straightened and put the car in park and jumped out, meeting Kim halfway up the drive.

"You can't come in," she said.

"What's wrong?" I asked. I lowered my voice and leaned in. "Need my gun?"

She shook her head, chewing on her bottom lip. My friend's eyes were red-rimmed and puffy. Her usually put together appearance was a disaster. She wore an apron covered in various colored splotches, she reeked of smoke, and it looked like only one of her eyes had eyeliner on it. She had a streak of black grease on her cheek and one curler hung from the back of her head.

"It's a disaster. One thing after the other has gone wrong." Kim's eyes filled with tears as she explained. "How am I supposed to help his mom make real Thanksgiving dinner when I can't … I can't even—" Her lip trembled, and she broke down in sobs. I pulled her in and let her shake against my shoulder.

But damn, I hadn't eaten all day. I'd been waiting for this meal.

"It's gonna be okay. Everything will be okay," I said. I shot a look to Vincent over her shoulder. He looked worried. "Let's get inside and assess the damage. Something has to be salvageable."

* * *

Vincent

NOTHING WAS SALVAGEABLE.

Absolutely nothing. How does one manage to both undercook and burn Brussels sprouts?

Gretchen and I meandered around the destroyed kitchen, taking stock. Pots and pans were stacked, covered in black goo, and the counters were covered in vegetable entrails and flour, and the air smelled of burned … *something.*

"We could have done it potluck style? Or catered?" Gretchen said.

The big guy, Devlin, scowled.

"I wanted to show that I could do it," Kim said meekly.

I stepped toward a giant covered dish. Maybe something in there was edible.

"No wait—" Kim called out.

Too late. The second I lifted the lid to whatever the food used to be, the contents exploded all over me. Literally exploded. Like something possessed. I had just enough time to turn my face away, but the steaming contents splattered all over my dress shirt.

Gretchen gasped.

Kim moaned.

Devlin was stoic, but if I had to bet, I'd put money on the fact that he probably smiled on the inside.

I stood there unable to process exactly what had just occurred.

"Shit!" I yelled as the heat registered. I pulled the sopping shirt away from my chest. It reeked of raw meat, gravy, yeast, and onions. And it was hot. "Ow, ow, ow."

Gretchen came over to scoop bits of what I really hoped was not partially digested food. She scraped off heaping clumps into another towel. "What is this?" she asked. "Or rather what was this supposed to be?"

"Oh," Kim moaned. "It was supposed to be a beef casserole. I thought, since everyone was having turkey tomorrow, I'd make something different."

Gretchen asked, "Why is it so angry?"

"I don't know." Kim tried to help but Gretchen shooed her away. "I thought I could just double the recipe, but I think … maybe that didn't work."

"We took it out when it started making noises." Devlin put a hand on Kim's shoulder protectively.

"Was the animal dead before you put it in?" Gretchen teased.

Kim's face fell. "Gretch. Of course. But maybe not totally defrosted? I dunno. I thought that it didn't really matter since the oven would cook it anyway. But then I added the biscuits on top and they made this sort of protective dome, trapping in the heat. It only got worse from there. We put the lid on when it really started to bubble on the surface. Shoot. Are you okay, Vinny?"

"Vincent," Gretchen mumbled quietly.

I nodded. My chest smarted a little, but no third degree burns as far as I could tell. "I'm fine, Kim. These things happen."

"No, they don't," she said. "Every single thing has gone wrong. I'm such a disaster. I can't even—"

"It's not your fault. I'll build you a new kitchen." Devlin pulled her in and held her.

He glared at me over her head like I had something to do with it.

Gretchen scraped a particularly meaty blob from me. I lowered to whisper in her ear. "The big scary guy keeps staring at me." I took pleasure in the little goosebumps that covered her neck.

"Don't mind Devlin. That's just his face," she whispered.

"I'll have to take your word for it." I looked closer at him. It was the first time I'd seen his face without something covering at least part of his features. His frown deepened and he reached for his neck reflexively but dropped his hand when he found nothing there. "Actually, he does sort of look familiar."

"He's a softie," she said and then touched my chin to get my attention. "But you probably shouldn't stare at him. Just to be safe."

"We're here with full bottles and empty bellies!" Sanders announced as he walked into the room holding up four bottles of wine, Roxy right behind him. Suzie, Ford, Skip, and Jack followed in after. Sanders's easy smile faltered when he surveyed the disaster behind us. When he saw me, his eyes widened. "Did you start eating without us?"

"Not intentionally," I said dryly. Though I could taste the uncooked bread and spicy meat that had flown into my face.

Roxy gasped and stepped forward, going to Kim who started moaning again. Suzie joined the women. Skip and Jack exchanged one wide-eyed look before backing up. "We'll just go wait in the living room," Jack said.

"Wait for me." Sanders chased after them. Roxy glared at his retreating form.

"Cowards," Gretchen called after them.

"Too many cooks in the kitchen and all that," Jack yelled, already safe in the living room.

Ford hovered near the door, looking longingly to where the guys escaped. One look at Suzie and he went to the counter. "I'll just start cleaning up a bit."

"It's not as bad as it seems. Nothing the SWS can't handle," Gretchen said. "We've dealt with much bigger messes than this."

Kim made a pathetic little groan.

"Look. There's got to be something left," Suzie said looking at a smoking pan. "Oh my, was that broccoli?"

"Brussels sprouts. They're still good." Devlin grabbed one and popped it into his mouth. He bit down once and stilled. A tiny muscle under his eye twitched as he swallowed. "Mmm. Good."

"Maybe we can see if the Front Porch is open," Gretchen said.

"The Lodge restaurant is open today," Roxy suggested helpfully. "Though, reservations are needed for the fixed holiday menu," she added after a thought.

"Y'all should just leave. Save yourselves," Kim said, tossing out her arms helplessly.

"Listen. This is fine. I'm sure we can scrounge some things up." Gretchen was already in the pantry grabbing a jar of olives. "We've got apps and 'zerts.

Those are the best parts of any meal anyways." Gretchen looked at the lost cause that was once my shirt and shrugged. She turned to Kim. "One day this will be a great story to tell."

"I don't want to be a laughing stock." Kim frowned. "We're still making fun of Ford for the Bruce Willis thing."

Ford opened his mouth, "Hey—"

Suzie elbowed him. He gave her a sheepish look and went back to wiping down the counter.

Kim slumped onto a barstool next to the kitchen island, completely deflated. A memory bubbled to the surface. I walked to Kim.

"This isn't so bad. I've seen much worse," I said as she looked up at me with watery eyes. I spoke low only to Kim but felt the rest of the eyes in the room on me.

"You're just saying that." She sniffed.

I shook my head with a laugh. "I wish I was. The first Christmas I met my first wife, Elaine's family, I caught the tree on fire with a batch of Baked Alaska and bad timing." Kim gasped and covered her mouth. I went on, "It was especially bad because it was a plastic tree."

Kim snort-sniffled. "Did they hate you?"

"Not even a little." I stepped closer and reached to put a hand on Kim's shoulder. When Devlin growled, I dropped it. "I was humiliated. Convinced I'd never be invited back. But they never brought it up. Well, not for a long time. Not until I made a joke about it many years later. Because they knew how important I was to her. I don't think a group of people has ever laughed as hard as we did when I casually mentioned the flaming Tannenbaum."

Kim laughed more, shoulders shaking, but that could have also been a sob.

"You know what I remember most about that Christmas?" I asked softly.

"The burning smell?" Kim asked looking up at me.

I laughed with a shake of my head. "No. I remember the love. The love from her family for her. That same love that carried over to me. It was a bond that only made us all stronger." My throat tightened at the memory. At how young we'd been then. How it was all so big and devastating in the moment but with time it became a funny memory. Especially now. "It feels overwhelming today, but it won't always feel so big. You know? In years, when you and Devlin are sitting around telling the story to your children or nieces and nephews, you'll only remember the love. I promise."

She glanced to Devlin who stepped closer. Her cheeks went fully red as tears balanced on her eyelids. "Okay."

"Devlin is clearly over the moon for you." I looked to the man. But he was only looking at Kim, hands balled at his side, obviously feeling miserable and helpless at the sight of her in pain. "That's all his family will care about."

Devlin came close and scooped her into his arms. "Mom and Dad, Wes and the girls, they all love you already. I told you. Definitely *you* more than me."

She smiled and let out a long breath.

"And the great news is you got all the bad luck out of the way with us. Tomorrow can only go better than today," I added and backed up.

"That's true." She sniffled and wiped a tear from her eyes.

When I looked up Gretchen was watching me closely. Her throat bobbed as she smiled at me.

"I'm sorry about your nice shirt," Kim said.

"No worries. It'll wash out."

"No offense, but you reek," Devlin said.

I took that as a cue to back up farther, especially when he wrapped Kim up in a big protective hug. "Thankfully, I packed an extra shirt."

"I'll go get this hot mess express cleaned up," Gretchen said, taking my hand. "Kim, you go take five to go decompress a bit, okay?"

Kim nodded and Devlin led her to the staircase. "I'll help," he grumbled, and she giggled with a blush.

"Suzie and Roxy?" The other two women stood straighter. "Get those hors d'oeuvres out."

Suzie saluted her and said, "Aye-ye, captain." Roxy rolled her eyes but got to work.

"Ford, get the guys and bring in the pies from my car." She tossed the keys at him. "And make those boys help clean up this mess. Hiding in front of the TV, the cowards."

I smiled at Gretchen. I liked bossy, assertive Gretchen. I guess that was redundant. I liked Gretchen.

I liked Gretchen so much I don't think *like* was the right word anymore. I looked at her and felt that same emotion tighten my throat when she first picked me up from the airport. I had been so close to telling her how much I missed her. How often I thought of her … but I hesitated. I didn't want to put pressure on this weekend when she was already feeling so much.

As Gretchen started to lead me away, Kim stopped before heading upstairs and turned around. "There's an extra shower downstairs, in the studio. In case you need it." She bit back a knowing smile at Gretchen before continuing on. Gretchen just shook her head and grinned.

What was that about?

CHAPTER 14

GRETCHEN

"Fast Car" by Black Pumas

Oh, I caught Kim's little look back there. I knew exactly what bathroom she was referring to. The infamous Eggplant Incident that started it all for Kim and Devlin. Not exactly sure what she thought would happen when I took him down here. It's not like schlongs just magically popped out in this bathroom.

At least not without prompting.

"Here. Take off your clothes." I leaned across Vincent in the tight space to turn the shower on.

"Well, if you insist," Vincent said from close behind me. The heat of him burned my entire back.

"Har har. There will be no shenanigans when you smell like you just had someone go exorcist all over you." I glanced over my shoulder as he unbuttoned his shirt.

This wasn't really a two-person job. I could leave any time. But I wasn't about to be the one to point that out.

"I could probably manage this alone," he said.

Dammit.

"I was gonna wipe some of those intestines off your pants. The steam will help keep them wrinkle-free." *Wow, smooth lie. Go me.*

He cleared his throat. "Sure."

When I turned around to face him, he had his shirt off, bare chest exposed.

"Lord help me," I said without thinking.

I had seen Vincent shirtless before, but had he always been this ripped? I felt like I would've remembered. His pectoral muscles were buff, dusted in dark hair. His shoulders and arms bulged with those little veins that only very fit men seemed to have. The ones that made you want to run your hands over the surface like a treasure map. He had strong flank muscles that would be very lovely to squeeze as I—

"What? More casserole catastrophe?" he asked. His abs flexed as he looked down. He smoothed his hands self-consciously down his front. Lord, to be those hands.

"You're just … You're very, uh, chiseled."

He shrugged but didn't deny it. *Cheeky little monkey.* "I have had some free time. And excess energy since we are … Well, since I'm not participating in bedroom activities."

"Oh. Makes sense." I sucked in my lips and nodded. The shower sure got it hot in here real fast. What was he thinking of now? And why was he looking at me like that?

I grabbed a washcloth and wet it in the sink, taking a moment to get my horn-dog eyes off his body.

"That was nice what you said to Kim. About Elaine." I turned around, grabbing his hand and pulling him closer.

He was quiet a moment then said, "Yeah. It was an unexpected memory that popped up."

"They do that from time to time, don't they?" I dabbed at something slimy on his neck. "What was she like?" I asked not quite meeting his gaze. I'd never been brave enough to ask about her before now.

"Elaine?" He looked over my shoulder into his memories. "She was wild. Always on the move. The definition of a free spirit. I could never predict how she was going to be or what she would want to do."

I stilled, a smile growing on my face. "Really?"

"Really." His own smile grew. "Why? What did you expect?"

"Beautiful, obviously." I focused on gently rubbing spots that weren't even dirty. He was literally about to get in the shower, but he wasn't exactly pushing me away either.

"That she was." His gaze remained focused on me, hard to read. We talked about most everything, but we didn't often discuss our previous spouses. Not really.

"But I guess I also pictured a very sophisticated socialite that dazzled at parties," I confessed.

"She could be that too. When she needed to be. But when we first got together, we weren't … I didn't have the success I have now. She and I met in design college."

"What were you like in college?" I asked.

"A nerd. Quiet. Painfully so. She dragged me around and forced me out of hiding."

"She sounds awesome," I said. It was hard to imagine Vincent as anything other than the confident man that I knew. Maybe his quiet confidence came with age and with Elaine's influence?

"She really was. So full of life. She lived … well, she lived like every day might be her last. Even before the diagnosis. Maybe on some level she always knew." His voice got tight and he cut himself off abruptly.

"She must have been so happy with you." I pressed a hand to his cheek. My own emotions were just there under the surface, making my heart race, stinging my eyes. His sadness cracked through the icy devastation I fought to keep at bay like a ship through arctic sea ice.

"I think so." He grabbed my palm and nuzzled into it. These touches would be the end of me. "Sometimes I still get so mad. I'll be fine and a wave of anger will slam into me. How completely unfair it was. She was so good and vibrant. My shooting star, bright and gone too soon." He looked away with a frown, still holding my hand.

I took him into my arms and squeezed with all my might. I couldn't offer any words of wisdom. There was no wisdom to tragedy far as I could tell. I knew the anger he spoke of. The helplessness of being the one left behind.

"I was a mess after Ephram was killed. I lost myself. Any sense of time. I forgot how to care for myself." He pulled back to listen to me but didn't let go. I focused on the little divot under his Adam's apple at the base of his throat. "It was a motorcycle wreck. But I knew, *knew*, that it wasn't an accident. I was caught up in some dumb shit as a kid. There was this motorcycle club Jethro Winston got me involved in."

"The Jethro Winston that SWS was founded around?"

"The very one."

"Am I going to have to talk to him?" Anger he'd never displayed flashed in his eyes, tendons in his neck flexed. It didn't seem like he wanted to just talk to poor ol' Jet.

I lay my hand on his chest. I rubbed a pec. *Oops*. "Nah. Jet's alright now. Married to Sienna Diaz believe it or not."

His eyes widened before narrowing.

"But he got out of the MC, the Wraiths. That's what Ephram and I were trying to do. We were getting older. We wanted to leave Green Valley, have some babies and raise 'em right. Away from all the trash, you know?"

He nodded. I still rubbed around his chest. Two handed now. How could I be talking about something so tragic while I accosted this man? But it was like being wrapped in a weighted blanket, it helped me get through it. He moved to rub my shoulders.

"But the Wraiths weren't letting Ephram go so easily. Man's pride and all that. He was killed the day before we were supposed to leave town."

He was killed because of my plans. I looked down when water splashed the back of my hand. I lifted a hand to my cheek, confused. I was crying. I didn't even realize it.

"I'm so sorry, Gretchen. Just so sorry." He wiped my other cheek.

"I used to think of nothing but revenge. But it was hurting me more than it was doing anything to the Wraiths. Plus, they're doing a pretty good job of killing themselves off."

He pulled me back into a hug. "You don't need to be mixed up with those lowlifes."

"I'm just saying, I get the anger thing. I have to force myself not to think about it or I get so damn mad," I said against his chest.

"Did you ever go to therapy?" he asked.

"Yeah. Group and solo. You?"

I felt him nod.

I let out a long sigh. "It helped. But, you know. People always describe it like you've lost your other half. But it's worse than that, isn't it? It's more like you're hollow. The only person who came close to seeing you completely for who you are was gone. So it's like you're walking around wearing a person-shaped shell. I'm not making sense."

He squeezed me. "You are. Because who are you when there's nothing left of you but the way strangers see you?"

I let out a long breath, tension melted out of me. "Exactly. I forgot how nice it is to talk about this stuff," I admitted.

"You can talk to me about him any time," he said earnestly.

"I want to hear about her too." I was surprised to find I genuinely meant it.

We poured our pain into each other—our healing too—into the other person who understood the breath-stealing unfairness of it all. We held each other until the steam started to curl the hair around my face and neck. I pulled back but he didn't loosen his grip.

He was looking at me in a familiar and yet confusing way. New but seen many times.

Desire wasn't a strong enough word, but it came close.

"I better go get your suitcase from the car. You'll need your shirts. At this rate you'll run out of hot water."

He tilted his head. "Or you can stay."

"What's that?" *Whose high voice was that?*

"You can stay. If you want."

"Are you asking if I want to see you naked?" I tried for nonchalance.

The tips of his ears were bright red, but otherwise he kept his features completely relaxed. As though it wasn't the most bonkers question ever. Then the barest twitch at the side of his mouth. What was he playing at? Trying to distract me maybe? He liked to fluster me. Sure. I was very clearly flustered but that's never stopped Gretchen LaRoe before.

"Aren't you curious too?" he asked.

The way he asked, the growl to his words, the implication that he was curious. I fought to match his carefree expression even as heat made my knees weak. I crossed my arms and scanned him head to toe. "Let's see." I shrugged like it mattered very little to me either way.

He kept his face neutral even as his hands went to his dress pants. Even as he slowly unzipped them. He held my gaze as he dropped them and kicked them off his feet and at me.

I had enough time to grab the pants before getting smacked in the face. They were still warm from his body. I folded them over my arm and looked pointedly at his briefs. I could already see the outline of him. His cock jumped as I studied it. This was a dangerous game of chicken.

"Keep going," I said.

This was it. This was when the tension was going to break with a joke. This was when he would turn around. Not me. A Scorned Woman never turned her back first.

He bent over, taking his briefs down with him before standing back up. Naked. Hands on his hips, eyebrows high waiting for a reaction. "There ya go."

Not a single muscle in me moved. Except my eyes. They flew everywhere. They moved from his strong thighs, his masculine bare feet, to his half-hard dick, to his chest, to his shoulders. Back to his dick. The dark hair from his chest leading down to his cock. Was it harder than the last time I looked? I always felt neutral toward twig and berries in general, but seeing Vincent now … I ached to taste him. The desire took me by surprise.

I was about to pass out.

"Your turn," he said. He took a step closer.

My eyebrows shot up. "I don't need a shower. Plus, my hair and makeup are all done."

He ran his hands down my exposed shoulders. I was wearing a simple, formfitting houndstooth dress, belted to emphasize my hips and cleavage. He'd not stopped looking at me since I picked him up. Not that I minded. Lord knew I hadn't worn this dress for the SWS.

"You don't have to shower." His Adam's apple bobbed up and down as he blatantly stared at my breasts. We stood inches apart. I licked my lips. Was I really considering this? With everyone upstairs? One zipper and he could get his eyeful. One zipper that might lead to so much more.

"You want to look at me?" I asked on a whisper.

"Just look. I'll keep my hands to myself." To emphasize the point he put his hands behind his back. The skin he'd been touching went cold at his absence. I looked down the length of him again. He was definitely getting harder. Desire curled like the steam around us. "You have no idea how long I've been dying to see your—"

"I brought down your suitcase so you could—" The bathroom door opened, letting in a blast of cold air and a clueless Kim. "Oh, God!"

Kim dropped the bag and jumped back out of the bathroom.

"Kim," I said, laughing at her mortified expression. Vincent's hands flew to cover himself.

"Shit. Sorry. Oh God. Not again." She slammed the door behind her. "I'm so sorry. This never happened." She yelled through the door.

We waited, staring at each other in shock but not without humor.

I glanced to the door. Vincent waited patiently. "I've traumatized her," he said quietly.

A quick peek confirmed I could still see her shadow under the door. "Kim?" I asked.

"I just wanted to say that I didn't really see anything. But also, congratulations, Gretchen."

I threw my head back and laughed.

"Believe it or not this is sort of a thing with her," I said, collecting myself. Welp, the mood was shattered now. "Get in the shower. I really am starving."

He held my gaze for a minute. "Don't think you're getting off that easy.

You owe me." He turned and walked toward the shower. I watched his ass, thighs, and calves as he went. I snapped his pants at him.

"Yeah, yeah," I said, simultaneously relieved and disappointed.

* * *

Vincent

"LOOK who was right about the pies after all?" Gretchen took a bite of apple pie. Her full lips sucking the fork clean.

"Mm-hmm," I said around another forkful of banana cream pie, taking my time. Gretchen watched me. I didn't have to look at her to know. I could picture the exact smug smile on her face.

"You're awfully quiet. Had a lot to say about all my pies earlier," she said.

"I would never complain about your delicious pie, Gretchen LaRoe."

One of the ladies to my left snorted. The desserts were spread out between the ten of us. Turned out there had been plenty of food, even though the main dishes were a lost cause. Plus, we had booze and pie and honestly, that's all anybody really needed.

"I'm so full of sugar, I could sneeze cotton candy," Suzie said pushing her plate and leaning back.

"Thank God for pie," Kim said.

"And water chestnuts wrapped in bacon," Suzie said.

"And charcuterie boards," Roxy added.

"And basically nothing that I made," Kim said. She looked around the room. "It's okay. I'm ready to be made fun of."

"I mean it was a disaster." Gretchen laughed.

"How'd you burned mashed potatoes?" Roxy asked.

"I lied. I'm not ready." Kim stood up. The others smiled at their laps but relented. "Let's play a game. Charades?"

"Can I be judge?" Devlin asked dryly.

"No. Everybody plays." Kim smiled sweetly at him in contradiction to the harsh demand.

"You can learn a lot about someone based on how they lose," Roxy said looking at me.

Message received. "I wouldn't know," I said looking back at her. "I don't lose."

She narrowed her eyes to hide a smile, which for her was as good as the real thing. "Oh, it's on now."

We moved to the living room, carrying our drinks and arranging ourselves on the massive wraparound couch that sat before an equally massive fireplace.

"No couples on the same team," Gretchen said. She was already passing around paper and pens to write clues on. We worked in silence for a while. Kim giggled madly before throwing her clues in the basket. She snorted at Devlin. He shot her a dubious look.

The first team was Jack, Kim, Gretchen, Ford, and Roxy. Sanders, Skip, Suzie, Devlin, and I made up the second team.

"Vinny first," Suzie called out happily.

"Vincent," Gretchen corrected but nobody acknowledged her.

"I should have known I'd be first," I grumbled good-naturedly. I grabbed a piece of paper from the basket and went to the front of the living room. I frowned at the clue. It rang a bell but I wasn't sure.

"I don't know what this is," I said.

"No talking," Roxy said louder than necessary.

I blinked at her. Sanders looked between us, smiling. If he had a tail it would be wagging.

"Let me see," Gretchen stood and came to me.

"Hey, no helping the enemy," Jack said.

Gretchen grabbed the paper, sticking out her tongue at him, before reading it. A devious smile grew on her face.

"Oh, who did this? This'll be fun." She looked around the room and chuckled. Everyone just looked confused, except Kim who looked like she was about to explode with giggles.

Gretchen leaned into me, breasts pressing against my arm, hot breath in my ear. "*Thoughts of you, my soul on fire …*" she whisper-sang.

It was too much, too soon after the incident in the bathroom. I could have cried at Kim's interruption earlier. All these weeks of temptation. All the months of wanting her. It was all reaching a boiling point. Throughout dinner, I couldn't take my eyes off Gretchen. We were so close to something, a next step.

"You think you can handle it?" she whispered and it brought me back to the here and now.

"I can handle it," I said out loud, focusing on my task before I made a fool of myself in front of her friends. Well more of a fool. Suzie had already asked how my nose was.

"No talking," Roxy said again.

I didn't even know how to do this. I frowned at the clue again.

"One minute, starting now," Roxy said looking at her phone.

I held up three fingers.

"Three words," Sanders yelled.

I nodded, pretending to hold a microphone.

"Singer? Song?" Skip asked softly.

I nodded as I started to hum, trying to remember the one-hit wonder. What a random choice.

When I looked up at my teammates, Devlin was glaring at me.

I looked back to the paper. Then back at Devlin. Then back at the paper. Everything clicked into place.

"Ohhhhh. I get it," I said louder.

"No talking!" half the room yelled.

I half danced, half hummed as I attempted to mime my way through the song. It was going terribly. I looked absurd but with Gretchen watching me with a smile that lit up her entire face, I couldn't care less. She was illuminating.

"Really?" Devlin looked at the rest of our team. Suzie had her lips sucked in and shook her head. Sanders and Skip shrugged. Devlin just sighed. "I'll put us out of our misery. 'Can't Look Back,'" Devlin said dryly. "By Erik Jones."

The whole room broke into laughter.

"I'm so glad you all find this hilarious," the big guy grumbled.

Kim went to sit on Devlin's lap and smacked his cheek with a loud kiss. "We do it because we love you."

He rolled his eyes but nuzzled into Kim, growling until she giggled.

The game went on and I continued to suck but it was fun. Everybody was having a good time. My heart felt full. I missed having this, friendships. I had cut myself off from many of the friends I'd shared with Elaine. But this reminded me how necessary this connection to others was. My gaze kept being pulled back to Gretchen. I couldn't take the distance anymore.

As the first round came to an end and groups broke off in conversation, I picked up my whiskey and moved to sit next to Gretchen.

"You're not on my team," she said with a tease.

Her cheeks were pink and her eyelids heavy. She was so full of life and beauty. I missed those lips. I needed to kiss her again soon. When she was ready. But I really hoped that would be soon. Before we were separated again.

"Search the rule book. I can fraternize with the enemy." I held her hand, running her fingers through mine.

"Why were you looking at me like that?" she asked with a curious grin.

I took her in again. She was just so damn breathtaking.

"Can you be more specific?" I asked. "Which time?"

She rolled her eyes. "Just now you were staring at me. And earlier."

I nodded seriously. My eyes moved pointedly over her throat, breasts, and shoulders, before returning to her face.

"What?" Blinking up, her smile slowly faded. "Is it pie?" She checked her cleavage. "I lose all sort of things to these girls."

I laughed and pulled her focus back. "You're just so beautiful," I said. "When you're laughing and smiling. Here among your friends, you're just so … astounding."

"Me?" She swallowed.

"Yes," I said seriously.

She looked to the side.

"Your huge smile. Seeing you laugh like that, with your whole body. Your hair, the way that dress fits your body, the way you tuck your legs under you. The arch of your eyebrow when you're trying to focus. Everything is just … really enjoyable to look at."

She rolled her eyes. Her cheeks were flushed, and it only added to her shimmer. She *shimmered.*

"Also." I leaned closer in to rub my nose up along the column of her neck, inhaling her scent. God, she always smelled so good. I couldn't get close enough, breathe her in enough. "Your breasts bounce a lot when you laugh."

She cackled and shoved my shoulder. "How much have you had to drink?" she asked jokingly but her chest rose and fell too fast and there was no hiding that gleam in her eyes.

"Just a little. After the moonshine incident, I'm going to take it easy."

"You just put it all out there, don't you?" Her tongue flicked out to lick her lips as her gaze moved over my face.

I didn't though. I kept so much locked away for fear of scaring her. If she knew how strong my feelings were, I didn't know how she would react. But I needed something.

"Gretchen," I used the voice. "We should go to bed."

Her slightly parted mouth closed as she swallowed before she nodded.

I grabbed her hand and stood, ready to give my goodnights. We were staying in one of several guest rooms upstairs. I'd have to make sure to keep her quiet …

Whispered conversation had Gretchen's head snapping to the left. She sat very still, focused, listening intently. I tried to find the source of her sudden interest, but it was just Devlin and Kim talking.

"I thought it was my water. I wasn't paying attention," Kim was whispering to Devlin.

He knelt in front of her, holding her hands. "It was just a sip. I'm sure it's fine."

Gretchen's eyes narrowed. I could practically see wheels turning. Earlier when I offered Kim wine, she declined saying she wasn't a big drinker. I didn't get what had piqued Gretchen's attention so thoroughly. Just a sip wouldn't really do any harm. As I watched Gretchen, her eyes widened. Slowly. Processing information I'd completely missed.

Kim must have felt the audience because she looked up and met Gretchen's gaze. Kim's eyes widened and her face went red. She fought to smooth her features, but it was too late. She gave Gretchen a half smile.

Gretchen sat stiffly, eyes flicking around the room, like she was checking to see if anybody else could see what was happening.

"Are you okay?" I asked her.

I squeezed her hand. Her mouth was pressed into a tight line. She brought her focus back to me. "Of course," she said lightly. Whatever connection there had been between her, and I was gone with whatever she just learned.

Kim whispered to Devlin, he looked at us and frowned. Or maybe that was his normal face. It was still hard to tell.

Kim gave one last look to Gretchen before standing up. "Hey ya'll, Devlin and I have some news."

The room went quiet, and everybody turned toward Kim. "We're having a baby!"

A gasp went up followed by a whirl of commotion. The SWS was wrapped around Kim a second later, the men clapping Devlin on the back and smiling.

"How far?" Suzie asked.

"About three months." Kim smiled, tears in her eyes. "We were going to announce it on Thanksgiving to our families. But shoot, y'all are just as much family too."

"I didn't even know y'all were trying," Suzie said, wiping a tear from her cheek.

"We weren't," Kim said.

"We were practicing." Devlin hauled Kim closer to him.

"It was a happy accident." Kim shrugged.

"Why didn't you say anything sooner?" Gretchen asked, brow furrowing. "Wait, were you pregnant in New York?"

"Just barely. I didn't know yet. I just felt punky." She shrugged again happily. "I didn't want to say anything too soon, just in case, and also because, well, I didn't want you to think I was trying to steal your thunder. With Suzie and Ford getting married." Suzie shook her head like Kim was crazy. "And you and Vinny, well. I know you're trying to uh, well … you know."

Gretchen shook her head and squeezed her friend's hand. "Don't even worry about that. We're all just so damn happy for you."

"Good." She sniffled with a little laugh. "I'm damn happy too." She wiped at her forehead and Devlin lowered back to the couch. "Maybe that's why I was such a mess today," she said.

"You're beautiful. Today and every day," Devlin said.

His raw honesty took me by surprise. Although after realizing that Devlin was the same guy that wrote "Don't Look Back," I guess I shouldn't be surprised by his soft side.

Kim looked back to Suzie. "Good thing the wedding is in December otherwise I don't think I'll fit into the bridesmaid's dress."

* * *

LATER THAT NIGHT, I held Gretchen close in the guest bedroom. Her head was on my chest. We'd been quiet a while, but she wasn't sleeping. Her fingertips lazily brushed my chest.

"Are you okay?" I asked.

She'd been effervescent the rest of the night, after the announcement. She must have thought leaving right after would have given a bad impression, so we ended up staying a few more hours. I was sure nobody else would think anything was wrong, but the second we came to the room, she had gone silent, like slipping out of one of her outfits, she changed completely. The heat that had taken over us earlier in the evening was replaced with silent introspection.

"Yeah," she said softly.

"How do you feel about the big news?" I asked.

It was hard not to wonder if she was feeling mixed up. When a baby had been our goal and yet we hadn't even tried. But speaking softly in the quiet night felt far more intimate than anything I'd initially planned. More important too.

"Thrilled. Kim and Devlin will make the best parents." I felt her smile against my chest.

I brushed my hand over her hair. Anybody seeing this would think we were a married couple. And we were in so many ways, legally of course, but also in our total ease around each other. Except the one big elephant in the room.

"But something's on your mind," I pressed.

"Yeah. Lots of things." She sighed and rolled on to her back. "I'm not really great at change. Kim pulled me aside later and asked if I was okay, like I would be mad. Am I really so terrible that people don't want to tell me happy news?"

There was a vulnerability to her that I doubted she'd share if the lights were on.

"Not at all," I said. "Your friends obviously adore you. Kim especially looks up to you. You're like their big sister."

"I have been a little hard on Devlin and the other guys in the past. I just wanted to make sure they were the right fit for my friends. They deserve everything wonderful, you know?"

I nodded, pulling her back to lie on my chest.

"It's everything I wanted, my friends being happy. But now things are happening so fast. We're all growing up."

"Growing up doesn't always mean growing apart," I said.

But I also knew the truth of friendship. When things got very bad with Elaine near the end most people stopped visiting and bringing food. I didn't blame them. It was hard to see her like that, a different person from the one so previously full of life, but tragedy was one of those things that revealed a lot about character. After she passed, I had no interest in maintaining those friendships. Not only because they reminded me of her but because a part of me never forgot their actions, regardless if I understood them. I guess I had been alone for a long time. Being here tonight had shown me just how much I missed that connection.

"I hope so. These girls, they're my life," she said.

I felt a slight sting of rejection, even though rationally I understood what she meant. I was in her life now. I was her family. Hopefully she would grow to feel that way. The way I felt about her.

She *was* my family now.

"And they still will be. No matter what happens," I said.

CHAPTER 15

GRETCHEN

"Such Great Heights" by Iron and Wine

I was back in Vincent's closet, sprawled out on the ottoman, staring at the beauty surrounding me. "I want to sleep in here."

He chuckled. "Feel free. But first, this one or this one?"

I brought my focus to the two ties he held up. "A tie? Is this that formal?"

I glanced down to my high-waisted plaid skirt, cream button-up, and sweater vest. Simple and understated. Except the delicious maroon plaid, full-length vintage trench coat I planned to wear over it.

"I always tend to dress up," he said.

"Even with family? I'm lucky if my uncles wear pants to thanksgiving," I said.

He laughed but I wasn't kidding. I came from a long line of backwoods folk. A sliver of unease coiled in me. What if this was a super swanky Thanksgiving complete with a catering crew and real silver?

"I have to stay on my game to keep up with you." *Damn, the things this man said.* He set down the ties and opened the top two buttons of his shirt. "But you're right. Ties are too much. They'll make fun of me. Plus, gravy on silk is never good."

I relaxed a little as I stood to examine my reflection next to his in the full-length mirror. I hadn't wanted to put too much pressure on today. Even if I was meeting the family of his perfect late wife. "Is this okay, what I'm wearing?"

He tilted his head, his eyes eating up the length of me. "Tall boots and a plaid miniskirt? Yeah, you look great."

"Okay but not like, sexy? I'm not going for sexy."

"Like you can help that?" When I blushed with a frown he added, "You look perfect. Classy and stylish as always." He pulled me closer to play with a strand of my hair.

Classy? I'd been accused of many things over the years but classy wasn't one of them. This man was delusional. And he was looking at me with that fire in his eyes again.

I fixed his perfect collar unnecessarily and said, "Hurry up. I don't want to be late."

We'd had to stop by his place on the way to dinner from the airport for a quick change.

"I only brought one other shirt to Green Valley. I didn't expect to have guts on me like I gave birth to an alien."

"Weird example," I said.

"That's what it felt like. But don't worry, they won't care if we're a little late."

"People say that but if they set the time, they care." I cocked my hip to give him a skeptical look. "Especially when a turkey is involved."

"Well maybe if you didn't have to check a bag for a long weekend trip, we would have more time now."

"Don't put this on me, mister." I stuck a finger in his face then dropped it. "Actually, no you're right." I stomped from side to side, whining. "But I had to make sure I wore the right thing. I don't want to look like I'm trying too hard, but I also don't want them to think that I didn't care."

"Gretchen. You look amazing. Always."

"Always? See, I know what you were going for there but now I just feel like average Gretchen. Not Gretchen meeting her in-laws." I flushed after realizing what I'd said. Really, I didn't want to make a big deal about this. I know I'm awesome, nothing to worry about.

"Technically, I'm not related to any of them," he said softly.

I chewed my lip. Oh right. Just the relatives of the woman's whose shoes I would never fill. I clamped my mouth shut.

"They're important to you. They *are* your family. I just want …" God, what did I want? They would never love me like they loved Elaine. I didn't want or expect them to. But I guess … shit, well I wanted to be good enough for Vincent. When did I even start worrying about that? Maybe when he put up with the humiliation of my friends? Or when he comforted Kim? Or when he looked at me like I was something wonderful. "I want them to approve," I admitted. And it was hard. I never cared two flying figs what people thought about me. It was hard to explain now, even as I admitted the words.

"Just be you. New Yorkers can smell insincerity."

"No pressure."

"Gretchen." He squeezed my hands. "I've never met anybody so sure of themselves as you."

The words warmed me, dissolving my worry. I lifted my chin. I was being ridiculous. "Tell me more about Elaine's sister."

"Nicole's a badass. She basically runs an entire children's unit at the ER. She raised Lauren by herself. She doesn't take shit from anybody."

"Okay, I like her."

"And she'll like you." He scratched his chin. "I just wish that she took more time for herself. I feel like she's been going since Lauren was little and then with Elaine, she did so much to help us. I wish she would take time for herself. I'm tempted to book a cruise or something and just send her."

"Would she like that?" I asked.

"No, she'd kill me."

I laughed. "Okay, so maybe we can think of something else we can do for her." The words had slipped out without thinking. I had meant them though. I didn't know this woman personally, yet I wanted to do something nice for her. I felt my superpower of getting involved itching already.

"Yes, *we* will," he said.

His eyes held that look again. That look that made my heart go ALERT ALERT! Danger, Will Robinson! Without meaning to my eyes flicked to the picture of Elaine on Vincent's vanity. He followed my gaze and then dropped his arms to his side.

He stepped back. "I just want you to be comfortable." He said it lightly, but he had tensed. Maybe he was thinking of Elaine now. I had to stop putting my boot in my mouth.

"Ugh, you're such a man." I teased, bringing the comfortable banter back.

I followed him out of the closet and downstairs. I grabbed my coat from the solid black oak coat tree.

"I'm sorry?" He chuckled. He pulled my trench closed and kissed my nose. "It's sweet that you're so nervous about this."

"I'm not nervous!" I frowned.

"Okay good, because they don't take kindly to strangers in these parts." I felt the blood drain from my face, and he threw his head back and laughed. "I'm kidding."

"I know," I mumbled. "And your Southern accent is still terrible."

* * *

OKAY, so I had freaked out for no reason. Vincent's family was amazing. Dinner was delicious. There were no glares, no probing questions. Not even passive-aggressive remarks about being good enough. I forgot how nice family felt. My own parents came sniffing around when they learned about Ephram's life insurance and vanished just as quickly when I made it clear I wasn't a viable source of cash. Dinner with Vincent's family was nice. Familiar but totally new to me. And oh my God, I had been so worried about fashion for no reason. I wish I'd worn leggings and an oversized sweater to fit in better.

Now we sat around Lauren and Troy's coffee table, digesting way too much food. The air was filled with the scent of spices and coffee. I sat in front of a gorgeous bay window that streamed in soft fall light while holding a sleeping baby Lainey. She was beyond beautiful. Perfect and round and mewing in her sleep. Vincent glanced to me from the couch with a sleepy half smile.

He looked so handsome. So at ease and different from that businessman I met so long ago at the Lodge. I loved how his dark trousers were cut just so that the absurd pumpkin socks he wore were visible above his shining dress shoes. Though he was relaxed and shoeless now as his long fingers drummed the back of the couch, listening to his niece, Lauren, talk about going back to work in two weeks.

Troy and Lauren looked tired but held hands happily on the couch. She was a beautiful young woman, not much younger than me maybe? She looked like her mother, with her slash of dark eyebrows, eyes that tilted elegantly, cheekbones to die for, and thin lips that had an air of being in on a secret. Troy was a handsome man who sported the same dark curls found on his daughter but cropped close, and a finely shaven goatee. Otherwise, Vincent was right, those Walsh genes were strong. I could see so much of their family in the little baby in my lap.

"She's beautiful," I said for the umpteenth time. I gently pressed my finger into her tiny palm so she would grip it tight. My chest ached with want. Basic, bone-deep desire that took me by surprise. Damn, Mother Nature. Damn hormones. Damn, perfect sweet babies that smelled so good. I inhaled her little head loudly and crossed my eyes in pleasure. "I feel bad that I have to steal her and keep her forever."

Lauren laughed. "You can take her. I'd love to sleep for more than three straight hours."

"Hey," Troy said without much fight.

"Just bring her back eventually," Lauren amended.

He tilted his head and yawned. "Okay, maybe just a few nights."

"Deal," I said.

Vincent came to stand above me. "Give me that baby. You're hogging."

I pouted but carefully handed her over.

Nicole sighed happily from the recliner. "And how is married life, newlyweds?"

She was a good ten years older than me, maybe more, but it was hard to tell. She aged liked I hoped to, with laugh lines and great hair. Hardly the stereotypical image of a grandma. Would her sister be as beautiful today? But I could sense that Vincent was right, she needed to remember the importance of taking care of herself, how therapeutic it could feel to pamper yourself for no other reason than to feel good. It gave me an idea. Which would have to wait as I fumbled with how to answer her question.

I looked to Vincent again, but he was lost in his grand-niece. If I felt a pull for procreation just holding her earlier, it was nothing compared to how my ovaries practically punched me in excitement now. Vincent's strong capable hands holding the tiny baby checked so many boxes I didn't even know were on the form.

I cleared my throat. "Good. We don't see each other terribly often."

I looked to Vincent to help but he was still lost in babyland. "I can't believe how different she looks already," he said.

When he smiled up at me his eyes gleamed with pride. My heart hammered with some emotion I couldn't figure out. Like hope? Longing? I was grateful for the subject change. I had expected it but still wasn't sure how to update our lack of progress.

"I know. She eats like it's going out of style," Lauren said.

"She gets that from me." Troy lifted his chin proudly.

Lauren raised an eyebrow. "I'd argue it's the several diaper changes a day that she gets from you."

He shrugged, looking at his wife in adoration.

"I'm not sure if we are allowed to ask this but, uh—" Nicole started.

"You can ask," Vincent said. He shot a knowing look to me and I stared down at the baby in his arms. No, this wouldn't be awkward at all.

"How goes your own baby making?" Lauren asked when her mother seemingly lost the courage.

"Things are fine," Vincent said.

I winced internally at the flat response. *Fine. Ugh.* I felt more than saw the exchanged look between mother and daughter as I brushed some fuzz off my skirt.

"What does that mean?" Troy asked. "Are you pregnant or not?"

"Not yet." I flushed despite myself. We haven't even had sex. Wasn't that *hilarious*?

"Well, don't put pressure on it," Lauren said. "I swear the more we wanted Lainey the harder it became. It was when we finally gave up that it happened."

I smiled at Lauren. I'd heard that before. Time would tell but there was a tiny voice that asked, *And if you can't give him a baby?* It was such an archaic thought. That my only value as a woman, as his partner, was to breed. I would have smacked anybody else that said that to me. And yet … and *yet*. Wasn't it interesting that our internal voices were the hardest to ignore? Our standards the hardest to meet? And by interesting, I mean incredibly frustrating. Because there was a part of me that thought the only reason that Vincent ever went for this bananas idea of marriage was because he wanted a baby. Though he made it clear that was not an issue for him. But how could it not be? Why me? Why now?

Lord, look at the man. He was built for this. He would be patient and calm. He would be stable and protective. More than anything, he would love that baby no matter who they turned out to be. I felt that truth in my bones like nothing else. I pictured him buying musical instruments, or styling hair with eyes narrowed in focus, or driving around to karate lessons, or getting into whatever video game they wanted. Whatever made his child happy, they would enjoy it together. They would be free to be who they were meant to be. And he would love them.

We went into this arrangement with the understanding that we wanted the same things, but … what if I wasn't enough? Just me.

"Excuse me." I stood and smiled. I went to the bathroom and took a few deep breaths in the mirror.

You are Gretchen freaking LaRoe. You kicked Iron Wraith ass. Grown men cower with one withering look. You don't take shit from anyone. You are a badass.

I glared at my reflection in the mirror waiting to feel the things I told myself.

We were going back to his house tonight. I was supposed to be here until Sunday but I felt like we were moving backward, not toward the same goal.

Vincent was waiting for me when I left the bathroom. One look and I knew he could tell something was off with me. He leaned against the wall, his dark brows furrowed, hands in pockets as he looked up at me. Could he see the worry and doubt warring inside me? It was supposed to be easy. This was the whole point. Or maybe that was the problem? Could something be too easy?

I opened my mouth to speak but he shook his head. He brought a finger to his lips to stop me. Maybe the baby needed quiet? I glanced to the living room where the others chatted happily.

When I looked back to him, he pushed off the wall. In one step he had me pressed against the wall, one arm leaned behind my head and the other pulled my hips against his. My mouth parted as he lifted my chin to look at him. "I can feel you all up in your own head."

I nodded once.

"Let's not talk for a while," he said.

He lowered his mouth to mine and finally, *finally* we were kissing again. God, he tasted better than I remembered. He was too good at this. Of course he was, he was amazing at everything.

I sighed and relaxed into him. Letting our mouths and tongues get reacquainted.

Except he wasn't perfect, was he? He was a little goofy, a little nerdy, a little handsy. I liked all that about him. I liked him *so* much.

He broke the kiss. "You're thinking too much. Have I lost my touch?"

There was a flash of vulnerability in the question despite his light tone.

"Not even a little." He was honest and so I would be too. "I was just thinking about how much I like you."

His eyes flared. He kissed me once softly, chaste. "I like you too, Gretchen LaRoe."

He lowered back to continue our slow and steady kiss. We spent time remembering how good this felt. We hadn't done this in some time. And in that time, we'd grown to know each other so well. It tasted sweeter, sexier, needier.

Just like his nearness, my worries melted away with his touch. This was what I needed. To feel his want for me, not the arrangement. I wanted to know … *something*. I couldn't put my finger on it, but we were getting closer to it. In the meantime, I needed him. Fully. Not a tease. Not a phone call.

We kissed as our bodies pulled closer, like we couldn't be close enough.

My arms wrapped around him. Desire blazed hot between us. I wanted more. *More*.

A throat cleared.

I pushed off the wall to straighten my skirt that somehow was now almost all the way up around my thighs. Vincent stepped back and adjusted himself subtly with a clenched jaw.

Troy looked between us, eyebrows raised.

"Gretchen and I need to head out," Vincent said, hands clasped low in front of him.

"Yeah," Troy said. He blew out a breath through his cheeks. "I would be jealous of all the heat coming off you two, but I have to pee. Also, I'm so exhausted and full of tryptophan I'm not even sure this isn't a hallucination."

He walked through us and into the bathroom.

"Gretchen."

Vincent waited until I looked at him. I was a little embarrassed but probably not as much as I should have been. I was too worked up.

"Time to go." It felt more like a command, thrilling me.

"Yes, sir." I winked and his eyes darkened. He crashed against my mouth again.

* * *

Vincent

I'D BEEN GOING about this all wrong. Not this kiss. This kiss was perfection. But this plan to take things slow. I'd been an idiot.

Gretchen was passion personified. She craved desire and fire. She was built to need and be needed. As we kissed, I formulated a plan. I said no dramatics early on. What the hell had I been thinking? Gretchen lived for the drama. For the thrill of the chase.

"Uhm, I'm coming out," Troy called from the bathroom.

I'd forgotten about him. I was taken away by the hot desire in her eyes. The second I took charge I remembered everything that made her hot. That's what I needed to be doing. Not taking it slow or giving her space. I needed her to see and feel how fucking wanted she was. I needed to show her that she was more than a contract or a plan. She was the air I needed to breathe. She was what kept me doing reps until my arms shook. I needed her and I needed her now.

I broke our kiss. Her lips were swollen and wet. Her eyes blinked rapidly to open. She swallowed, gaze moving over my face.

"Let's go. I have plans," I said flatly.

She swallowed and nodded.

It took me a minute in the bathroom before we could go say our goodbyes and thank everybody. Troy was already snoring on the couch by the time we left. It took another eternity to get back to my house. We took a taxi even though we could have walked the short blocks.

In the foyer of my house, Gretchen looked up at me, more subdued. Her nerves were getting the best of her again.

I didn't comfort her.

I put space between us and flattened my voice. "Give me your phone."

A crinkle of confusion appeared between her brows, but she did as I said.

"You're going to go upstairs and change into the sexiest outfit you packed."

When I looked up from working on her phone, she was chewing her lip, holding back a grin.

"And don't pretend like you didn't pack something sexy with that suitcase." I plied my tone with cold aloofness but only because I knew it would drive her wild. Her eyes narrowed but she didn't stop me.

"Then, when you've gotten yourself all done up for me, you're going to meet me here in an hour." I handed her phone back, the map app open.

There was nothing quite as satisfying catching Gretchen off guard. She opened her mouth in confusion, but I spoke first.

"I didn't say you could ask any questions."

Her narrowed eyes went hazy. I was going to drive her so out of her mind, there wouldn't be room for doubt. There would only be begging.

She hesitated, like she wanted to test this new side of me.

"Go," I said sharply.

She sucked a tooth before deciding better or arguing. She turned and left. I watched her ass as she went up the stairs. She stopped to look back, catching me in the act. Her mouth curved in a satisfied smile knowing she still wielded her own fair share of power.

"And Gretchen?"

The light at the top of the stairs back lit her perfect figure like a dame in a film noir. She tilted her head in question. She didn't speak though. She was good at following directions. She was going to be so much fun. I ran a hand over my mouth. "Don't be late."

She bit her lip before continuing on her way. Though she moved a little bit faster.

CHAPTER 16

VINCENT

"Need You Tonight" by Welshly Arms

The bar was packed for a holiday. Businessmen sat around smoking and chatting as beautiful women mulled about or sat in laps. This establishment was not a cheap place to get into. I called ahead to let them know to expect her. But luckily, this was also a place that didn't ask any questions. Worry gnawed at me when I didn't immediately see her. Gretchen was the first place my gaze always went in any room. What if I went too far? What if she couldn't find—

A blond woman at the bar caught my attention. She stirred her drink, her foot tapping with impatience. But it was her knockout figure that kept my focus. Breasts and hips and curved waist. A softly pointed chin and heart-shaped face, full lips, and smooth skin. My blood thrummed in excitement.

She wore the wig from Halloween. I fought a smile. Only Gretchen LaRoe would pack that "just in case." It was a confirmation that she wanted these games as much as I did. Her makeup was dark and smudged around her eyes. She wore that dress from the night of the engagement party. That *damn* dress. She packed that too knowing what I'd confessed to her. Knowing she could torture me with it. A simple black dress high on her thighs and with a square cut neckline that barely contained her breasts. It was a second skin, showing every beautiful line of her curvy body. With her new hair, the skin of her neck and shoulders were on full display. I was going to lick every inch of that skin before the night was over.

Several businessmen around the bar shot her looks, gazes lingering on her figure. I had to act quick before the circling sharks moved in. I ran a hand over my face, collecting myself before I made my way over to her. I leaned behind her, trapping her by placing my arms on the bar on either side. She stiffened but didn't turn. I dropped my mouth to the shell of her ear, watching as chills spread down her arms. Her sweet scent of roses and something sharper like spice heated my blood.

"You think I wouldn't find you," I whispered in her ear. Her head turned toward me slowly, she opened her mouth to speak. Our mouths were so close her warm breath caressed my lips. "Don't bother," I said. "I know exactly who you are."

The bartender shot us a quick glance, but they'd probably seen much weirder things than this.

I spun her on the barstool until she faced me, still trapped by me. She watched me skeptically but not stopping me. I pushed her knees wide so I could stand between them. Her dress scrunched up her smooth thighs. I gritted my teeth but let her watch as I devoured every inch of her until I met her gaze. Her head was tilted back to look up at me exposing the long smooth column of her neck.

"What—"

I grabbed her chin and tilted her face up to mine. "I didn't say you could talk."

I felt eyes on us. When I looked up a group of businessmen watched us with greedy eyes. I glared at them, practically snarling, until they looked away.

Gretchen quickly hid a smile when I brought my focus back to her. She wanted this. The fierce overprotectiveness. The wildness of the chase. She wouldn't have admitted it out loud but her blown pupils said enough.

"Get your hands off me." She glared but color rose to her cheeks. My fingers curled around the long column of her neck as she looked up at me.

"I know you're working undercover on …" I hesitated. "Project *Cattywampus*." I emphasized her absurd safe word, reminding her that she could stop this at any time.

She bit back a smile. "You won't get me to admit that." Her swallow moved under my thumb, her gaze burning into mine. "I've been wanting this meeting for a long time."

I lifted my chin, running the pad of my thumb over her lips. I was wildly aroused with this game, and she slid perfectly into her role. The hardest part was going to be, well, walking with *my* hardest part.

"This is what's going to happen," I said quietly in my most commanding voice.

Her nostrils flared.

"We're going up to my room. You're going to do exactly what I say. Trust me, you don't want to cause any scenes."

"Or what?" Her defiant gaze flicked to my mouth and back to my eyes.

I leaned closer to her ear and brushed my lips up the column of her neck. "I'll be forced to teach you a lesson."

She trembled under me.

I threw money on the bar. The bartender nodded.

I grabbed her arm. She roughly pulled it out of my grip. "I can walk on my own."

"Don't get any ideas," I warned.

As we waited for the doors of the elevator to open, I put a hand around her waist, pulling her close to me. *Mine*.

Even my internal voice was getting into the game now.

Once inside, I pushed the button for the floor with the room I had booked last minute. As soon as the doors closed, she broke out of my protective hold and went to the other side.

"Get off me." She gripped the handrail behind her, her chest heaved, breasts practically spilling out of her dress.

I was on her in a second. I caged her in, not quite touching. "You will listen." I glared down at her. "You may be able to tempt the others, but you can't distract me."

Her eyes widened a fraction before she freed one hand from behind her. She slid her palm up my chest, before grabbing the tie I put on when I changed to meet her. She tugged it free and wrapped it once around her hand, holding my gaze as she roughly pulled my face closer to hers.

"Is that right? You seem pretty tempted to me." She flicked a look to my dick, pressing hard against her hip, giving me away. I wasn't even sure when I'd leaned into her. Her coy smile taunted me. My growl was the only warning before I slammed my mouth against hers, swallowing her gasp of surprise. A fraction of a second later she responded in kind. Mouths wide. Tongues pushing and teasing. Always battling for dominance.

This was the opposite of the kiss I greeted her with at the airport. This was rough and wild and yet still part of who we were. I kept in character, pretending to be going against my orders, overtaken by how bad I wanted this temptress. I groaned as I rocked into her. She writhed against me as I fucked her mouth with mine.

The elevator dinged as the doors opened to our floor. I stepped back, glaring and panting.

"Fuck," I swore and wiped my mouth with the back of my hand. "Let's go," I grabbed her and dragged her out as she pretended to be mad about it.

"I'm not going anywhere with you." She dug her heels in, crossing her arms.

I curled my lip. "Have it your way."

Her eyes widened as I came at her. I scooped her easily up onto my shoulder, so her heels kicked in front of me and her ass was in my face.

"Put me down," she squealed with a laugh.

I smacked her ass. She gasped but then moaned when I rubbed to soothe the area.

"I did warn you."

I clenched my jaw as I carried her to the room, resisting the urge to bite her. This was going to be harder to keep up than I thought. I was ready to take her, games be damned. But I had planned hours of exquisite torture. And I never cut corners.

* * *

Gretchen

VINCENT SET me down in the threshold of the hotel room. He smoothed his tie back in place and attempted to fix the hair I'd roughed up. Not that I fought him, not really. I was heavy with longing. That kiss almost broke me. Being carried like I was no more than a sack of flour … well, let's just say yet another *new kink unlocked.* Part of me wanted to call off whatever this role-play was and beg him to hurry and get inside me already, but I was having way too much fun.

I stepped farther into the hotel suite. Behind me the deadbolt locked with an ominous click.

"Get on the bed," he said in that raspy demanding voice he'd used when he came up to me at the bar; still him but with a hint of ferocity that buzzed just under my skin.

I crossed my arms and shot him a look.

"Umm." I looked to the two queens that filled the space. "Which one?" I asked laughing a little. Too many beds for once.

Vincent shot me a secret smile. "Sorry it was last minute," he said lightly. "They were out of kings."

It was nice to share this moment of humor, even in the middle of this role-playing. It was a reminder that under it all, it was still just us. *Us*. When had I even started considering Vincent and I, an "us"?

Seriousness hardened his features, and any hint of smile was long gone. His mask was back in place. "Sit."

He pushed my shoulders until I sat on the bed closest to the window.

"Yes, sir," I said.

Was it archaic and wrong? A part of me wondered if I should be ashamed to be manhandled and bossed around. But more of me fucking loved every second of it and told that voice to go sit in the corner for a while and cover its ears. And since when did I worry about feeling shame? I loved his commitment to the character. I loved that safety in feeling completely lost to this pretend fantasy. I was an evil seductress, he was … well, I wasn't exactly sure who he was trying to be but I didn't care. This was fun and sexy as hell. I really liked his whole evil mafia boss vibe.

Vincent took his time taking off his suit jacket, then hanging it in the closet. He wore a fitted gray vest over his crisp white dress shirt, both were tailored to perfection, emphasizing his cut physique. I thought for sure we were going to get naked soon, but he was delighting in this slow torture. He walked to the small bar and poured himself a couple fingers of whiskey. The dress pants and vest were even a sight to see from behind. I sighed without meaning to, tilting my head as I took in my fill. He turned around and raised an eyebrow at me. I straightened into a scowl as he took a long sip. His Adam's apple worked the column of his throat as he swallowed.

He set the glass on the table, never taking his eyes off me as he spun a chair to face the bed. I shivered in anticipation for whatever he had planned. I loved having control in every situation but this. Now, I wanted to lose all control to him. I wanted to do everything and anything he demanded of me.

He unbuttoned the cuffs of his white dress shirt that pulled tight across his shoulders and biceps. Tortuously slow, gaze still on me, he rolled them up to just below the elbows. Veins popped out of the back of his hands as his fingers worked deftly. Those beautiful strong fingers were calloused but manicured with clean trimmed nails. Another example of how Vincent was a contrast of the uber masculine mixed with sophisticated class. I wanted to suck each one of those long fingers. I wanted to watch as they explored me.

He cleared his throat, breaking my hypnosis.

"Stand up and spread your legs," he said.

My chest rose and fell. The evil man was already torturing me. I scowled. "You can't tell me what to do."

Even though he kept the mask of the angry mafia boss—or whatever—his cheek twitched in what felt like humor or approval. He wanted games? I could play his games. Fuck, I would always play his games.

"You're wrong about that." He pulled me off the bed and kicked my legs apart, pushing my dress higher up my thighs. "You'll learn."

I growled even as heat pooled at my core. If the very clear evidence of his own arousal wasn't between us, I might have been embarrassed at how hot this was for me.

He caught my gaze and lifted my chin. "I'm only a man."

His calloused hand wrapped around the back of my neck, sending chills through me, hardening my nipples. His nostrils flared as he licked his lips. He held me in place as his other hand moved from my shoulder, down my arms, before he dipped his fingers in between my breasts. He splayed his hand across my rib cage and down my hips, exploring every possible inch.

"I'm not wired," I said, managing to catch on even though my head was fuzzy with want.

"I'll be the judge of that." He dropped to his knees in front of me. As he went down, he brought the zipper on the back of my dress with him.

My dress remained held up, but it wouldn't take much for him to tug it off. I stepped back. Looking down at him, I placed a heeled foot against his chest. His nostrils flared. He looked up at me as his rough hands smoothed around my ankles, unbuckling my shoes. His thumbs brushed the arches of my feet, shooting electricity straight to my core. He tossed my heels to the side. "Those could be dangerous," he said.

He continued to slide his hands higher up my calves. With my legs spread, it felt humiliating, intrusive, and so fucking hot. We both knew that I was the one with the power here.

After all, he was the one on his knees.

His hands continued higher. When his fingertips tickled the back of my knees, they almost gave out. I reached for purchase but only found his head to hold on to. His dark hair stuck out between my fingers as I gripped.

He looked up at me, watching my every reaction, as his hand moved higher and higher, teasing every second out of this. His hands encompassed my thighs and when one fingertip brushed along the super sensitive skin of my upper thighs to brush against my wetness, we both gasped.

Surprise. No panties for me.

"Gretchen." It was a curse as he temporarily broke character. He cupped my ass and dropped his head to my pelvis. His thumbs kneaded my hips as he held me for dear life. "I need a minute," he said in his regular voice.

I smiled in victory, as he collected himself. I scratched my nails through his hair, loving the vulnerability of this position. After another few seconds, I said, "I don't know who Gretchen is, but you're falling down on your job, sir," I said sharply.

He glared up at me, mask back in place.

He stood, adjusting himself with a wince. Good Lord, I knew the man was packing but I'd never seen him this hard. The shape of him was clear against the dress pants that could hardly contain him. I couldn't wait to see him free of its confines.

Roughly he palmed his pants, as though willing control. "Eyes up here."

He backed up to sit in the chair now facing the bed. He lounged, legs sprawled, eyes hazy. He grabbed his drink with lazy indifference and waited. One casual finger lifted from the glass to point to the area in front of him, at the foot of the bed. "Stand there."

I stepped forward. He sat there like a spoiled prince on a throne.

"Take off that fucking dress." He sat perfectly still, but his jaw was clenched tight.

I debated my options but to be fair, I did owe him a show after the tease in the shower. One arm at a time, I slowly pushed the tight dress down my body, wiggling maybe more than necessary to get out. I arched my back, legs straight as I bent over to push it off the final inches. I rolled back up and kicked it off and at him like he did with his pants yesterday.

I thought he'd try to catch the dress, but he'd set down his drink and both hands now white-knuckle gripped the arms of the chair.

Chin lifted, I stood in front of him in only a sheer black bustier. It cinched my waist and pushed up my breasts. It was an expensive purchase but the look on his face made it worth every penny. I was even more aware of how ready I was as the cool air reached my wet core.

"Are we going to keep pretending you have any control here?" I asked as I ran my hands down my body and hissed in pleasure as I passed my exposed center.

If he heard me he showed no signs. He sat wound as tight as a spring staring at my breasts. I think I may have knocked him out of the game. I ran my hands over the tops of them where they spilled out. I luxuriated in the way my soft skin felt but more in the way his eyes went wild at the action. The muscles of his arms twitched from holding on so hard.

"Things not going as planned?" I stepped forward and straddled his lap, one leg on each side of him, breasts under his nose, my wet heat pressing hard against his erection through his pants.

He went mysteriously silent.

We both moaned as I ground against him.

I lifted my hips up to make room for my hands to get to work. I undid his belt, unzipped and found him through the layers of clothing. He panted as he watched me work. I grabbed his incredible length and pulled him free with effort. I gently caressed the soft tip with my thumb.

"Gretchen," he ground out, dropping his head to mumble against my chest.

I was too far gone now to realize the game had paused. He grabbed my wrist to stop me from stroking up and down.

"I can't—" he broke off.

"You don't have to." I kissed his temple, his forehead, down his nose, until I reached his mouth. He kissed me back with fervor. I directed his hands to my backside, breaking our kiss before I made room for him. I lined him up, teased myself with him. Got us both wet and ready.

"I meant to—hours of—" His hands gripped so hard it was sure to leave bruises on my waist and I couldn't care less.

"Shh." Our eyes locked as I slid down onto him. "You did perfect."

"Jesus," he swore. "You're so good. You're so—"

He lost coherent speech. I lifted up and dropped back down. I rocked forward and back.

"Thank you," I said.

His hand gripped me harder as he thrust up to meet me. He palmed the tops of my breasts, but it wasn't enough. "More," he grumbled as his hands fumbled with the hook and eye clips on the back of the bustier.

A second later I sagged in relief as I was freed. He'd gone quiet. When I looked down to him, his eyes were wide, hands hovering in front of my now free chest. He looked like he'd finally found the hidden treasure.

"I imagined … so many nights … even better." His fingers flexed impatiently.

I looked down to where he still *wasn't* touching me. My back was arched because of the position on his lap, pushing them up, my nipples were hard from having him inside me. I had to admit, I did look spectacular.

"Aren't you going to touch me?" I asked breathy.

He made a sound somewhere between a defeated sigh and a groan. He attacked me. I held his head, trying not to laugh as he devoured me. He cupped and sucked. He pressed them together to rub his face in them. He licked them like ice cream. At first it was funny, but soon I couldn't sit still. To see him so obsessed with me, to know he went through all this trouble with the hotel, somehow knowing it was exactly what I needed to get out of my own head. It was all too much.

"Vincent." I ground against him, feeling full. "More." I needed more, deeper.

"What do you need?" He left my breasts to pull my hips snugger to his and lifted his own hips to hit that perfect spot.

"Yes. That." I tried to chase that spot he was hitting, but the angle was too hard to sustain in this chair, with my knees digging into the uncomfortable sides. "More."

"What?" he asked. "I'll give you whatever you need."

"Arugh." I rode him harder it wasn't enough. My knees began to ache. "I don't know." I grew frustrated, but I didn't want to ruin this moment. It was a slippery slope when I started to think.

"I've got you," he said.

He stood up, carrying me by my ass, to drop me back against the bed. He never left me for even a second as he set me back against the pillows. He pressed his whole weight on top of me, pushing himself deeper. It was instant relief. There was nothing else in the world except everywhere our bodies met.

"Yes," I called out.

He sat up and grabbed my ankles and hooked them behind his back.

He lowered his hand to tease me. The sensitive nerves reacted but it wasn't what I needed. He needed to get on top of me again.

"Too much." I brushed his hand away. He brought his hand to grab my foot instead and hook it over his shoulder. He bent forward to lay on top of me, stretching me, pushing deeper into me to hit the spot.

I gasped in relief.

"Like this?" he asked, panting with focused determination.

"Yes," I called out.

There was no shame as he discovered what I needed. There was no hesitation to tell him. He was still in his clothes, and I was naked and writhing against him.

It was impatient and perfect.

This set him off, his hips pumping into me. "Fuck, Gretchen."

"I know." I dug my nails into his shoulders and back, rocked to meet him. We slammed against each other. Taking what we'd needed for months, sweaty and uncoordinated and loud. We were ravenous and greedy. We used each other. The more pleasure he took from me the more I gained.

"Oh God," I screamed and came hard without warning.

He was a second behind me, like he'd been holding out as long as he could and my pleasure broke the final thread.

He collapsed onto me and I *oofed* with a little laugh. He rolled off me but pulled me on top of him as he went. As we panted, he softened and slipped out of me and the kinky little perv that I was, loved the feel of him leaking out of me. I slid against him. We were hot and it would get uncomfortable soon but right now I relished in feeling used and marked.

"You'll never learn my secrets," I huffed out between breaths.

He chuckled, nuzzling into my neck. "Eh. I was never very good at this job."

CHAPTER 17

VINCENT

"I'm On Fire" by AWOLNATION

It was spectacular. Finally being with Gretchen had been everything I'd been waiting for and then so much more.

Maybe it'd been way too long since I had mind-blowing sex, but I doubted it was just that. It was her.

I rolled Gretchen onto her side so I could spoon her. I hooked my leg over her and buried my head into her neck.

"I miss your hair, can you take this off?" I asked, tugging on her wig.

"Hmm. Yeah, but underneath is horrifying," she said slurry with sleep.

"Please." I whined. "I want to see the real you. It can't be comfortable to sleep in that."

"Fine. But only because I have to get up to pee." She ran to the bathroom, legs crossed awkwardly. I chuckled before cleaning myself up, stripping down to my briefs, then pulling the sheets back on the bed we hadn't defiled.

"Perk of multiple beds," she'd said when she returned.

She stood there naked, unabashedly. Her hair was in fact frizzy and wild. It reminded me of how girls had styled their hair in high school. Adolescence desire came back in a flash. Just like it had when she first revealed her breasts to me.

I devoured the image of her from head to toe. "Are you done?" She pretended to be annoyed by my obsession with her body, but I could tell she loved every second of it.

"No." I kneeled and shuffled toward her, cupping her breasts to nuzzle her chest, feeling myself harden already. "I feel like I'm fourteen and I just discovered my first JC Penny catalog."

She snorted. "JC Penny, huh? You dig old lady bras and high-waisted jeans?" She pushed me down onto the bed and got into the sheets next to me with a contented sigh.

"Hey, it was pre-internet and I had to work with what was available. Plus, some of those models—" A pillow hit me in the head.

I pushed it away to pull her into another spooning position. I couldn't help it. My hand squeezed her breast before running up her thigh and ass and waist.

"Argh," I ground out. "I want you again."

"Okay, just don't wake me." She yawned before chuckling. "Aww, we're like a real married couple now," she said.

I felt fevered again. It couldn't be normal to want her this bad so soon. Sex with Gretchen had the opposite effect that it was supposed to. I was supposed to feel some relief to this constant aching desire for her. Instead, it was like only having just one lick of ice cream on a hot day. I just wanted to devour her.

"You really are a boob guy, huh?" she asked and smacked my greedy hands back.

"I didn't think I was. I think it's more that I'm a your body guy."

"You," she said with a smile I heard more than saw.

"I'm also a Gretchen's ass guy," I said squeezing her bottom to prove my point. "And a Gretchen's stomach and hips guy." My hands roamed there next. "And a Gretchen's …" My hand went lower as she gasped out.

"Vincent," she begged but I wasn't sure if she wanted me to stop so she could sleep or keep going.

"I don't know who Vincent is, but I'm not done with you yet." I lowered my voice, lacing it with demands.

She stilled, waiting to see what I'd do next. Maybe I should let her sleep, it had been a long couple of days. But I wasn't feeling so kind. And I didn't think she wanted to be coddled.

"You can try and stop me, Miss Cattywampus, but I always get what's owed to me."

I moved my fingers in and out of her, as my erection nestled in between her backside.

She gasped, I felt her grow wetter with my words. "God, I need a better safe word," she said but she was gone in a haze of desire again. It made me feel a million feet tall to bring her to this point so fast.

"Nobody else can take what I want," I growled.

She shook her head, eyes closed.

"You're mine. And nobody else can fucking touch you."

"Just you," she gasped.

I gently bit her shoulder then sucked the area roughly. I was playing a character, but I also wasn't. I was free to reveal this dark side of myself to her. If she only knew how much of this playacting was true. "I get you any way I want and whenever I say."

She nodded, before she threw her head back, turning her mouth toward me so we could kiss. Our tongues clashed. She was hot and soaking. It took no effort to slide back into her and take her again.

Later, when we were done and sated, for now at least, we cuddled back in the first bed. She ran her hands through her hair—now even more wild. "We ran out of clean beds."

"There's at least four back at my place. Just saying," I said.

"Oh, that's true." She smiled against my shoulder.

"Listen, I've been thinking," I said, tracing the mark I'd left on her.

She gasped. "I'm so sorry. Are you okay?"

"I walked into that one, didn't I?"

"You really did."

I sat up on my elbow to look at her in the dim light of the bedside lamp. I took in her soft blinks and flushed cheeks and lips puffy from kissing. Her brow furrowed when she saw my serious look.

"I thought I could do this whole back and forth thing. It doesn't feel like it's working." I wanted to say more, that I couldn't stand being away from her. So, I told her some, but only part of it. Baby steps. We could manage these feelings with baby steps.

Her eyes widened a fraction before she schooled her features. Realizing she may have misinterpreted what I meant, I added, "It might be easier if we didn't have so much distance between us."

She nodded and chewed her lip, casting a worried glance to the side. Then seeming to decide something she said, "It's hard for me too. I feel like we're starting new every time. Or maybe not new, but like we have to re-walk the same tracks."

"What if you stayed in the city for a while? I don't have to be in Green Valley as much for work, but I want you here with me. Just until we get closer to Christmas and the wedding. I know it's a big ask, with all your properties and driving—"

"Okay." She sucked in her lips. "I mean I think I could make it work. I'll check my schedule."

I couldn't help my giant grin. Her quick acceptance stroked an already inflated ego. "And on that note." I was a little more worried about my next request. "How do you feel about maybe not trying so hard to conceive? I want to spend some time getting closer to you. And maybe more of this." I shrugged. I acted casual, but inside I wanted to scream, *I just want you.* The baby wasn't the point. I would tell her. Eventually.

She smiled. "We just had unprotected sex but who am I to point it out?"

"If it happens, I'd rather it be because we are enjoying each other," I said. "Not because of a schedule. I know that may not always be an option but for now let's just take more time for us."

"As it turns out I've really been enjoying us," she said softly.

"So, you're okay?" I asked. I hadn't been sure what to expect. I of course would love to make a family with Gretchen, but to think we could attempt it so casually had been naive.

"To be honest, I feel some relief. I was putting too much pressure on it. Because how could I not? It's a *baby*." Her eyes widened on the last word.

"I know. We've been a little too clinical." I squeezed her closer, also feeling a measure of relief. "Let's spend time together and just have a little fun. I don't have to travel for a while, at least until January, and I know you'll have to do things for the wedding."

"As long as we're back in Green Valley by Christmas." Her eyes widened as she sat up. She chatted excitedly which caused her newly revealed breasts to bounce. She mentioned something about getting more clothes shipped out. I missed most of what she was talking about because my brain short-circuited.

"Vincent, are you listening?" She used a finger to lift my chin.

"Absolutely." I pulled the sheet over her chest. "What did you say?"

It was a little disorientating. I don't remember ever being so obsessed with somebody. It must have been like this with Elaine in the beginning and I just forgot. We were so young when we met, maybe it was just different. There was a lot more hesitant exploration and quiet fumbling under blankets while my roommate snored in the bed next to mine.

There wasn't this primal desire that only came with the confidence of knowing exactly what you needed to get off, or the all-consuming goal of bringing the other person pleasure, not just trying not to come too fast.

"It's Christmas time in NYC. Can you take me to all the touristy places?" She clasped her hands under her chin with big puppy dog eyes.

"Touristy places, huh? I dunno." I speculated for show but honestly it sounded nice. I imagined Gretchen in a cute red hat and snowflakes falling on her lashes as we stood in front of the Rockefeller tree. My heart raced. I *really* liked the idea of it. "I suppose. But you'll have to make it worth it."

"Yes, sir."

I groaned and flopped back onto the pillows. "You have to stop saying that in that tone of voice or we may never sleep."

"Yes, sir," she repeated. She shoved me away when I reached for her. "I'm too giddy to sleep now. I feel like you're asking me to go steady. It's all happening so fast," she teased in an over-the-top voice, fanning herself.

"Says my wife after our kinky spy-roleplaying sex."

Her eyebrows raised. "Oh, is that what we were doing? Spies?"

"Yeah. Double agents. What did you think?"

"I thought you were mafia, and I was like a classy hooker or something."

"Damn." I scratched at my chin. "Next time, we should plan ahead."

She nodded seriously. "Next time. Yes. Definitely."

"I'll make some character profiles. Give some background and motivation to really get in the role."

She threw her head back. "I'm just focusing on the 'next time.'"

"Oh yeah, we've just begun."

CHAPTER 18

GRETCHEN

"La Vie En Rose" by Lucy Dacus

"I already regret this," Nicole said dryly as we crossed the threshold into the vintage shop.

I, on the other hand, had to keep from skipping down the racks of clothing, screaming in joy.

"Trust me." I squeezed her arm. "There ain't many things I take pride in, but this is one of them."

Vincent helped me coordinate a clothes shopping trip with Nicole a few days later as a thank you for hosting and to get to know her better. Not at any of those big box stores, because *boo*, but at some great little locally owned vintage shops.

"It's better than Saks at least," she said looking around, feigning boredom.

"That isn't really my speed either." I gestured to the outfit I wore. "As you probably guessed."

Today I wore a brownish-tan flower patterned long-sleeved, pilgrim-collared dress over Burgundy leggings and bright blue chunky platforms.

"You look like you'd fit in anywhere." She waved me off. "Vinny has tried many times to get me to shop where he does, but those bougie shops just feel pretentious and overpriced to me." She pulled a shirt from the rack pretending to study it but I could tell she wasn't fully present. She seemed a little put out. That was the look of someone who felt uncomfortable. I had work to do.

"Hang on, let me look at you. So. You have an amazing figure. These great eyebrows and your cheekbones! People actually pay money for cheeks like yours."

She shrugged and bit back a smile. She was wearing worn jeans and a T-shirt that while comfy had clearly seen better days. Girl needed to treat herself.

It's not that I thought appearances made people more important. It was quite the opposite. When someone took care of themselves, it indicated that they had found their own self-worth. After Ephram's death I completely stopped caring how I looked, I hadn't even showered. Maybe that's why it felt so important to me. That's what I feared Nicole was lacking. Years of taking care of other people meant she had put herself aside for too long. That changed today.

"Just trust me," I said.

She nodded and followed me as I browsed the racks.

I wasn't planning anything too extreme for Nicole. I didn't want to freak her out but some more color and some better fitting tops and bottoms would do wonders.

She followed behind, bored, but I was used to that with Roxy, so I didn't mind.

"Have you been having a nice visit?" she asked as I added to my growing pile. "You two have gone awful quiet." Her tone was heavy with implication.

Thank God, I was facing away because there was no way to hide the blush that spread over my cheeks.

"Oh yeah, things are great." *She said, super vaguely.*

"He seems happy. Happier than I've seen him in a long time," Nicole said, causing me to smile.

You should have seen him this morning before he left for work ...

He'd been sprawled out on the bed, dazed and content. His hair was ruffled, his eye shone with pleasure. We'd played a quick game of "who's ticklish and where?" and it ended with his face between my legs.

"Lauren and I had been worried about him." She stopped me with a gentle hand on my shoulder until I turned to her. "I don't want this to be weird for you. I just want you to know that we're glad you've come into his life. It's been a long time since he looked so ..." She searched her mind for the words. "Hopeful for the future?"

My heart hammered recognizing that same feeling in myself. I thought of him all the time. I looked forward to seeing him again whenever he went away, though admittedly that hadn't been a lot the last few days. But even when we paused our sex-a-thon so he could do some work, I felt myself scurry to his office to curl up on his couch just to be near him. He'd looked up at me over his computer with his glasses on and made a comment about needing copies made. Needless to say, he didn't get much work done after that.

I smiled genuinely back at her. "Thank you. It means a lot." And it did. I was lucky to have been accepted so easily. Despite what she said it had to be hard on some level for them. "But you guys should also know that I don't mean to replace her. Obviously," I added quickly. "I mean, that's not even possible. That's the point." I held up a blouse to her before smiling and throwing it over my arm.

"The point?" she asked, her brow raising skeptically at the stack.

"Obviously the best thing about this whole arrangement is that it's not complicated. I know Vincent could never love me. And he knows that I can never love again. At least not like our first marriages—but we can still have something else."

Wow, I sure was talking a lot. But it felt important to say it. Set things clear. He and I were … well, things were physically accelerating at an amazing rate. We fit so well. Really, so well. Vincent hadn't been kidding when he said he had loads of ideas. If this was a movie, the director would now insert a montage of all our crazy sex from the last several days. Cut to Vincent dressed as a cop as I handcuffed him to the bed. Cut to me in all black leather as I poured wax on his chest. Cut to him asking me how much I cost for a night I would never forget as I walked down the street.

Every day I got to explore this amazing city and play housewife in his gorgeous home and every night I got to unleash a part of me that I had never previously explored. Ephram and I had loads of fun back in the day, but these adventures with Vincent were like amusement park sex after only ever having national park sex. Both great experiences but one with crazier costumes and thrilling drops.

The best part was there was no guilt or weird sense of misguided betrayal to Ephram. I was playing a role, scratching an itch and so was Vincent. Maybe I shouldn't be proud of all the different scenarios we'd come up with. Surely we were capable of straight-up vanilla sex. Who was I kidding? I was extremely proud of our freaky-deaky love life. We were little weirdoes and I loved every damn second of it. Being a freak only sucked when you felt totally alone in your freakiness. When you had a willing, equally wild partner it made life all the more exciting and adventurous.

"He and I are extremely compatible," I finished with.

As I spoke, a little crease deepened between Nicole's eyebrows. "That's what he told you? That he'd never be able to love again?"

I could sense her worry. I held up my hands. "Don't worry. It's not a sad thing. I mean it is because of your lovely sister, but this arrangement isn't sad. I'm not waiting for him to fall in love with me or anything. We know exactly where we stand with each other. And that's what we both wanted. That's why this all works so well."

"Right." She nodded slowly.

"And we've put the having a baby thing on the back burner for a bit. We realized now how crass it was to talk so casually about it. Especially in front of Troy and Lauren."

"They're excited. They don't have many couple friends with kids, they'd hoped it would work out actually."

"Oh. Well, we're taking things a bit slower in that department." Although, *actually*, we were having more sex than ever. I didn't feel like I was explaining the situation right. "It's all good things. I promise."

She gave me a weak smile. "He seems happy and that's what matters. And if you're both on the same page," she lowered her head to scrutinize me closer, "and it seems like you are, then we're happy for you guys."

"Vincent and I are—" My feet moved me before I even realized I'd stopped talking.

I was drawn like a baby to a sparkling light. A magnificent ball gown hung from the back wall. It was a formfitting golden yellow floor-length gown, art deco style, and finely embellished in oranges and golds. The sleeves had tiny, beaded details that hung in tiers off the shoulder. Completely stunning and just a little over the top. It really was made for me. I reached a hand out reverently but couldn't bring myself to touch it.

"Wow, that's a gown," Nicole said at my side.

I closed my mouth to swallow and blinked back to the present from being hypnotized by the world's most perfect dress. "Yeah," was all I could muster.

"You should get it." She nudged me with her shoulder.

"It's probably not my size." I checked the tag. It was perfectly my size. "Well, it's a bit pricey."

That was true at least. Though to be completely honest it was worth far more than they tagged it. Normally, a splurge for gorgeous fashion was my favorite thing. I never needed to be talked into buying something. But this. It felt too important. It was a genuine vintage gown. I imagined the life this dress must have led. All that it had seen. It deserved some grand finale. What could I offer it? A closet in Green Valley? I was still living mostly out of a suitcase at Vincent's. Things were too all over the place right now.

I shook my head again and stepped away. I cleared my throat feeling strangely emotional over a gown. "We aren't here for me," I said. "We're here for you. Stop trying to distract me." I smiled brightly and led her away.

She flicked one last look to the gown before following me.

All in all, we only needed to go to two shops, and we did damn well. Nicole ended up having a hairstylist friend who could fit her in for a roots touch-up and a fresh cut and she looked magnificent.

That night we had a grand reveal of her new look as baked shells and garlic bread cooked at Troy and Lauren's. Nicole showed up in one of her newest outfits: nice fitted high-waisted trousers that flared out and a lovely lavender printed blouse tucked in. Some heels and accessories took it to the next level. She really was a stunning woman. I could only imagine how Elaine and she must have looked side by side strolling down the streets.

"Mom!" Lauren's eyes welled as her hands went to her cheeks. "You look amazing. Ugh, hormones." She wiped away a tear. "You were already lovely, but this just lets everyone else know too."

"Very nice," Troy said with a nod.

"Stunning," Vincent said. He shot me a look of such genuine appreciation that my heart skipped. After we stuffed ourselves as full as the pasta shells, and a little bit of tummy time with baby Lainey, Vincent and I made our goodbyes.

Nicole pulled me aside as I pulled on my coat. "I don't do mushy shit well, so just know I appreciate this, okay?" She looked away as her eyes glistened. "I guess I haven't been caring about myself lately. I sort of forgot—" She stopped abruptly. "Shit, I'm getting weepy over new pants. This is your fault." She sneered at me with false menace.

"I have heard that quite a few times in my life believe it or not. Honestly, this is what I love to do. It was fun."

She chuckled and gave me a quick hug. "Thank you. And now we can never talk about it again."

I nodded once. "Deal."

"And I'm glad that you and Vinny found each other. You're both good people who deserve another chance at lo—happiness," she said.

"I'm glad to have met him too." Thick panic rose in my chest. "And you all too. It's been a lovely visit."

Her comments made me nervous. It was like she was hoping to hear that Vincent and I were falling in love. We were not. We were falling into a rhythm.

That was different. We weren't supposed to complete each other. We were supposed to complement each other. Neither of us wanted love again. We just wanted company. Forever. In my head it made sense but there was no point in explaining it.

That night Vincent and I played a game of strip poker—I'm pretty sure he cheated—and then went to bed. I lay in the dark studying the ceiling. My heart hammered so loud in my chest as I tried to identify why. Everything was right on track. Everything was going smoothly, so why did I feel like things were spinning out around me?

CHAPTER 19

GRETCHEN

"(You Make Me Feel Like) a Natural Woman" by Caitlyn Smith

The faces of the core four filled up my screen. "Hello, hello," I said.

Everyone said their greetings and we complimented each other on how cute we all looked.

"How are you feeling, Kim?" I asked.

"Much better. I feel like I could lift a bus. The first trimester is over and I feel alive." She shook her fists in the air showing off her "muscles."

We laughed at her enthusiasm.

"I still cannot believe there's going to be a tiny Devlin around soon. I wonder if they'll come out all broody," Roxy said.

"Wearing a teeny tiny little bandana over their face," Suzie said, and we cackled.

"It's gonna be crazy. I have no idea what to expect. My mom basically told me that I have no control over anything from here on out." We all nodded as Kim spoke. "As you can imagine, Erik did not take that well. He's already researched the top brands of strollers and car seats. He's custom ordered organic cotton onesies in every possible size leading up to a one-year-old. I'd be worried but honestly it's nice to let him take the lead."

"Are you guys going to do any more performances?" Roxy asked.

"A few here and there. As long as I can still reach the strings of my cello, I don't see why I can't play. Though Erik doesn't want me traveling so they'll have to be local."

She went on to explain how he played almost every instrument in his studio every day for the baby, so that they had "options" when they came out.

"Does he think that the baby will come out singing and make you a touring trio?" I asked.

Kim nodded. "I really think that's his dream. But enough about me. How goes the wedding planning, Suze?"

"All's well on my end." Suzie shrugged. "I think we're just about done with everything. It's going to be a pretty small ceremony. There really wasn't much to do. The trip to get the bridesmaids dresses was the most extravagant aspect of the whole thing. Roxy's been handling everything like the freaking angel that she is."

Roxy fussed with her bangs. "It'll all be really nice. The Lodge will look beautiful, but nothing compared to you, Suzie."

"Aww." Suzie waved a hand. "Obviously not," she said with a wink.

We chatted a little bit more and it wasn't long until the inevitable questions came.

"And how are things in New York with Vincent?" Roxy asked.

She was doing that thing where she watched me a little too close for comfort. Damn lifelong friendship and not being able to hide anything.

"Oh my goodness, is Gretchen LaRoe blushing?" Kim cackled.

"Am not." But I was. I *totally* was. "Things are progressing nicely," I said as though this were a business meeting.

"So, you're finally doing the horizontal hanky-panky?" Suzie asked.

"And vertical," I mumbled.

"Shakin' sheets?" Roxy asked.

"And windows … and walls …"

"Knockin' boots?" Kim added.

"Among other things."

"Buttering that biscuit?" Suzie asked.

"Bam-bam in the ham?" Kim said.

"Kim!"

"Squatting in the cucumber patch," Roxy said.

"Oh my God, stop. Y'all are out of control." I crossed my arms and rolled my eyes. "That was just terrible."

"Bumpin' uglies?" Kim covered her hands over her face. "Okay, I'm done. I hate that one."

"But yes. We have discovered a creative outlet for our energy," I said.

"And how is it?" Roxy asked bluntly. I was surprised she'd ask that detail considering Vincent was her former boss.

I raised an eyebrow at her and asked, "You sure you want to know?"

She shrugged. "Nothing we can't handle."

"I bet he's so sweet and romantic," Kim said.

"No way. He's probably loud and freaky." Suzie shook her head. "It's always the suits that have the craziest fetishes."

"You would know," Roxy teased.

"Bet me," Suzie said.

I chewed my lip. Vincent was loud and domineering. But I got the distinct impression it was all an act for me. Of course, he loved it, wild sex wasn't exactly a chore for him, but I suspected that he was playacting for me. And that made me feel … unsettled?

"I wouldn't say that," I said.

Suddenly, I felt weird about this conversation. Since when had I ever held anything back about my sex life, *especially* from the girls? But Vincent and I were, well, we were having a lot of fun but we weren't exactly romantic. I bet he was though. I bet he would love slow and steady, eye contact, and cuddling. We had an incredible sexual connection, but I had to admit there was a time when I still felt a lot of distance between us. Even when he was balls deep in me.

"So?" Suzie prompted.

"It's really hot. He's really hot. But I don't want to talk about it. I just wanna hear more about what I'm missing." I didn't like the look the girls exchanged. Well, it was hard to tell on the screen who was looking at who, but it felt very pointed, I could tell that much.

"No worries. You don't have to spill the beans," Kim said. "As long as you're having a good time."

Oh, we were having a good time alright. But was that all we were having? That's all I wanted though. We agreed that this thing between us would be easy. And the sex was very easy … except when it was a little rough. *Heh.*

And yet, there was this nagging feeling in my gut. A voice that told me there was a reason I hadn't told the girls about all our sexcapades. Maybe I was a little worried about their opinion on the matter. Maybe because they knew me too well.

"Okay, y'all. Fill me in on Green Valley," I said. "I need the deets."

* * *

WE HAD plans to go out on the town after dinner. There was a fancy wine bar opening. A few months back he helped renovate its sister bar in Chicago. I was going to wear a new little number—sans panties—and see if he wanted to get a freaky somewhere. I cleaned up the house and waited for my husband to return home. I stopped midway through wiping off the counter and looked up.

"Huh," I said to the room.

I hadn't called him that in my head yet. *Husband.*

For so long Ephram held that title. I didn't want to feel the guilt that swept over me. I loved Ephram. I always would. Vincent was my husband by law but that didn't have to mean anything. Especially after the talk with the SWS it felt extra important to prove that to myself. When he came home tonight, I would prove that … that Vincent was the man I had wild sex with and we happened to be married, that was all. Things wouldn't get any more complicated. My heart of course, would always belong to Ephram.

When I heard Vincent's key in the outer door, I ran to pose on the stairs where he would see me in the tight-fitting purple number upon entering. But as soon as he walked through the door, it was clear that something was off. His shoulders were slumped, eyes bloodshot, and his tie was loose around his neck.

"Hey, what's wrong?" I shuffled down the stairs to greet him in the foyer. A cold wave of air came in with him, snow dusting his head and shoulders. I brushed off some of the snow, purposefully pressing my breasts into him, hoping to make him smile, but he just slumped onto the bench.

I grabbed an extra jacket to cover myself, but he didn't even seem to notice my racy outfit. If Vincent wasn't ogling me something really was wrong.

"Just a rough day," he said. He leaned forward to let me take off his heavy outer coat and cashmere scarf to hang on the hall tree.

"Talk to me. What's going on?" I asked. "Is everybody okay?"

"Yeah." He shook his head with a frown. "Nothing happened really. I just had a bad day. From the second I left you in bed it was one thing after another. I forgot a hat and it flurried earlier as I was walking. I missed the train by seconds. Work sucked—we lost the bid on that mansion in South Carolina I was telling you about."

"Oh yeah. I'm sorry," I said and knelt to take off his soaking shoes. These were his favorite pair and the salt and snow had not done good things to their sheen. Another example of what he was talking about.

Something I'd grown accustomed to with Vincent was his relatively unflappable nature. Little things never ruffled him. He was mature and stoic when it mattered. He balanced me out. To see him so brought down by his bad day, flared all my most feminine instincts to nurture and cherish him.

He ran a hand through his hair, it came away wet. He shook the excess water loose. "Still snowing." He shivered.

"Come inside," I pulled him away from the draft of the outer door and closed the interior one.

"Then Nicole called to say that Troy and Lauren had to take Lainey to the urgent care. She had a really high fever, and they were worried."

My hand went to my mouth. "Is she okay?"

"Yeah. Just a normal kid thing, I guess. But still scary. I'm not trying to sound so …" He frowned. "I know none of it's a huge deal. But it's just one of those days."

"Of course. It stacks. No matter how you try to shake it."

"Exactly. I'm sorry. The house smells amazing. Did you cook?"

I raised an eyebrow. "I ordered food that was cooked by a person."

He gave a weak smile and lifted a thumb to brush my cheek. "I'm absolutely beat. I don't even think I can eat yet."

"Don't worry. It's just curry. It'll reheat."

"Thanks. I feel bad. I know you were looking forward to tonight but …"

"Everyone has shit days. Let's stay in, okay?" I pushed down the mild disappointment but knew there were plenty of nights to come and he was truly out of sorts.

"Thanks." He sagged into the chair near the fire I had thankfully thought to start before he got home.

"Here. You sit here and warm up for a minute." I poured him a quick drink and handed it to him.

"You're the best." He leaned his head back and closed his eyes after he took a sip.

"I'm gonna go make you a bath. I'll come get you when it's ready, 'kay?"

"Mmm." He nodded but his eyes were already closed.

I made my way up to the owner's suite bath and started the water. I poured in some soothing lavender bath salts and bubbles. Everybody liked bubbles right?

It wasn't until I was changing into comfy pjs that I realized what I was doing. I was putting amazing sex to the side to run Vincent a bath. I was racing around to make him feel better. Tonight was supposed to be about me proving that this was just sex. But he needed me to show up for him. All these nights, since the beginning really, he'd gone out of his way to make sure I got what I needed.

It was time I stepped up and did the same for him.

I didn't even stare at his ass later as I helped him get in the tub when it was ready. Maybe just a peek.

He let out a long sigh as he sunk into the deep claw-foot tub. I pulled up a stool and sat behind him. After pushing up my sleeves, I scratched my nails through his hair. I rubbed the tight tendons in his neck and shoulders. We didn't talk much, I just comforted him with my touch. It felt like the most natural thing in the world. I rubbed my thumb into the base of his skull. He groaned.

"This is amazing, thank you." He reached up and squeezed my hand with his soapy one. "Exactly what I needed."

There was a knot in my chest that started to loosen the more he relaxed. I could help him. I helped people. That was fine.

When the water grew cold he let me guide him out of the tub. I wrapped him in one of his luxurious towels. I mussed his hair to dry it only to get a smile out of him. It worked this time.

"Come here," he said.

He pulled me to him. My pajamas stuck to his warm, still-damp skin. He wrapped his arms around me and tucked me under his chin. "Thank you."

"It was just a bath." I couldn't handle the thanks for doing the bare minimum when he'd been the one who had done most of the heavy lifting in this marriage so far.

I had gone into this wanting to be married but I didn't actually want my life to change at all. He was the one who traveled to Green Valley the most. He was the one that put up with the borderline terrorist actions of my best friends. He was the one who figured out just what I needed in bed so we could move forward. And he took the pressure off trying for a baby, so that I knew he wanted me for me.

I squeezed him back tightly. A bath and some head scratches felt like nothing in comparison.

"Want to eat now or get some sleep?" I asked as he pulled on his briefs.

"Bed." He yawned.

I noted that he didn't say *sleep* exactly.

As soon as we laid down, he tucked me against his side, holding me tightly. Usually if we were in bed together, his hands roamed my body endlessly. I felt the absence of it now.

This man. He cared so much for me. He had done so much for a practical stranger from the beginning. We were much closer, closer than friends. Definitely the partners we'd both been longing for when we began all this. Before he came home tonight, I'd been so set to prove that what was growing between us was nothing but sexual, but I'd been lying to myself. We were partners now. I looked forward to him coming home all day long. I did things with his needs in mind. More often than not, my thoughts went to him more than anybody else. This was exactly what we'd been discussing that night months ago. And it was pretty damn nice.

My head rose and fell with his gentle breaths, and I felt more at peace than I could remember feeling in some time even with his chest hairs tickling my nose.

"What're you thinking about?" he asked, surprising me. I thought he'd fallen asleep.

"I was just wondering what else I could do to make you feel better."

"You did everything." He kissed the top of my head. "Consider my day turned around."

"Good." I nuzzled my face against his chest.

He let out a long, contented sigh. "Want to go see the Rockefeller tree tomorrow? I could play hooky."

I smiled up at him. "Yeah?"

"Yeah. It's almost Christmas. Things have slowed down at work," he grumbled.

"That would be great."

I wasn't tired yet, but I decided I could lay here just a little bit longer. I must have fallen asleep at some point because I woke to hands cupping my boobs and ass. *Ah*, it was good to have my man back.

I lay still for a moment to determine if it was sleep-groping.

"Gretchen?" he whispered. His nose bumped against my chin. He kissed my neck. "I need you."

The words sent a shudder through me.

I turned to search for him in the dark. I placed a hand on his cheek before kissing him gently on the lips. "Then take me."

He groaned. Only the rustling of sheets filled the dark room. We were silent as we stripped off our clothes under the covers. We were silent as he moved on top of me save for the soft sounds of our kiss. It wasn't until he slid inside of me that we both broke the silence.

"Yes," he said as I gasped out.

As my eyes adjusted there was just enough light from his alarm clock to see his profile as he moved above me. He held my gaze and rocked to hit the spot that I needed. He dropped to his elbows to brush the hair out of my face. He kissed me with reverence and gentleness. Like he *needed* to kiss me. No more masks or role-playing. It was just Vincent and I now. And it was good. So damn good and intense. He held my gaze as his movements got faster and faster.

My orgasm swept over me like a gentle rolling wave, taking me by surprise.

"Oh," I gasped.

"Yes."

It had never been like this with us before. Something was shifting. Blooming like time-lapsed flowers all around us.

I closed my eyes to fight the strong emotion flooding my chest.

Then I realized what was happening, why guilt and anxiety were swirling within me despite the amazing orgasm.

We weren't having sex. We were making love.

CHAPTER 20

VINCENT

"Can't Help Falling in Love" by Beck

New York City did its very best to impress Gretchen LaRoe. It was a perfect winter day as we made our way toward Manhattan. Heavy dark clouds made it cold enough to need to be bundled up, store windows sparkled with festive displays that had her drooling, and nowhere to be seen was a man with his pants down pissing in the streets. *Ah, what a time to be alive*. She was absolutely smitten.

However, just as we suspected it would be, Rockefeller Center was madness. There were crowds in NYC and then there were *crowds*. There was the everyday congestion, the herds of people commuting back and forth that kept their weary distance, jamming themselves on to the subway, avoiding eye contact and conversation at all costs. And then there were the tourist crowds that were unpredictable and frustrating. People stopping to take pictures with no warning. Groups, five people across, blocking the flow of traffic. Chaos.

But surprisingly, I wasn't bothered. Not surprisingly, actually. I had Gretchen on my arm. She wore a cream knit hat over her lovely red hair and a heavy plaid peacoat. Every time we were jostled or annoyed, we'd share an eye roll then grin.

She looked around in wide-eyed wonder. It was thrilling to experience my city from the eyes of somebody I cared about. It created a specific type of excitement I hadn't felt in a long time. Like sharing a song with someone and listening to it again just to experience it in tandem.

"Want to ice skate?" She looked up at me with eager eyes, her red hair spilling out over her shoulders.

"If you want to." I kissed her pert little nose tipped red from the cold. She could have just as easily asked, *Can I have your kidney?* and my answer would have been the same.

Gretchen's enthusiasm for ice skating lasted exactly as long as it took for her to learn that reservations were necessary, or the wait would be hours.

"There are too many people on the planet. Don't have this problem back in Green Valley, I'll tell you that much," she grumbled as we continued to walk around Rockefeller Center.

"They have ice skating rinks in Green Valley?" I teased.

"Oh, very funny. We're such hicks to you, aren't we?" Then her eyes squinted, and she tilted her head to think. "Actually, I don't think we do. Still, shutty. Take me to see the tree."

We made our way through more crowds to get closer. Gretchen leaned her head all the way back. "I can't even see the top. Is it really just one tree?"

I nodded. "Usually, a family donates it. This one is about sixty years old and from Florida."

She looked at me surprised that I knew. "Seems a bit of a waste. I can't imagine it's cheap or easy to ship from there. And for it to just die."

"Well, they donate the tree to Habitat to Humanity for the lumber after."

Her eyes narrowed. "Who are you even?"

I chuckled. "What? It's a thing everyone knows."

"I doubt that. But it makes me feel better at least. And it really is so beautiful. I suppose you know exactly how many bulbs there are."

I shook my head. "I could Google it."

"Let's keep the mystery alive." She grabbed my arm and snuggled closer to me.

Two little kids shoved in front of us.

"Sorry about the heathens," a dad said a moment later. "Kids, say 'excuse me.'"

A little boy and girl rushed out a, "'Scuze me" before their heads tilted back just as Gretchen's had a moment before.

"Okay. That's the biggest tree I've ever seen. It's got to be the biggest tree in the world," the little boy said.

"It's probably like a thousand hundred feets tall," his little sister said in awe.

The brother widened his eyes and nodded seriously. Gretchen and I shared a smile. There was a tug in my chest so sharp, I worried it was a heart attack. But no. It was extreme fondness for Gretchen. All things Gretchen. She made me feel young. She made me *feel.* It was a miracle I never thought I'd get to experience again. It was a longing for a life with her. A real life. Not whatever this was that we were doing. Last night when we made love, it was the first time I felt like she'd actually let down her guard with me during sex. It was my favorite time with her yet. I wanted more of that.

I'd fallen in love with Gretchen LaRoe. If I was being honest with myself, it happened a while back. Probably before we even started sleeping together. But I kept it locked down. Partially because it wasn't something I could ever dream of having twice in a lifetime, and partially because it would freak her out.

But this was love, without a doubt. It was a different sort of love than my love for Elaine, which still held a place in my heart. Elaine's love was what had kept my heart beating all these years. Kept it from collapsing in on itself like a black hole of despair. My love for Elaine made way for Gretchen.

Now. I needed to decide how to tell her. I needed to pace myself, I needed to present it in a way that wouldn't cause her to panic. Just because I loved her, didn't mean I expected anything to change. People should know that they're loved, shouldn't they?

"Hey, let's get hot chocolate," I said after a few minutes.

We walked a few blocks away until the volume of the crowd was a little more bearable. I paid almost twenty dollars for two cups of shitty hot chocolate—extortion—and found a little bench near a gazebo. There was a moving light display as music from *The Nutcracker* played over the loudspeakers. People were still everywhere but it was peaceful.

"Oh, this is just too much. This is a perfect New York holiday. The whole area is buzzing with festiveness. I feel like my brain is going to explode from all the mental pictures I've been taking."

"Have you heard about camera phones? It's this new-fangled—Oof." I rubbed my ribcage.

"You're lucky you're so damn cute." She pulled out her phone. "But you're right. This is selfie worthy. Hold up your cup and say, 'cuckoo for cocoa.' *Ugh* my arms are too short to get us both in the frame. Try and get the lights or something too." She handed me her phone.

The image on the screen showed a man looking with complete adoration at the woman he loved. I snapped a picture.

"What?" she asked after it clicked. "You have a look. But listen, there are children around so keep your hands to yourself." She scanned the crowd, neck arching as she searched the area. "Although maybe if we go behind those trees? It's a little cold but we can work fast."

I pulled her closer to me until she was half in my lap. I nuzzled my head against her hot neck and cool cheeks.

My feelings were overflowing out of me. Instinct told me this was too big to tell her here and now. But I experienced this overwhelming emotion here and now, it was the most organic and real time possible. A sharp wind brought the first sign of snow.

"I love how the wind announces a storm is coming." Gretchen tilted her head back and the first flurries started to fall.

My throat felt tight. I had to tell this woman how I felt about her. I could tell her, knowing it could go either of two ways. She'd roll her eyes and tell me I was an idiot, or she'd freak out completely. Either way, I knew I wouldn't hear that she loved me back. And that was okay. Loving her wasn't contingent on being loved in return. My love was enough to carry us both until if and when she ever felt ready.

"Gretchen—" A large crash shook through the crowd, drawing the entire area's attention.

Dozens of heads snapped to our left where a cloud of dust—I hoped—rose into the air.

"What was that?" she asked me already slipping out of my arms. We both stood. I shook my head, unsure.

There were screams. People started running. Parents grabbed their children.

I looked toward where the sound was but the snow was falling harder now. I couldn't see that far. "It sounded like something fell."

We weren't thinking when we started toward the confusion. Had I been, I would have told her to stay right where we were. To stay in that exact spot until I checked it out and came back for her.

"Gretchen. Slow down," I called out.

She was running toward the chaos as others ran away. As we got closer it looked as though scaffolding had fallen, causing a scare. Sirens wailed and the crowd grew thicker. She should be moving in the opposite direction. I should have kept her where it was safe.

"Gretchen," I growled louder. She was getting harder to track. So many hats and heavy coats. Wind and snow.

Of course, moments after I understood that I was in love with her, things start to crash to the earth. I looked heavenward as snowflakes fell fat and thick.

When I looked back, I'd lost her red hair. "Gretchen!" I yelled louder.

Fear started to make me panic. I needed to calm down. It wasn't like she couldn't find me. She could just text me. She had her phone—

I looked down realizing I still held it.

Gretchen would be fine. She was level-headed. Okay, maybe level-headed wasn't the right word. She tended to act first and then think. But she wasn't an idiot. She was incredibly capable. There was nothing to worry about.

A scream to the left caught my attention but it was just a woman calling for someone else.

Gretchen, where are you? My heart raced harder now. Fear gripped me and clouded rational thought.

I understood she was an adult. But the panic took over. It swallowed me whole.

Cannot lose her.

Cannot lose her.

"Gretchen!" I yelled above the crowd. Her name was instantly lost in the surge. Besides a few questioning glances nobody even seemed to hear me. There was no way she could hear me.

The crowd was too much. The snow swirling in the wind made finding her all the more impossible.

The panic felt like someone was standing on my chest. Like the whole damn crowd was pressing in on me. I couldn't calm my racing thoughts.

I had to find her. I couldn't lose her.

"Gretchen!" I called until my voice went hoarse.

* * *

Gretchen

I'D GOTTEN PULLED AWAY from Vincent in the madness. It was like being swept up in an undertow and probably equally as dangerous. I climbed up onto a short wall to look for Vincent in a sea of dark coats and black beanies. He was easy enough to spot—being the best-looking guy in the crowd by far. I kept my eyes locked on him as I swam upstream like a trout to get to him.

Vincent was pale, and his voice was rasping by the time I made my way back to him. He'd been yelling for me, wild eyes searching all around. I hadn't heard him until I was right in front of him.

"Hey." I tugged on his sleeve. He didn't react to me. His eyes were glossy bouncing around and searching. This close up, I noticed his skin was actually tinged a little green and there were beads of sweat on his forehead despite the cold. "Vincent. Hey, it's me."

He looked at me, but it took him a second to register my face. When the information sunk in that the person he was looking for stood right in front of him, his face crumbled. He pulled me into a hug so tight his arms cinched almost painfully even with the layers of fluffy coats between us.

"It's okay. I'm okay." I had to fight to push out of his embrace enough to grab his face and hold it in my hands. He looked on the verge of tears. "Are you okay? Are you hurt?"

His mouth opened and closed like he couldn't manage speech. "I thought —I thought I lost you."

His emotions were raw and right at the surface. I grabbed his gloved hands and nuzzled them. The leather was icy against my cheeks. I hated seeing him worried like this. I needed to fix it.

"Nothing would have happened, okay?" I took off a glove to allow him to nuzzle my palm. Skin to skin. I pulled his forehead down to mine. "I would've found my way back to you. We would have been okay no matter what."

His jaw clenched. The rawness of his expression had my stomach clenching. He looked almost devastated. I'd never seen him like this. He was sturdy. He was the rational one.

"You don't know that," he croaked.

I opened my mouth to argue but I didn't know that, did I? Things happened all the time out of nowhere. Freak accidents. Healthy people got sick. Good people got caught in the wrong place at the wrong time. There was no accounting for the randomness of tragedy.

"You're okay." I lowered my head back to his chest. His heart slammed against my ear. "I'm here now. It's all okay."

His arms pulled me closer. After his heart returned to a normal rhythm, I said. "Let's go get some soup and warm up."

* * *

WE'D WALKED in silence away from the crowd at Rockefeller once we learned that everything was okay, and nobody had gotten hurt. It had just been loud. The snow was falling beautifully all around. Holiday decorations hung everywhere we looked. I enjoyed the walk, but Vincent was more withdrawn than I'd seen in a long time. It reminded me of how he was when we first met which made me realize how well I really knew him now. How close we'd grown. And I fully understood that the look of terror on his face when I found him was genuine. It hadn't been role-playing or part of a game. He was terrified to lose me.

He held my hand tightly the entire walk to the diner, refusing to let it go until he took off my coat and lowered me into the booth. There was a jukebox in the corner with actual records and a giant board with those plastic letters listing the limited menu above the kitchen. The booths were vinyl and squeaked like farts when we sat down, especially with our wet jackets.

Outside the snow continued to fall but already snowplows were coming out in droves.

I wasn't even sure that Green Valley had a snowplow. The rare times it snowed enough to warrant one, they were probably borrowed from the forest rangers.

"So," I said a while later, watching the cheese melt in my cup of chili. "That was quite a reaction to losing me back there." I took a spoonful and blew on it, watching Vincent.

He'd still not spoken more than to order a cup of coffee and a grilled cheese. He hadn't even laughed at my booth fart joke. Sure, the humor was lowbrow but usually it got me a smile at least.

He pulled off his knit cap and smoothed a hand through his dark hair. "Yeah. Maybe a bit of an overreaction."

"Want to talk about it?"

He let out a breath and said, "I don't know. I'm afraid if I do, you might freak out."

I swallowed the bite of chili feeling instant heartburn. "Why would I freak out?"

But I saw his face right before the commotion broke out. It was the same face he made during our amazing sex last night. Vincent was looking at me with adoration. Not the lust he normally had—little pink hearts practically floated from his eyes. My palms began to sweat.

"Listen," I said cutting him off at the pass. "Your reaction was totally normal. It was a lot. It was hard to see. Who wouldn't get scared? I'm sorry that I ran off like that."

"I'm usually very good in high pressure situations," he said to the table.

"Well, you're a New Yorker. Loud crashes mean something different here now."

He tilted his head like he was disappointed in my weak excuse. "You know that's not why I freaked out."

I watched my spoon sink into the chili. "No, I don't."

He let out a breath. "I know we talked about keeping it simple but I'm in love with you, Gretchen, okay?" He nudged my bowl until I looked at him. "I love you."

His eyebrows furrowed with earnestness. My heart took off like a bucking bronco but not because I felt happy. Shouldn't I feel happy? Instead, I panicked. Sweat prickled under my arms.

"You guys need anything else?" our waiter asked, appearing out of nowhere like an angel to break the tension. Or add to it, the way Vincent tensed.

We both shook our heads, still maintaining eye contact with each other until he slapped down the bill. "Pay up front. Have a Merry Christmas or whatnot," he said before walking away.

"You're just confused. With the sex and the scare. The holidays. It has your brain all muddled." I grasped at straws, trying to explain this curveball. He couldn't be in love with me. Sure, we made promises and commitment. But we swore that when we got married it would never be about love. I'd been ignoring growing feelings just fine, thank you very much.

He shook his head. He wasn't even listening to my rambling. "Gretchen?" he said. "I know you can't love me back like that. I know your heart still belongs to Ephram. I didn't tell you to make you say it back or anything."

I ground my teeth together. Why had he said it then? Because there was no way at least one of us (mostly likely both) were leaving this diner now without feeling like a bag of shit.

"We were on the same page," I said, shocked at how normal my voice sounded for the circus act of thoughts jumping around my head.

"We are. Nothing has to change," he agreed.

"Okay," I said. Not buying that BS for a second. *Everything* had fucking changed. Why couldn't he just go on pretending? Why did he always have to say what was on his goddamn mind instead of burying it deep under coping mechanisms like the rest of us?

"You told me you couldn't fall in love again. You said that." This time I couldn't control how my voice rose.

"I didn't think I could." He grabbed my hand.

I pulled my hand back into my lap and he frowned. But I couldn't think clearly when he touched me. How could I think when he looked at me with all those little pink hearts flying everywhere? I didn't want to be this person. I didn't want to be the heartless one that couldn't love him back. He was perfect. There were a million women in this city alone that would die for the chance to have a guy like Vincent. And me with my preoccupied heart was the one that had to go and marry him.

But we had a plan! I'm not the bad guy. He was the one that changed up the rules.

"Dammit, Vincent. What am I supposed to do here?" Moisture burned my eyes. I couldn't love again. I wouldn't. That was the plan. He'd broken the rules of the game.

"Sorry. I was just trying to make you smile."

I tried to smile for him.

"Are you okay?" I rolled my eyes at his teasing. "There you are. Come on, Gretch. Honestly. Nothing has to change. It's just you and me."

I nodded. But of course, everything had changed.

* * *

Gretchen

I WASN'T FREAKING OUT. I wasn't going to do the thing where I freaked out and ran away just because I couldn't process or talk about what was happening. This was me reacting to a situation in a calm and healthy manner. Which was more than I could say for Vincent. He was confused. He needed space from me. I couldn't help the awesome power of me. Men were simple creatures, easily confused. He just needed some distance to realize that the stuff in the park, the holidays, all the sex—it had all built up to make him feel like he was in love, but it was a trick of the lighting. A really good filter. It wasn't real.

I shoved my clothes roughly into the suitcase, without using garment bags or even folding them. I would mourn this decision later, but for now I had to pack.

I had to get back to Green Valley. It was too cold here anyway. Winter in the city was way less fun than fall. I needed to get home and check on my tenants and help Suzie and check on Kim. That was all. Really, there was so much I'd been neglecting.

I explained all these things to Vincent as I packed my suitcases. "Honestly. I'm fine. Everything is fine."

He nodded from the doorway, hands in pockets, mouth twisted to the side. "Okay. I trust you to be honest with me."

Ughh. Why did he have to say shit like that? It's like when your teacher said they weren't mad about you not doing the assignment, just disappointed.

I went to stand in front of him and grabbed his hands and smiled brightly. I hoped it looked authentic.

"I just have to go help with the wedding. Roxy has a lot on her plate."

"You said that," he said.

"You aren't mad?"

He scratched his eyebrow and sighed. "I'm not mad. You could wait until the weekend, and I could come with you."

My heart launched itself into my gut. "No. No. I've already made you miss work for the Manhattan outing. I don't want to screw up anything else."

"You didn't screw anything up." *Really, VINCENT? Because it feels like I did.* "I could at least take you to the airport."

"No. You have to get to the office." I gestured to his suit and tie. "I'm totally fine. Plus, you know I love chatting it up with cabbies." Wow, look at how light and breezy I sounded. See, everything was just fine.

Except last night when we came home, I went to bed first, pretending to be asleep by the time he brushed his teeth and joined me.

He didn't say anything, but I felt his need to discuss things. It was a physical weight between us as we lay there in the darkness.

I needed to get home. That was all. I had a whole life in Green Valley.

"I'll see you on Christmas Eve right? You're gonna fly out and stay through the wedding still?"

"Yes, Gretchen. Nothing has changed for me." Oh, that tone of his.

Except, uh hello, you were the dingbat that "fell in love" when we were supposed to get married and have babies and never *ever* talk about our growing feelings for each other.

Suddenly my coat was too tight. The air in this house is too stuffy.

I hugged him. He hesitated a minute before squeezing me back. When I lifted to peck him on the mouth goodbye, he held me in place and deepened the kiss. He found his way into my mouth and kissed me until I submitted to him, and my knees almost gave out.

Now I was really hot. I was sure my face was bright red. I pressed cool fingertips against my cheeks. He looked down at me, cupping the back of my head. His look was … knowing. I didn't like it and I didn't trust it.

"Okey dokey, artichokey!" I reached for my suitcase, but he beat me to it, and we walked downstairs.

"I'll see you later," I said.

"One week." He nodded, hands in pockets, face serene. He leaned down and kissed me again. "Have a safe flight. I love you, Gretchen."

I babbled something incoherent and ran down the stoop to the waiting taxi. I didn't look back. It was the shame that kept me focused on the road ahead.

"Parting is such sweet sorrow, eh?" the driver said.

Sweet sorrow. I squeezed my eyes shut and took a deep breath. This was fine. I was not freaking out.

CHAPTER 21

GRETCHEN

"The End of the World" by Sharon Van Etten

"Why is Gretchen freaking out?" Suzie asked, looking at Roxy.

Roxy shrugged watching me closely, her dark-lined eyes narrowing.

"I'm fine," I insisted in a high voice.

We were back at Genie's for our SWS meeting. It was packed as always.

Several people had already come up to me.

"Missed seeing your red head bobbing around, Gretch," said Genie.

"Gretchen, where you been?" asked Patty.

"Hey, I needed to use a stupid taxi the other day and missed your pretty face," said Joe the bartender.

It was good to be back. This was home. This felt right. NYC was nice but it was too much. Too many people but still so lonely. Too much noise, not enough Smoky Mountain magic.

I sighed and leaned back in the chair. This was my home. I made the right choice. Everything was fine.

"Why do you keep making that face?" Kim asked.

I schooled my features.

She leaned closer. "Do you need to go number two?"

Suzie cackled. “Look at you already sounding like a momma.”

Kim blushed and rubbed her tiny bulging belly seemingly without realizing.

“I’m fine, y’all,” I insisted though my stomach had been in knots since I got back last night. Probably just the plane rides. Airports always made me queasy.

“So, this has nothing to do with Vinny?” Kim asked.

“No.” I laughed with a shake of my head. “*Vincent* and I are doing fine.”

“Yeah, you keep saying that but then you make the constipated face Kim was talking about.” Roxy tossed back a fried pickle.

I frowned at her.

“Last time we talked, you seemed all flush with sex,” Suzie said.

“I’m telling y’all it’s f—We are great.” My voice went high, and I forced it to a normal register. “I just needed some space.”

“You needed space from your doting husband? Or that gorgeous house? Or that amazing city with endless things to do? Or the great sex or—” Roxy asked dryly.

“Okay, I get it.” I sighed. “Just space. Don’t you ever just need to get away from your guys?” I asked.

“Not really,” Suzie said.

“Nope.” Kim shook her head.

“Yes.” Roxy bit back a smile and a blush. “But he refuses to give it to me.”

“Well, I guess we’re just a different type of couple,” I said, feeling defensive.

“We couldn’t stay apart those first few weeks.” Suzie tilted her head. “Months,” she amended.

“Same.” Kim shrugged sheepishly.

“No comment,” Roxy said. But then her phone buzzed on the table with a text showing Sanders’s goofy grin. She read the message, biting her lip as she furiously typed a response.

When she finally looked up, we were all watching her.

“Shut up,” she said, as she fixed her bangs. “He’s just checking in.”

Suzie gestured to Roxy. “Case in point.”

“I missed you guys and Green Valley. I wanted to help with the wedding.”

Roxy set her phone screen facing down as she glared at me. “No offense, but I have things under control. I literally do this for a living.”

“More of a moral support thing.” The gals exchanged one of those looks. I knew I had done my fair share in the past, but it was super annoying to be on the opposite side. "Stop doing that. I can see when you do that, you know that, right?"

"Why didn't you just bring Vincent?" Kim asked.

"He'll be here in less than a week."

"So then nothing happened? Nothing caused your 'not freak out?'" Roxy asked using air quotes.

"Not really. Well. I mean." I played with the condensation on my drink I'd hardly touched. My stomach really was in knots. "Now it's gonna seem like a big deal because y'all made it a big deal."

Three sets of eyes waited patiently.

"He told me he loved me." I shrugged. "That he was in love with me." My voice cracked inexplicably.

I glanced up. I'd expected eye rolls. I expected teasing remarks like *Oh, poor Gretchen found someone who loved her.*

I had not expected the pity I saw reflected in all their gazes. And turned out that was much, much worse.

"Oh, Gretch." Kim squeezed my hand.

"It's fine. I'm—"

"Fine," they all chorused.

I sighed. "We had a plan. As long as we stayed on the same page nobody would get hurt."

"It's not a hostage negotiation," Roxy said.

"He's just confused," I clarified.

"Confused?" Suzie asked.

"We've been very intimate lately. We're too much in each other's pockets. It's probably just messed with his head and when he realizes that it was just the sex endorphins, he'll remember that Elaine is still his only true love."

I tracked each of their reactions.

"Well now *you* look constipated," I said to Kim.

"I'm trying really hard not to look at Roxy and Suzie." Her words spilled out in a rush and she let out her breath.

"Just say it." I crossed my arms.

"If he said he loves you, then he loves you." Kim shrugged.

"He's confused."

"Don't do that." It was Roxy who snapped to my great surprise. "Don't project what you want on to him. He's a grown ass man who can decide if he's in love. We've already established that you're the one who got all weird and ran home."

I slowly closed my mouth that had been hanging open. "We did not establish that."

"Yeah. We did." Roxy held my glare until I broke eye contact first.

"Maybe because now I find myself in a much worse situation," I said without looking up from my hands.

There was a murmur of agreement.

"And there's no way, that maybe you could love him too?" Suzie asked.

It must be real love if it hurts this much to be apart. I ignored that voice in my head. The pain in my stomach seized tighter. I shook my head. "Ephram was it for me."

This time when I said the same words I'd said over and over they fell flat to my own ears.

"Is it possible," Roxy hedged cautiously, "that maybe what you feel in regards to Ephram is a misplaced sense of guilt?"

My head shot up. "No. I loved him."

Roxy held up her hand. "Of course. I know. I just mean. Plenty of people love more than once. There isn't any shame in that. He wouldn't be mad."

I frowned at the tabletop. They didn't understand. I had loved, wholeheartedly. I had done everything I could to get Ephram out of Green Valley and it was because of me and my selfishness that he died. I pushed and pushed. It was my fault. It wasn't that I thought if I loved a man, then he would die. It was more that I had loved a man and he *had* died. Because of me. Because of what I'd done. I'd spent years trying to help others find love to try and balance out my wrongdoing. But another chance at happiness? It wasn't in the cards for me.

"He told me that he loved me, but he also told me he would never love anyone like he loved Elaine," I said.

"People fall in love in many different ways. I'm sure when he said that it was true. Both times," Suzie said.

I didn't see how it could be. Or I refused to admit it.

"You know, he had more time to say goodbye to Elaine too. They had months knowing she wasn't going to make it," Roxy said. "He had more time to heal. More closure maybe?"

"Whereas …"

"Yeah. I know." Whereas Ephram was ripped from my life without warning. "Maybe that's why." But what if I *could* love again? I never even allowed myself to think about it. I wouldn't even know how to go about it now.

"You know we just want to make sure you're as happy as you helped make all of us," Suzie said.

"I am happy. I have y'all."

"And just remember you're never alone, Gretchen," Roxy said. She moved to swing an arm around me. "No ex left behind."

I smiled at the SWS. I could focus on these friendships and worry about Vincent later. If my brain gave me a break.

"Ooh girls. Y'all are not gonna believe who just walked in," Kim said and in tandem all our heads turned to the door.

"Well, ain't that something," I said.

* * *

Vincent

I DIDN'T REGRET my honesty with Gretchen. I would never regret telling someone that I loved them. Life was too short. I did regret her absence. Her scent lingered on the pillows. Clothes she hadn't taken back still hung in the corner of my closet. Her extra toothbrush and products lay scattered around the bathroom.

Despite these small things, I lamented that there weren't *enough* signs of her. If anybody were to come in, they'd think that I lived here alone. My apartment looked the same as ever.

Our marriage could be so easily forgotten. But what could I do? I'd been honest with her and she left. It hurt. I was hurt. But we'd played enough games. If she wanted to talk to me, it was up to her.

These and other lies, accompanied me as I made the short but cold walk to Lauren and Troy's the day before Christmas Eve.

The door opened and Nicole gestured me. "Hurry up, you're letting the cold in."

"And Merry Christmas to you!"

She took in my arms laden with gifts. Her dark eyebrow raised. Ah, that Walsh stare. "You think you went a little overboard?"

"For Lainey's first Christmas ever? Hardly."

"Good point. Come in, come in, and Merry Christmas Eve *Eve*." She kissed my cheek, and I was pulled farther into the warm apartment. Cinnamon and pine competed with the smell of fried seafood creating an instant tightening of sentimental longing. But for the first time in as long as I could remember, it wasn't Elaine that instantly popped into my mind. It was red hair and full-body laughter.

Our Feast of the Seven Fishes had been scheduled a day early this year as I was leaving in the morning. Though throughout the years we'd cut out many of the dishes we didn't like and now the menu was only fried calamari, shrimp, and some baked cod. It was our family tradition and Gretchen's absence sat heavy in the room. I imagined her lip curled in disgust as I wiggled a fried smelt in her face.

We'd made it all the way until the cannoli dessert until the women decided to further investigate why Gretchen was missing.

"Come on. You can do it." I shook the softly ringing rattle in front of baby Lainey. I was on my stomach for tummy time with her. She grunted and gurgled as she struggled to keep her head up.

"Why did Gretchen go back to Tennessee already?" Lauren asked. "I thought you guys were doing good. Really good." She wiggled her eyebrows.

"She freaked out." I rolled onto my back taking Lainey with me. She trilled happy sounds as I lifted her into the air. "I told her I loved her, and she went running."

The silent tension in the room caused me to sit up, the baby on my shoulder.

"I'm sorry, what?" Nicole asked.

I focused on lying Lainey on her back, watching her kick her little legs. "You heard me just fine."

"You think you can just drop a bomb like that and not elaborate?" Lauren said.

"If you told her like that, no wonder she ran for it," Troy said. He looked up and away when I glared at him. "But what do I know."

"Right? They were probably just sitting around eating soup and he's like 'I need to check the mail and oh, by the way, I love you,'" Lauren teased.

A flush burned up my neck. "It was chili actually."

When I looked up Lauren and Nicole had the exact same face—somewhere between horror and disgust. Troy shook his head, laughing into his palm. "Oh man," he said.

"What?" I asked. I explained the disastrous night in more detail. It did little to fix their unimpressed expressions.

"You told her you loved her at a shitty diner?" Lauren scoffed.

"Oaky, hang on," Nicole said. "First, congratulations. I'm happy to hear that you love her. Honestly. I know my sister would be happy too."

I smiled at her.

"But, *dude*, really? Just like that?"

"You're trying to make me feel bad. It won't work. Gretchen ran because she's freaking out. She just needs space, she'll come around." But even as I spoke a little spring of doubt twisted in my brain. I'd thought they'd be on my side on this. Wasn't honesty the best policy?

"My friend, she does not need space," Troy said.

"And don't act like you're being the bigger person here," Nicole said.

"What? She's the one who left," I defended.

"What did you do to make her want to stay?" Troy asked. "How welcomed does she feel in your life? You opened your heart a teeny tiny bit. Got shot down and now your pride is hurt. You can't put this all on her."

We all blinked at Troy. I'd honestly never heard him speak so much at once. Between Nicole and Lauren, Troy didn't often get a word in.

"What?" He shrugged. "I know things too. How do you think I landed someone so totally out of my league?"

"Awww." Lauren snuggled closer to her husband.

"I'm just saying you're acting like you're being open, but you're still just a man with a fragile ego."

I frowned. I didn't like that. Had I been scared? I told myself that Gretchen needed space when she got distant. But actually, thinking back on our interactions whenever she freaked out and I'd forced her to open up to me, it usually made us both feel better. The worry was fully lodged into my brain now.

"You haven't talked to her since she left?" Lauren laughed.

"Let me ask you a question, seriously, don't get all defensive." Nicole threw a ball of used wrapping paper at me. "How many times did you tell her that you loved her?"

"Twice," I answered instantly.

It was weird that I knew that. When you were with somebody for a long time you didn't remember the specifics, the firsts. You were just a "we" as far back as you could remember. It was strange to be back at firsts again, being able to recall exactly when and what I'd said to her. I'd probably told Elaine a million times before she …

The understanding was starting to settle in.

"And how many times did you talk about Elaine? At first, at least. How many times did you two convince each other that neither one of you would ever be able to love again?" Nicole asked.

I scrubbed a hand down my face. "Ah, shit."

"When I went shopping with her—not that long ago, mind you—she very much seemed convinced that you two were on the same page. That page being 'I will never love again.'" Nicole spoke with air quotes.

I pushed up my glasses to rub my eyes. "I may have said that in the beginning a lot because I knew she needed to hear it. She wouldn't have ever even given me a chance if she thought that I—"

They all looked at me expectantly. Even baby Lainey stopped gnawing on her toes to give me what felt like a very pointed look.

"I knew if I had admitted that I had strong feelings for her she would have never agreed to all this." I let out a long sigh. Not to mention the thought of her casually giving her life over to somebody who wouldn't value her was too much to take. "You guys know I play things close to the chest. Gretchen is so convinced that we wouldn't be able to love each other … I don't know what exactly but there is some block for her still that she needs to work through."

They all groaned. "What?" I asked.

"You *both* need to work through," Lauren said. "How is she supposed to know any of this if you don't tell her?"

I started to speak but Nicole cut me off. "And not over freaking soup or when she's leaving. Jesus, Mary, and Joseph."

"Maybe you need to show her you're serious about her. That maybe you've been feeling this way for a while," Lauren said.

"She probably thinks you're still in love with Elaine," Nicole said softly.

I frowned. "I think I am. I love them both."

Nicole smiled. "We know that. Your heart is very big. One of the many things we love about you. But she may not know that yet."

"Show her. Tell her," Lauren said.

"I don't know that I'm a grand gesture kind of guy."

"But is *she* a grand gesture person?" Nicole asked.

She very much was. Gretchen was vivacious and spotlight stealing. She was hilarious and caring. She was so many things, and I didn't know that I'd even once let her know all the things that I loved about her. Of course, she didn't trust my confession of feelings. Of course, she thought it was all confusion due to all the amazing sex. But I knew the truth. Gretchen was my person now. And I knew what I had to do to show her.

CHAPTER 22

GRETCHEN

"Hurt" by Johnny Cash

The core four turned their heads as Jethro Winston walked into Genie's and went to the bar to talk to Joe.

"No protection from his brothers tonight," Suzie said with an evil grin.

"He's probably picking up food for Sienna and the boys," Kim said. "They've got their hands full these days."

"Oh good, so he has a second to chat." I grinned.

"I see those wheels spinning, Gretch. What're you up to?" Suzie asked.

Jethro went to the back to use the restroom. "Just follow my lead," I said.

We caught him on his way back out, still adjusting his fly.

I stepped out into the hall, blocking him from returning to the main floor.

He stumbled a little before slowing to a stop. "Gretchen LaRoe. Looking fabulous as always." He said it smooth as ever but his whole body tensed.

I raised an eyebrow and crossed my arms. Suzie, Roxy, and Kim came to stand by my side.

His swallow was audible.

"And the rest of the Sco—ladies. How are all y'all doing tonight?" he asked lightly. His forced smile melted off his face as we surrounded him.

"We know what you did," I said.

Suzie crossed her arms. Jet looked around, side to side and behind him searching for an exit. He had nowhere to go.

"You have some serious explaining to do, Romeo Junior," I said as his eyes widened comically.

"You thought you could hide it?" Suzie said, catching on first.

"All these secrets." Roxy tsked.

"Uh." He scratched at his hair. "Not sure …"

"The donation," Suzie said.

"The note? Rehab?" Kim asked.

"All that stuff to get me out of the Wraiths and into school. The work reference at the Lodge." Roxy's face was impeccably smooth.

Color rose above Jethro's beard. He studied his shoes. "I'm not sure what you mean."

"Alright, ladies, I think we've scared him enough," I said.

A huge grin broke out on Kim's face before she wrapped her arms around his waist. His hands shot up in the air, like touching her back would get him in major trouble. He glanced to the bar but nobody would see this.

"Thank you," Kim said.

Suzie shoved his shoulder. "Really. Thank you."

"You've changed all our lives," Roxy said, still not smiling.

"And I'm really sorry about all that." Jet frowned looking honestly wrecked.

Roxy rolled her eyes. "For the better."

"Oh, I don't know about that." He lifted his head to hold their gazes one at a time. "If it weren't for me—"

"Don't give yourself too much credit," Roxy said. "We made our own choices."

Jethro swallowed, his jaw clenched tight. He looked to me, like he wanted to say something.

"Can y'all give me a minute?" I said to the others.

Kim hugged him one last time, Suzie waved goodbye as Roxy turned and walked back to the table.

"I started the SWS because of you, Jet," I said. "I was hurt and frustrated with everything that happened." As I spoke worry furrowed his brows again. "But none of us have any hard feelings toward you anymore. I just wanted to tell you that." I smiled. "You don't have to leave buildings if you see us inside anymore."

"You noticed that, huh?"

I winked. "Honestly, you took way too much of the burden on yourself. You more than made up for everything, helping out my girls over the years."

Jet's dark brows furrowed. "And what about you?"

"I'm fine." I smiled and shrugged casually. "I'm Gretchen LaRoe."

He nodded, not buying my forced cheer. He cleared his throat. "I was real sorry to hear about Ephram. I've been meaning to tell you for, well, for a while now."

My throat tightened.

"I'm sorry he got caught up in all of that because of me," he said.

I growled. "Stop taking the guilt of the world on your shoulders, Jet. People make their own choices, just like you have. You've done real good. There're no more hard feelings."

"I know but we worked so hard to get you out of the Wraiths. And then the accident."

"Right," I said acidly. "The *accident*."

Jethro frowned. "It was an accident. The rain and a blown-out tire, down Tail of the Dragon. I was there at the scene." He tucked his hands under his arms and shook his head, gaze dark with memories.

The floor seemed to tilt as I fell back against the wall. "No. No. Someone told me it was the Wraiths behind it."

The world narrowed down to a point as I delved into memories long locked away. Jet was still talking but it sounded far away and underwater.

"It was Rooster or Cueball," I said.

"They rode for the Black Demons, Gretch. They were probably just trying to stir things up. Trust me, Ephram came to me asking to help him get out. I had someone help me and I thought I could pass it on. But the Wraiths didn't do that. It was just a horrible accident."

I felt the color drain from my face. My knees felt like they might give out. For so long the anger kept me going. The anger and the guilt …

"Hey, are you okay?" Jet lowered his head to get me to look at him.

"I went to the Dragon Bar with a gun," I said, my hand going to my mouth.

"You sure did. Yeah, that took some work to untangle." He chuckled with a hint of nerves.

"Sheriff James still won't let me carry a gun. Legally." I blinked up at him. "You helped him try and get out?" Had he also convinced Ephram to take out the last-minute life insurance policy that'd been funding my life? I couldn't ask that. I couldn't even think about that.

"It was the least I could do for you and Ephram. All the ladies I'd scorned," he said pointedly. "Y'all don't ever have to worry about the Wraiths. Not as long as there are Winstons around."

I couldn't speak. I couldn't breathe. We were definitely going to have to rename the SWS.

"Ephram was a good man," jet said tightly. "He always told me, back when we rode together, that he was gonna love you until his last breath. And I saw that he meant it. He said he'd always be taking care of you."

My face crumbled. I placed a hand to my chest to try and breathe. I hiccupped a sob.

"But he'd be proud of you. I know it. How you've helped so many people. What's that thing he always said?"

I looked up to Jethro. He was blurry from the tears balancing on my lids. "'Love is just shit unless you treat it like manure and spread it all around.'" I coughed out a sob-laugh.

Jet chuckled and shook his head. "You're good people, Gretchen LaRoe. Even if you and the gals scare me a little. I hope you're able to find some peace."

"You too, Romeo Junior," I teased. "Time to stop feeling like you owe us. We're good now."

We smiled at each other briefly before Jet squeezed my shoulder. With a last smile, he went to the bar and picked up his to-go order.

I stayed staring at the wall. For so long, I'd held onto the guilt that I was responsible for Ephram's death. Thinking it was my machinations, my constant meddling, and getting in people's business that had caused it ultimately.

I'd felt so guilty for surviving when he hadn't. I'd stayed in Green Valley. I'd done everything in my power to help those around me because I knew there was no hope for myself.

It was just an accident. It was a horrible accident.

It only took a moment, and everything had changed.

Something released in my chest, like a fist finally relaxing open. Actually, it started in my toes and traveled up through my whole body. All the knots in my belly untied and evaporated. It was like … I was released from so much guilt I hadn't even known I'd been carrying. I hadn't believed that Vincent could love me. I couldn't grasp that I was worthy of love. This guilt was like a chain around the iron box surrounding my heart and it just broke free.

"Oh Ephram," I said quietly. "I think I made a mistake."

CHAPTER 23

VINCENT

"Hallelujah" by Rufus Wainwright

"It's bad then?" I said, sliding into the passenger seat.

Roxy gave me a flat smile. "Gretchen said she had to get some things ready and asked me to come get you."

"Shit." I sat back in the seat and ran a hand down my face. "I really need to talk to her."

"That you do. And you will." She flipped on her blinker and moved the car onto the freeway, heading back to Green Valley.

It was Christmas Eve and Gretchen was supposed to pick me up from the airport. Her flimsy excuse made my anxiety even worse. How could I fix things if she wouldn't talk to me?

"I do love her," I said.

Roxy kept her eyes on the road. "I know."

Always the quietest of Gretchen's friends, Roxy and I spent many months working together. This could be weird for her. I wouldn't make the situation any more uncomfortable by prodding her for information about Gretchen. Even though I was restless with questions. We drove in silence until I felt her look at me pointedly before glaring at my leg.

"Oh. Sorry." I stopped shaking my leg. I let out a slow breath. "Guess I'm a little nervous."

She grunted in understanding. The longer she remained quiet, the more my thoughts had time to spiral out of control. I had assumed talking to Gretchen would bring back the woman I'd fallen in love with. But what if I'd well and truly misread the situation? What if I had done irrefutable damage to the months of trust and care we'd had built? Gretchen never actually needed this marriage. She didn't need anybody. She made that abundantly clear. But then she had said yes to our marriage, however convenient it had been. Of course, now she could have realized the trouble wasn't worth it. She could want to end our arrangement as easily as it had come to pass. We could dissolve as easily as sugar into tea. There was so little actually tying us together. We had signed contracts to ensure that. We hadn't even really moved in together. What had I been thinking?

"Vincent," Roxy said, breaking me of my thoughts.

"Shit. Sorry." I had been shaking my leg again.

She sighed loudly. "Listen. I don't do all this, uh, chatting well."

"We don't have to—"

"But I feel like another forty minutes of this—" she nodded to my leg — "might cause me to drive into a ditch." Her profile twitched with what tried to be a smile.

"I've noticed in media that women tend to be portrayed as hopeless romantics." She spoke slowly like she was trying to find just the right words. Roxy wasn't prone to speaking without intention, so I waited as she found her way. "Women are depicted as reckless and desperately searching for love. In my experience, at least, I've found that the opposite is true. The women I know guard their hearts fiercely, knowing it's a precious commodity. Once broken we fortress ourselves against ever feeling that level of pain again. It's men who, conventionally, fall hard and fast."

"When we know, we know." I shrugged.

"How nice for you," she said dryly. "Women don't always have that luxury. We bear the emotional burden more often than not. If something happens, men pack up and leave and women are left behind trying to pick up the pieces of our lives."

I was starting to feel really shitty for being a man.

She gripped the steering wheel even tighter. "When Sanders first told me he loved me, I didn't believe him. How could he possibly know that? I think I actually ran away from him."

I smiled. Poor Sanders. Always did wear all his emotions on his sleeve.

"I thought I had done such a good job of being patient for Gretchen," I explained. "Not revealing too much, too soon. I wanted her to see in her own time that we were right for each other."

It was a cold and dreary day, with heavy gray clouds blurring out the Smokys in the horizon. Fitting.

"I think you did that too well," she said. "Gretchen and you both know how preciously short life is. Maybe it's time to stop with the games and just admit that being with each other is what makes you happy. Maybe Gretchen just really doesn't believe it's possible that you could know that you love her. It doesn't have to be more complicated than that."

It really was that simple. And here I'd been trying to come up with an elaborate scheme to get her back. "I'm done with the plans and the scheming."

"I've heard that before." She sent me a quick smirk. "The irony that you're the scheming one in this relationship is not lost on me."

I smiled and relaxed back. I loved Gretchen. I wanted to be with her as often as humanly possible, and I thought, no, I *knew* she felt that way too. We are too good together for it to be one-sided. If she needed time to understand that our connection was real, then I would give it to her. But no more distance.

"I thought you would have some trial by fire for me," I said to Roxy.

She was suspiciously quiet. Even for her. Suzie had grilled me and "accidentally" accosted me. Kim had set up that little rendezvous for Gretchen and I in the bathroom—the more I thought about it, the more I was sure that was her plan all along. I had been waiting for Roxy to ambush me and test my loyalty.

"I thought about it," Roxy said. "Maybe make you go bungee jumping to prove something. But I worked with you. I know you're a good guy. I was never worried about you. I was worried *for* you."

"How's that?" I cleared my throat.

"I was surprised at first when Gretchen told us about y'all. Looking back, it's obvious. All those times you wanted to hang out were just a way to get to see her, weren't they?"

I made a sound that neither confirmed nor denied her suspicions.

"All the long looks. I thought maybe you were like so many others starstruck by the persona of Gretchen. But you were so patient. So eager to just be in her presence. You never pushed. When I saw you together. It made sense. You fell for the person, not the shine.

"Anyway. I'm not super comfortable talking about this. But I know that Gretchen has cut herself off from love. She says it's because she won't love again. That she *can't*. But we all know that's bullshit. Hearts are perfectly capable of loving again. She's just scared shitless." She shook her head.

"She's really no better than the rest of the SWS," she said quietly, almost to herself.

I was desperate for any additional glimpses inside Gretchen's mind. "What scares her? That I'll leave her?"

She shook her head. "You're not that stupid to lose someone like her."

She was right. As much as I could control anything, I would never lose a chance to be with her.

"Simply put, survivors guilt? But you should really be talking about this with her." Roxy fussed with her bangs. "I think she just can't stand the fact that she survived and Ephram didn't. She was the planner, you know? She was getting them out of the MC. I wasn't great at the time." Her brows pinched. "I learned about all this later because when it all went down I was still mixed up in the MC. But she saved me."

"She said you saved *her*." On one of our many talks, Gretchen told me all about the night she went to the biker bar, gun blazing. It had scared me to hear how close I had been to never meeting her. If anything had gone different that night all those years ago, she may have been taken too soon. It reaffirmed the burning drive to find her and talk to her and cherish every minute we had together.

Roxy rolled her eyes. "No. She saved me. I should have been there for her when Ephram died. I was her best friend most of our lives. But I was not there. I was checked out." She took a breath. "But she was the one who showed me that we aren't what we endured. That how we live and love now is what matters."

I smiled.

"It was the courage I needed to open my heart to Sanders. And I've never looked back." Her cheeks flushed.

"Is it hopeless?" I asked. "To think she'll let me in. I wouldn't expect … I mean, maybe in time …"

"I think she already does love you. Gretchen doesn't do anything a little bit. She may not talk about things as easily as you do but she shows her love in her actions. She always has."

I thought of how Gretchen cared for me. How she made love to me. How she made an effort with my family. I thought of all the tiny things she'd done. Maybe there was hope after all.

I didn't realize until the car was stopped that we had arrived at the Lodge.

"Mind if we go in really quick? I need your opinion on the new fireplace," Roxy asked.

I unbuckled, glancing at my watch. "Of course." Though to be completely honest, I was more than ready to find Gretchen.

"I just need to swing by my office to grab something." She led me briskly down the hallway to the back office that had been mine but was now hers as the main events planner. She gestured me in.

"Ah, home sweet home," I said walking passed her and into the space. I barely had time to register the rearranged furniture before I heard the door slam shut.

I turned around sharply. "Roxy?" I reached for the door, but sure enough it was locked.

"I lied," she called through the locked door. "I did have a plan. You'll thank me later." After a moment, she added, "Consider this payback for all the times you *accidentally* interrupted Sanders and I."

I turned around and found I wasn't alone. Gretchen leaned back in one chair, legs up on the other, like she'd been there a while. I hadn't seen her when I first came in and now my heart hammered at the sight of her, beautiful as always. My fingers itched to reach for her.

"Might as well get comfortable," she said, gesturing to the free chair behind the desk. "They aren't letting us out any time soon."

* * *

Gretchen

"WELL. She thinks she's so clever." I stood up to pace with arms crossed. "Locking us in a room together. Amateur!"

Vincent watched me without speaking as he moved to sit in the chair. I looked at him. His long leg crossed one over the other revealing stupidly cute little Christmas ornaments socks peeking out from his charcoal trousers. He looked adorable. My entire body missed him so acutely it took everything I had not to launch myself at him.

God, I had missed him. It hadn't even been a week but I ached with it.

"Why do you think Roxy did this?" Vincent asked calmly. Always so calm.

"Oh, this is her way of getting back at me for the whole Sanders thing." I rocked my head side to side. "And like twenty years of my constant interfering."

He snorted.

"It was a waste of time though," I said watching him closely.

His jaw ground together. "Yeah. I'd wondered about that."

He looked so defeated. I had done that to him. There were bags under his eyes and even his suit was slightly less pristine than normal.

Then he stood and stalked to me in two steps. “No. I can’t do this.”

I blinked up at him. “I think—”

“No.” He grabbed my shoulders and then forced himself to let me go. “I’m not going to sit here and pretend this is okay.” He scrubbed his hands through his hair sending it in all directions. “I’ve been trying to keep it together. I’ve been doing my best to take things slow. But I can’t do this anymore.”

“Vincent, I—”

“Look, Gretch, it’s okay. I understand that you think you can’t love me. But thankfully, I love you plenty for the both of us. I do love you, Gretchen. I love you so much. I feel constant burning here.” He fisted his hand and rubbed at his chest. “I know you don’t believe me, but my love isn’t limited. It’s not pie. It’s more like a garden or something that can grow. I’m sorry I’m not great at metaphors. The point is the more you have, the more it grows.”

“Like manure,” I whispered.

His words were like a sign from Ephram. Maybe. And I wasn’t even sure that I thought such things were possible, but maybe it was my Ephram who helped. He always told me to mind my meddling ways but look who wasn’t much better. Not that I hadn’t already decided, but it was nice to know he was looking out for me. My whole body tingled. It took every ounce not to tackle Vincent there and then. I smiled at the ground. This sweet and loving man. How did I ever get so lucky to marry him before I knew how much I could love him?

He frowned at me. “Love is shit?” he asked. “That’s what you think?”

I looked up to the ceiling, tears stinging my eyes. A sense of peace had completely soothed my jittering nerves. He, on the other hand, was more agitated than I’d ever seen him. Except maybe in the bedroom. He always got real worked up there.

“Remember that time we were talking about group therapy?” he asked. I nodded, waiting patiently. If he was going to keep cutting me off, then I could at least hear some more sweet words. “You said how it felt like you were walking around hollow? Pretending to be some empty version of yourself? I agreed.” He shook his head. “I don’t feel that way anymore. I used to. I thought I would never know what it was like to find myself in someone else again. I have that with you. I didn’t want to scare you. I thought what we had was easy compatibility. Maybe because we’d both dealt with so much loss. But I’m understanding that everything I felt now from the very beginning was love. I'd just forgotten how it felt. Or maybe it didn't feel this way the first time. But I know this is love. I know it is. So don't tell me that it's not."

Oh, he was getting really cranky now. His fists were balled at his sides but the look in his eyes as they moved over my face was filled with frustration and helplessness and … adoration. "Vincent—"

"I know you don't like to hear these things." His voice shook. "But I can't keep my feelings locked down anymore. I should have told you every moment from the second I suspected. We know the preciousness of time. We are married. We belong to each other. You are my person. And I think I could be yours. No." He shook his head. "I *am* yours. However you will have me. Our form of love can just be different." My head was shaking as he spoke. His nostrils flared and he swallowed back the tears that shimmered in his eyes. "You can't ask me to stop loving you. You can't ask me to end this marriage. I won't do it. I can't do it." His voice broke. He slumped into the chair, like all the wind had gone out of his sails. He put his feet flat to the ground and leaned forward, elbows on his knees, chin on his clenched fists.

Was it possible he'd really had these feelings the whole time? My mind reeled. All these truths that came spilling out of his mouth. So much to process. All the ease of being with him I'd assumed was because of our shared loss. But it wasn't. I understood now. That was the connection of finding my person.

It wouldn't be like the first time. It couldn't be. But our love was its own very wonderful thing.

"Vincent. Stop." My own voice was hardly more than a rasp through my tight throat.

He shook his head against his fists, refusing to look at me.

I dropped to my knees in front of him. I grabbed his hands and held them. He continued to shake his head not looking at me. This sweet, loving man.

"Vincent. If you would have let me get in a damn word edgewise, I could have told you it was a waste of Roxy's time because I already planned on finding you, locking you in a room, and telling you that I love you."

His eyes shot up to mine, bloodshot and watery.

I took a deep breath in before I started to explain. "I'd been so tied down by guilt from what I thought I did and didn't deserve. I thought the best I could settle for was a life without love. For so long, I thought it wouldn't even be possible to find someone like you. I thought I had a shot and I ruined it. But I understand that's absurd. Even if I'd lost Ephram another way, I can still love and be loved. I love you, Vincent. I love you like a best friend. I love you like a partner. I love you like a crazy sex-fiend. I love who I am with you. I love who you are. I love everything about you. And I love us. Together."

Tears overflowed and ran down my cheeks.

I shuffled on my knees closer to him. "I thought the most I could ever hope for was the friendships I captured and cultivated. I never thought in a million years I would ever be so lucky to love again like I love you."

He coughed out a relieved sob. I had done this to him. I had wrecked him with my confusion. This man who gave so much, so freely, after losing his whole world.

"I wasn't brave like you," I said. I tugged on his arms until our foreheads pressed together. He came to the ground next to me, our upper bodies holding on for dear life. "I couldn't handle loving this hard again. I'd be afraid all the time of losing you. And I am. But I also know that I'm more afraid to not have you in my life. I'm more afraid of getting so comfortable being alone that I'll miss the real thing right in front of me."

"Gretchen."

"I thought I lost my chance at a family. You are my family now, Vincent. I don't feel like a hollow shell walking around anymore either. I know who I am. And I am a person who loves you. I mean among many other things, but that's a big one. You're so much more than I ever dreamed possible. You have shown me so much about who I am and what I want. You have taught me to be brave. And I love you so much."

He held me so tight as our bodies shook.

"There will always be tragedy and broken hearts. There will be things we have no control over." He held my face as he spoke, and I nodded. I couldn't speak. My throat was too tight. "But there's this too." He placed his hand on my chest.

"My boobs. I know," I rolled my eyes. Tears spilled over with a sniffling laugh.

He shook his head. Then nodded. "Well, yeah. But also this connection." He pulled me close again. "This love."

"We have to find that and focus on that. There will always be the light to balance out the dark. I forgot that for a while. But we know how fast it all goes. We need to cherish the good things while we have them. Like you." I allowed myself to collapse into his embrace.

"And things like baby Lainey and baby Devlin," he said. "There will be weddings and parties that last until the morning. There will be impromptu Christmas concerts in the park. There will be music and laughter and love and community. It's all part of it."

I nodded. "And kinky married-people sex."

"Oh yeah, lots of kinky married-people sex," he agreed.

We kissed then, the salty tears mingling with the taste of his mouth. He sat back into the chair and pulled me into his lap. When we broke the kiss, we smiled in tandem.

"I want you to live with me. Or I can live here," he said fiercely.

"Both," I said. "We need to actually be together."

We sat in silence for some time, my head on his chest. Just breathing. "Hey." I sat up suddenly. "Remember that time on the phone? You told me about this office. And the things you wanted to do?"

He reached for me. We melted into each other. It was like no time had passed. Our bodies were perfect together. "I'm miles ahead of you," he growled.

CHAPTER 24

VINCENT

"Ave Maria" by Chris Cornell featuring Eleven

My hand slid up Gretchen's thigh as our mouths moved together. The relief of having her back in my arms was so intense my hand shook even as I teased her. Why had I ever thought to keep my feelings at bay? I had been a chickenshit. From here on out, I would tell her everything on my mind.

I broke the kiss. "I'm sorry that I told you I loved you … like that, the first time. It wasn't enough. I should have hired a plane to write it in the sky."

She laughed and it warmed my whole body. "I'm sorry I freaked out. I totally did by the way, you were right. You have just always been so open and honest this whole relationship. I felt like a fraud."

"Are you kidding me? I don't say half the stuff I think. I was so worried about coming on too strong. I've never been great at sharing things. I knew when we first met, I came off so stuffy. If I had told you how long I'd crushed on you—since the first time I saw you at the drive-in movie last summer, by the way—you'd think I was some sort of creep."

"I forgot about that. That was the first night we met, wasn't it?" Her gaze grew distant as though pulling up the memory. "Oh yeah, I was wearing that cowgirl outfit."

"That *amazing* cowgirl outfit." I growled and squeezed her ass. "I just remember wondering how everyone in this town wasn't tripping over themselves to get to you. You have such a big personality, and I was just this stick-in-the-mud that never really spoke."

She shook her head and rolled her eyes. "I loved your style from the second I saw you. I was attracted to you too and it bothered me a little. I always wanted to mess with you." She ran her hands through my hair, smoothing it. "I didn't understand. It irritated me. You may not know this, but I have control issues."

"Me too," I growled against her neck.

"God, I love that too." She threw her head back, cupping my head to her. "The way you dominate me in the bedroom. It thrilled me. I was afraid of that too. I told myself it was okay because it was role-playing." She tugged at my hair until I looked at her. "But that was always me and you."

Tension released from my chest. "I love you," I said again.

She smiled and let out a long breath. "It only took a single moment, and I knew we'd be in each other's lives forever," she said. "I felt it sure as anything, but I pushed it down. Because damn, it scared me to feel anything that strong again."

"Anytime you get scared, you let me know," I said. "I will hold you like this. Tell you to breathe. And remember to be with me here now."

She nodded and we kissed again. Soon it grew too hot. She pushed off my suit coat. I tugged her shirt out of her skirt. My hands roamed her greedily as my mouth kissed her.

"Uh, guys," Roxy said through the door as she knocked. "Super happy about the reunion," she said in a flat tone. "But this is actually *my* office now."

"Should I tell her it's revenge for all the times I caught her and Sanders?" I whispered against Gretchen's ear.

"I would also like to point out," Roxy continued, "that there are literally hundreds of beds in this building, that again, are not my office."

"Party pooper," Gretchen yelled.

"Also, we are going to be late for dinner if we don't skedaddle."

Gretchen and I frowned at each other, and mouthed *skedaddle*?

"Gross. Now I'm doubly annoyed because you made me say skedaddle. Twice."

"I think all that is just to say, it's time to go, mates," Sanders yelled through the door. His smile was audible. Their mumblings and a small giggle followed.

Gretchen and I stood up and straightened our clothes. As we were leaving the office, Gretchen brushed by and said to her friend, "That's twice now you've box-blocked me."

Roxy snorted. "You'll survive."

The four of us made our way to Devlin's house for Christmas Eve dinner.

"Wow," Gretchen said after we took off our outerwear and made our way to the living room. A massive Christmas tree stood by the fireplace. It was even bigger than the one that had been at the Lodge. The whole house was decorated professionally with pine wreaths, stacked candles of various shapes and sizes, silver mercury glass trees, and candleholders. Silver and pine carried over to the table where a gorgeous feast was laid out.

Soft classical holiday music drifted through the air along with the smell of roasting turkey and stuffing mixed with cinnamon sweetness.

Devlin and Kim welcomed us. Kim quickly mentioned the food had been catered with a bashful smile. Suzie, Ford, Jack, and Skip were already inside sitting on the couch, drinks in hand. I felt welcomed and content with my arm around Gretchen. This was perfection. This was my newfound family. Gretchen radiated with joy. I never thought I would feel this again. I never thought I could love this deeply again. Life was beautiful and tragic. There were ups and there were downs. It was unpredictable and it was constant. It was chaotic and it was boring. Life was full of paradoxes. I wanted all of it just as it was, with Gretchen by my side. Smiling up at me.

"What?" she asked as we sat down for dinner.

"Just thinking about how much I love you."

She unfolded a crimson napkin and put it in her lap. "I love you too. But you were staring at my boobs again."

"Ah. That." I leaned in and inhaled her just to watch the goosebumps play up her chest. "I was remembering that we have unfinished business downstairs."

She turned to brush her lips against mine. "I didn't forget." She winked.

Outside a trickling rain fell softly on the great pines outside Devlin's massive windows. It was a perfect moment. A series of perfect moments. My heart was so full.

We ate, drank, and were merry. After dinner Kim and Devlin played several Christmas songs—him singing on the piano as she played cello and harmonized sweetly. Their talent knocked my socks off.

"I had no idea," I whispered to Gretchen.

"Good, right?" She rested her head on my chest as we sat on the couches to watch them perform. He switched to acoustic guitar as Kim played cello, starting the familiar notes of "Ava Maria." As he sang, my throat tightened and the whole room went speechless with emotion. His voice was rough and deep, but his range sent chills down my arms. Kim sniffed and wiped her eyes during rests in her playing. We all watched on with glistening eyes.

After that, the mood shifted to a more party atmosphere. We sang silly Christmas carols and drank and played games until it was time to go to bed. Gretchen and I took a guest room because the mulled wine made it too easy to stay.

I reached for her and we held each other, swaying slightly.

"What a perfect night," she said on a sigh.

"The only thing that would have made it better, is if I could have given you your gift."

She leaned back eyebrows perked high. "Oh?"

"Unfortunately, it's back in New York."

"Boo. I guess I can be patient and wait until *after New Year's*. Sigh," she said loudly. "A hint?"

I shook my head and kissed her.

"That's fine." She pouted. "I didn't get you anything. Just me. Pretend I have a bow on."

"That's all I want."

* * *

Gretchen

I HADN'T BEEN ENTIRELY truthful with Vincent. But in my defense, some little white lies are good. Other than this last thing, I was done with interfering and game playing. I would focus on my own happiness and love.

"And you're sure it's okay that it's just you and me?" I asked him, the next day, as we sat in front of my tiny white LED Christmas tree.

"I couldn't want anything more." He leaned forward and kissed me. "This is perfect."

We wore matching buffalo plaid PJs and sipped hot toddies. The other core four were with their families or extended families to-be.

"That's a shame."

He raised an eyebrow at me just as there was a knock on the door.

I couldn't contain my grin as I jumped up and ran to answer.

"Merry Christmas!" Nicole, Lauren, Troy, and baby Lainey stood there grinning, arms laden with luggage and baby accessories.

Vincent's jaw dropped. "You guys!" He hugged them each in turn.

"Hopefully, this is genuinely good news, or this is the lamest gift ever," Lauren said, handing over the baby to Vincent. He grabbed her with a huge smile.

It helped ease a little of the pain that arrived with my irregular period yesterday. Part of me secretly had hoped for a big Christmas surprise. Everybody exchanged hugs and came inside.

"This is amazing." He looked around to me, pulling me over for a kiss as he hefted Lainey to his other arm. "You planned this?"

I nodded. "We have to be with family on the holidays. It's a rule. Whether we want to or not." I winked at Nicole. She did the same back. "The renters next door are out of town and offered their apartment for the week," I explained.

"It's great. I'm so glad you guys are here," Vincent said beaming.

"Now we can learn about the magic of Green Valley," Lauren said.

"What's the deal with all the hot bearded guys here?" Nicole asked. "I swear we passed at least five sexy mountain men just driving down Main Street."

Lauren nodded eagerly in agreement. Troy pretended to grimace and covered his ears.

"Well, I'm out of the matchmaking business. But since you asked and we have time, I may have a story or two. It all started with the Winston family ..."

CHAPTER 25

GRETCHEN

"What Are You Doing New Year's Eve?" by The Head and The Heart

It worked out well having Vincent's family around because the week leading up to Suzie's wedding flew with a million final preparations. We spent the evenings making love, and somehow the sex was better than ever. And it was really, *really* good before. I didn't feel guilty having to leave him alone for final maid of honor duties. Suzie and Ford had put him to work as an usher and even invited his family, but they had to leave before the big day. Soon it was New Year's Eve and the core four were in a titter!

We started the day early, at the Lodge in the biggest suite, all getting ready. We sipped mimosas—OJ for Kim—and we all breathed a sigh of relief when Kim's dress zipped up. Suzie wore a gorgeous lace dress that hugged her figure and was just sexy enough to cause jaws to drop. Her makeup was elegant and her hair, now past her shoulders again, flowed in soft waves with a jeweled clip pulling one half up.

Her father, sober over a year, walked her down the aisle before joining his neighbor Mrs. Albensi in the front row. Many young adults and teens from Triple F filled the chairs. Several of the regulars from the Stripped classes too. Blaire and Blithe waved from the seats, giving us thumbs up as we passed. Ford cried when Suzie entered the room. And again when he said his vows.

"I don't know how I got so lucky to be here today. But thank you for making me the luckiest man on the planet," Ford said with a shaking voice.

I found Vincent in the crowd and winked at him. He gave a small shake of his head and pointed to himself. I grinned at him before bringing my focus back to the happy couple.

The ceremony was short and sweet, the whole thing over in a half hour. Ford had asked Jack, Skip, and Devlin to be his groomsmen. Skip and Vincent were ushers. It appeared all the men of the women of the SWS had grown quite close over the past few months. Again, I wasn't saying it was thanks to me but if the shoe fits …

The Lodge's grand room had been transformed into a winter forest wonderland. Gorgeous without being hokey. Simple pine trees and white votives. Twinkling white lights covered the ceiling. Roxy had absolutely nailed it. As guests sipped on cocktails and hors d'oeuvres, the bridal party went outside for photos.

"It's colder than a witch's titty," I said as we made our way to the patio that stretched along the side of the grand room providing a perfect view of the forest valley.

Kim rubbed her arms, nodding, the tiniest bulge in her belly was covered by the flowing fabric of her royal blue gown. My own emerald green dress worked beautifully with Roxy's crimson. We looked damn good, as always.

"Good thing I got us these," I said. Vincent appeared holding four gold-wrapped gifts.

Inside were leather jackets for each of the core four. Vincent had a designer friend create SWS logos that resembled the circular pattern of a motorcycle club printed on all the backs. I had really wanted to stitch "No Ex Left Behind" across them but felt like maybe Ford wouldn't appreciate that for the wedding. So instead, the words had been discretely embroidered on the inside. Suzie's had an intricate rose pattern that matched with her gown and read "Happily Ever After" on the back under the logo.

"These are amazing. I can't believe you did this." Suzie fanned at her face as Kim helped her into the jacket and Roxy held her flowers. "Duck, my makeup."

"The SWS doesn't mess around." I hugged my girls but had to cut it short before we all ruined our makeup.

Inside the guests grazed the bar and munched as the ballroom was transformed into an epic New Year's party. More and more townspeople showed up for the reception. It was the end of the year event for all of Green Valley.

As soon as my bridesmaid duties were done, Vincent and I snapped together like magnets. The only time we had left each other's side was when Suzie led us all in a line dance. Apparently, that was where he drew the line. He waved from the sidelines, chatting with Skip. Sanders made a goofy show of trying to match the steps, yelling something about a bush dance. Ford and Suzie spent most of the night arm in arm, staring into each other's eyes in a way that tightened my throat every time. And the whole night, I lived in the moment. I didn't take any mental snapshots to replay later. Life had its peaks and valleys, and it was okay to enjoy the highs as they came without worrying about when they would be gone again. I would never be alone again. I never had been.

When the countdown to midnight began, our group met at the center of the dance floor. Time slowed as the lights flashed and the music rang out. I watched my people count down as overwhelming joy bubbled up in me. All the pain and suffering in life, all the beauty, and joy. It somehow always managed to find a balance. I looked to each of them. Kim's tearful joy. Ford's adoring gaze on Suzie. Jack and Skip arm in arm. Roxy rolling her eyes as Sanders peppered her with kisses. Vincent as he brushed back my hair to kiss my neck. But these loving glimpses didn't fill me with fear anymore. I didn't see our happiness through the future lens of loss and change. I looked at these wonderful people in my life and stayed exactly in this moment. Surrounded by love.

"Happy New Year!" the whole room shouted and before I knew it, Vincent had dipped me low to plant an epic kiss on me.

"Happy New Year," he said.

"I love you." I squeezed him so tight I thought my heart might explode.

The SWS women hugged each other and when I grabbed Roxy she whispered in my ear, "No ex left behind."

How could I ever think that I wouldn't love again? I was in love and surrounded by love every moment of every day. I was the luckiest person on the planet. Love may not always be a choice, but you can decide whether to cut yourself off from it or be open to it. And I was done living in fear. I was open to receiving.

After a few more dances and many more goodbyes, Vincent and I eventually made our way to the exit.

Hand in hand we walked to the room we rented for the night.

"Are you happy?" he asked me.

I leaned my head on his shoulder as we walked. "I'm *so* happy."

"Ready to go home tomorrow? Ready to really live as husband and wife?"

"Which home?" I teased, knowing he meant New York. "I'm so ready."

He stopped and grabbed my hands, turning me to him. "Thank you for marrying me. Thank you for loving me. Thank you for choosing to grow old with me," he spoke tightly.

"Thank you for showing me how to let love in again. Thank you for finding me and holding on tight. Thank you for loving me too," I said back.

"As if I had any choice in the matter. It only took one moment of knowing you."

"Oh, you," I said and pulled him in by the lapels for a kiss.

"That being said," his face transformed into something darker, "you've been late on your weekly reports."

I bit back a grin before blinking up at him with innocent doe eyes. "Oh dear. Whatever can I do?"

Heat rushed through me as his nostrils flared. "You're going to go inside this room and find a way to make it up to me." He was already loosening his tie and I watched the action, transfixed.

"Yes, sir."

He growled and was on me a second later. And that night I learned all the joys of kinky married-people sex when both parties came together with open hearts.

And it was very, *very* good.

EPILOGUE

VINCENT

"Heroes" by Peter Gabriel

I crept silently into the kitchen of our New York home, following the sound of Gretchen humming lightly to herself. Our unloaded suitcases were still by the door, but I instructed her to wait downstairs while I got her belated Christmas gift.

I crept closer, distracted by how her ass looked in her pants.

"Ready?" I asked.

Gretchen screamed and pivoted; a hunk of cheese wielded like a weapon in her hand. "Dammit, Vincent!"

"Never sneak up on a woman scorned! That was your final warning." She dropped the cheddar and lunged for me.

I had just enough time to catch her as we slammed back into the wall with an *oomph*.

She attacked me with kisses all over my face and neck.

"Oh no. You sure showed me. This is torture," I said flatly. "Please. Stop."

She ran her hand down the front of my pants. My cock responded instantly. "The torture is only just beginning." She bit the bottom of my ear.

I growled but when I went for her pants, she stopped my hand. "Nuh-uh. I want to see this gift."

"I see now where the lesson lays," I said. I grabbed her hand and brought her to the staircase that led up to the owner's suite. *Our* bedroom.

I smiled to myself as she gasped. "Oh, Vincent."

We slowed so she could examine each and every one of the framed photos that lined the staircase. Her eyes gleamed as she reached out and caressed a picture of her as a baby. Then one of her and Ephram laughing together. It was the only one of the two of them I could find.

She laughed at the picture of her and Roxy standing side by side, in identical poses of sass even though they couldn't have been more than twelve. And on and on it went up the stairs. Couples from the SWS. The core four dressed up and dancing. Our families. The Walsh women. Baby Lainey. My favorite photo with Elaine. We climbed through our lives' history. Every moment captured that had brought us to this exact moment.

There was the picture of us the day we got married. We seemed so young even though it was only a few months ago. In hindsight, we had so obviously been lying to ourselves. She paused to study us on the steps of the courthouse.

"I was so happy to marry you," I said. "That day it felt so right the moment you walked in.

"I'm glad one of us was." She laughed then added, "You know what I mean. I was a wreck, even if I couldn't understand why. My heart knew exactly what it was doing. My rational brain just needed to believe it."

"I'm a patient guy."

"Thank goodness." She kissed me.

The second to last photo was a picture of Gretchen, Suzie, Roxy, and Kim, arms linked, smiling at the camera, heads leaning on one another. She reverently touched the frame.

"It's all too much," she whispered.

"I figured since I won't be traveling so much for work now with this permanent position, we should bring some of Green Valley and our life together here," I explained.

"It's wonderful." She stopped to shake her head at me. The last picture was the selfie we took at Rockefeller Center. Her rosy cheeked and me staring at her with total adoration. The moment I realized I had to tell her how much I loved her.

"There's only one problem," she said.

I frowned and waited.

"There aren't nearly enough pictures of the two of us," she said, as she pressed a hand to my cheek.

"We have forever to work on that." I gestured to the other side of the stairs.

"That's what that wall is for. And whatever our future family looks like. You and me is all I'll ever need."

Her lip trembled and she let me hold her.

"This is the best Christmas gift ever," she sniffled.

I laughed. "That's not your gift." Her head snapped up. "That was just me decorating."

Her eyes grew wider.

"Vincent. You know I'm already in love with you. I physically don't know that I could possibly love you anymore."

She stopped dead when I pulled her into the closet off our bedroom. "I was wrong. I love you even more."

She jumped and squealed as she took in every detail. I had the closet reorganized professionally, moving most of my rarely used clothes to the extra bedroom closet. There was now plenty of room for Gretchen's stuff and room to grow. In fact, I had Roxy start shipping clothes out even though our time would be mostly split equally between the two cities.

"It's too beautiful. Look at all this stuff."

"Still not your gift," I said, leaning against the doorway, alit with her joy.

"What?" She turned and looked at me.

"Gretchen, having space in *our* closet is part of sharing my life with you. You should have more than the bare minimum. You should have everything. My love for you isn't a gift, it's a given."

She came up to me and kissed me. "Thank you." Her eyes glistened.

She went back to exploring the closet. "Oh my god, my very own ball gown rack." She was hopping up and down and I was thoroughly enjoying the view when she spotted it.

She stilled and her hands flew to her mouth.

"Now, that's the gift," I said.

Nicole had told me how her eyes had bugged out when she saw the yellow dress on their shopping trip. The very next day I went and bought it.

"Oh, Vincent." Her head shook, a hand over her mouth.

"A little birdie told me how much you loved it."

She nodded as tears flowed down her cheeks in earnest.

"But she told me the craziest thing." I stepped closer and grabbed her hands. "That you said you wouldn't have any place to wear it."

"I don't care. I'll wear it to check the mail."

I laughed. "Or I was thinking, we should renew our vows. But with a big party. You deserve to be the star of the show, Gretchen. You deserve a day just to celebrate you."

"Not just me," she said, and I smiled. "Me and that dress." She nodded seriously.

I pulled her close as I laughed. "So, is that a yes?"

"Of course. I would love to marry you, Vincent. Again. I mean, you'll never have to twist my arm to throw an epic party."

I brought her close and kissed her. I would never tire of the ease in which she slid into my arms or how perfectly we fit together. I must have been a saint in a previous life. How I got so lucky to love not once but twice, I would never know. But I would spend every day showing my gratitude. I would love Gretchen with all my heart and not take a single moment for granted.

"I would take you right here, right now," Gretchen said, seemingly reading my thoughts. "But I can't risk any harm to fashion. It's not in my nature."

"Don't ever change, Gretchen." I kissed her head.

"As if I could."

She hadn't changed. She was still the woman I met and loved all those months ago, but she had evolved to let me in. And I grew just by knowing her and being near her. Somehow, we both ended up becoming better together than we would have been on our own.

"Time for bed," I growled.

"Yes, sir." Her serious tone melted into giggles as I chased after her.

We celebrated our plans to be married by making love all night long. Our relationship may not have progressed in the typical order, but it had worked out just as it should in the end.

And now, I got to marry my wife.

* * *

Gretchen

Some years later

SUZIE, Kim, Roxy, and I sat side by side on the bench. A warm breeze blew through the flowering trees as we watched the drama unfold in front of us.

"Five bucks on Aria," I said.

Devlin and Kim's oldest was across the playground, with a look of pure intent on her face as she stared down an older boy.

Our focus was brought back to right in front of us as the twins came barreling toward their aunt.

"We found a bug, Aunt Roxy!" Caroline yelled, pulling her twin sister behind her.

Josephine nodded enthusiastically, before shoving a roly-poly under her aunt's nose.

Roxy grimaced and recoiled. "Uh. Nice. Do your dads let you play with bugs?"

They squealed out laughter before running off.

"I thought that was a fair question." Roxy shrugged. "I don't know what three-year-olds can handle. Jack and Skip just handed me their bags and basically shoved me out the door with them. I'm not equipped for this."

"They're fine," Kim said confidently, hands resting on baby number three currently percolating in her belly. "I mean, maybe if you see them try to eat it, step in. But they're probably fine."

The SWS, *the new class*, was at the park for a playdate on this wonderful spring day. The warm weather had also brought out most of the town.

"Any news?" Roxy asked me.

I grinned. "Any day now. We won't really know until we get a call. But we were approved and all that. Now we wait."

"You're going to be a momma soon. Can you believe it?" Suzie asked.

I shook my head. "Not really. But the room is all set up and ready for the baby whenever they arrive. We're so excited."

After years of trying, Vincent and I decided adoption would be the next right path to try. The application process went smoothly, all things considered, with my past life. Apparently, Jethro helped to clean some things off my record at some point and I wasn't about to bring up anything.

"Half of us are married and half of us have babies. What has happened to the wild women of the SWS?" Kim asked.

"I have no idea. Probably somewhere under all these diaper bags," I teased. "But I wouldn't go back. Not for a million years."

"Me neither," Kim said.

"Heck no," Suzie agreed.

"Nope." Roxy sighed. "I'm probably gonna give in and marry Sanders already."

She let her hair fall forward to hide her blush as Kim squeaked in joy.

"Ever since Jack and Skip adopted the twins. He's been dropping more and more hints," Roxy said.

"Please." Suzie waved her off. "He was dropping hints at our wedding."

"He was dropping hints the night you met in Denver. Put the man out of his misery, would you?" I put up my hands. "Not that I am interfering."

"I wouldn't even recognize the old you," Roxy teased me. "Anyway. Just so you know. Get ready for more bridesmaids dresses."

"Are you asking us to be your bridesmaids, Roxy?" Suzie nudged her with a growing smile as Roxy blushed.

"Ugh. Not again. Tell me the wedding is after the summer?" Kim poked her protruding belly. "First, this one gets married with Ari in my belly." She thumbed at Suzie. "Then I manage to be pregnant during your and Vincent's second wedding and for Jack and Skip's. I'm really starting to think y'all are doing this to me on purpose."

"Not our fault you keep getting knocked up. Ouch," Suzie rubbed her arm after Kim pinched her.

"I'm making Devlin get snipped." Kim crossed her arms. Then her gaze moved to where Aria was helping her little brother up off the ground. Her eyes went soft and she smiled. "Maybe not. *Ugh*, hormones."

"We might have another kiddo for a while too." Suzie frowned. "A good kid, but things are rough at their home."

She and Ford never had their own children, but they often helped with fosters or other kids in the system. They frequently had their hands full with the older kids that weren't as easily adopted. Taking them in and having their hearts broken after they left each time, even though the kids always left better than they'd arrived.

I squeezed her hand. I was in awe of her and Ford, the strength it took to foster was incredible.

There was a shout and all four of our heads swung to where a group of kids were playing tag or something. Aria had her hands on her hips, brows furrowed, and looked ready to pounce.

The boy standing between her and her goal was in trouble.

The little boy cracked a smile and raised his eyebrows. What was this kid, eight? And he had already perfected the suave pout of a grown man? From behind his back, he flourished a bouquet of obviously hand-collected dandelions. Aria's stance relaxed as she hesitantly took the flowers.

"Well, well, what have we here. A little Romeo, huh?" I said.

The moment the words passed my lips, I leaned closer. "Wait." My eyes widened. "Isn't that Benjamin Winston?" A couple years older than Aria, he already had his mother's good looks and his father's charm. I had been right when I said Romeo. Romeo the third.

We all looked at each other. "Oh no, I think it is," Kim said.

"Nope," Suzie said.

"Not gonna happen," Roxy agreed.

"If he thinks—" Kim started.

All four of us stood as one—well, Kim took a little longer having just hit her third trimester. Four formerly scorned women strode across the playground. Faces following us as we moved with focused determination. We were halfway across the playground when I reached out my arms and stopped the others.

"Wait," I said.

Kim had the face of the fiercest momma bear but she too, stopped to watch. Aria took the proffered flowers, turned, and divided them up between the twins, her little brother, and another girl she'd been playing with. She pointedly turned away from Benjamin but not before shooting him one last smile over her shoulder.

"I love that child," Suzie said.

Kim groaned as Roxy patted her shoulder.

"Should we step in?" Kim asked.

A soft wind blew through the air as I looked at each one of the women next to me, beautiful in the mid-day light.

Each of us had transformed into such powerful women. We'd taken the pain of our pasts and made ourselves into something more. We worked through our fear and hatred, insecurities and trauma, to forge new lives and new loves. Our lives were more wonderful than any of us could have possibly imagined.

We had our partners who we grew and changed with. We had full lives and careers. We had new families and communities. But more importantly, we still had, and would always have, each other. The SWS. No longer women scorned, but something better and stronger, connected by the deep roots of our histories.

"Nah," I said. "She's going to be okay."

They looked at me before turning back to the field where the kids played. The children would grow and get hurt. Love and lose. And in the end, they would always be okay. They would always have people who loved them. I grabbed Suzie's hand, and she grabbed Kim, who reached for Roxy, pulling her down to put an awkward arm around her shoulder.

"After all," I said, "no ex left behind."

"No ex left behind," they all repeated.

The End.

ACKNOWLEDGMENTS

You can't see me but know that I'm already tearing up writing this. I cannot believe this is the last of the Scorned Women. I am so incredibly thankful to everybody who I've met on this journey and to those who I've known that helped me get here.

I can never remember everybody and inevitably forget to include somebody special to me because I'm an emotional mess with a shoddy brain. But if you know me, you *hopefully* know how important you are to me.

To my husband whose unwavering support got me through more dark moments than I'd care to admit and who manages to encapsulate each of the best qualities of all my heroes.

To my daughter who makes me want to make the world a more loving and caring place.

To my family members who know I'm a writer and support me unconditionally. (Even though I will never want to talk about my books.)

To Nora for all the texts and pep talks and for just getting it.

To Ellie for all the soul-quenching conversations and laughter.

For Tracy for having read more of my words (published and still in drafts) than any other person on this planet, save myself, and somehow still not being sick of me yet.

For Lynsey for fighting to be here so I can bug you with daily voice memos.

To Brooke for all the things. ALL OF THEM. You are an inspiration.

To Fiona and Smartypants Romance for allowing me to write 4.5 books and not kicking me out and helping me reach people I never would have otherwise.

To Nicole who has given me so much support through this whole series. I honestly don't feel worthy to even have you read my books and am incredibly flattered that you do.

To my Peeps, I dedicated this book to you and am eternally flabbergasted by and thankful for your support.

And of course, to Penny, for allowing me to write in her world, a world that so many of us have found escape and joy in. We are all here because of her generosity and faith.

ABOUT THE AUTHOR

Piper Sheldon writes Contemporary Romance and Paranormal Romance. Her books are a little funny, a lotta romantic, and with just a little twist of something more. She lives with her husband, toddler, and two needy dogs at home in the desert Southwest. She finds writing bios in the third person an extreme sport of awkwardness.

Sign Up for Piper's Newsletter!

Find Piper Sheldon online:
Facebook: http://bit.ly/2lAvr8A
Twitter: http://bit.ly/2kxkioK
Amazon: https://amzn.to/2kx2RVn
Instagram: http://bit.ly/2lxxV7H
Website: http://bit.ly/2kitH3H

Find Smartypants Romance online:
Website: www.smartypantsromance.com
Facebook: https://www.facebook.com/smartypantsromance
Twitter: @smartypantsrom
Instagram: @smartypantsromance
Newsletter: https://smartypantsromance.com/newsletter/

ALSO BY PIPER SHELDON

THE SCORNED WOMEN'S SOCIETY

My Bare Lady Book 1

The Treble With Men Book 2

The One That I Want Book 3

Hopelessly Devoted Book 3.5, A Scorned Women's Society Novella

It Takes a Woman Book 4

THE UNSEEN SERIES

The Unseen Book 1

The Untouched Book 2

STAR CROSSED LOVERS

Midnight Clear - an introductory Novella

If the Fates Allow

You can find all of Piper's books at pipersheldon.com

ALSO BY SMARTYPANTS ROMANCE

Green Valley Chronicles

The Love at First Sight Series

Baking Me Crazy by Karla Sorensen (#1)

Batter of Wits by Karla Sorensen (#2)

Steal My Magnolia by Karla Sorensen(#3)

Fighting For Love Series

Stud Muffin by Jiffy Kate (#1)

Beef Cake by Jiffy Kate (#2)

Eye Candy by Jiffy Kate (#3)

The Donner Bakery Series

No Whisk, No Reward by Ellie Kay (#1)

The Green Valley Library Series

Love in Due Time by L.B. Dunbar (#1)

Crime and Periodicals by Nora Everly (#2)

Prose Before Bros by Cathy Yardley (#3)

Shelf Awareness by Katie Ashley (#4)

Carpentry and Cocktails by Nora Everly (#5)

Love in Deed by L.B. Dunbar (#6)

Dewey Belong Together by Ann Whynot (#7)

Hotshot and Hospitality by Nora Everly (#8)

Love in a Pickle by L.B. Dunbar (#9)

Checking You Out by Ann Whynot (#10)

Scorned Women's Society Series

My Bare Lady by Piper Sheldon (#1)

The Treble with Men by Piper Sheldon (#2)

The One That I Want by Piper Sheldon (#3)

Hopelessly Devoted by Piper Sheldon (#3.5)

It Takes a Woman by Piper Sheldon (#4)

Park Ranger Series

Happy Trail by Daisy Prescott (#1)

Stranger Ranger by Daisy Prescott (#2)

The Leffersbee Series

Been There Done That by Hope Ellis (#1)

Before and After You by Hope Ellis (#2)

The Higher Learning Series

Upsy Daisy by Chelsie Edwards (#1)

Green Valley Heroes Series

Forrest for the Trees by Kilby Blades (#1)

Parks and Provocation by Juliette Cross (#2)

Story of Us Collection

My Story of Us: Zach by Chris Brinkley (#1)

Seduction in the City

Cipher Security Series

Code of Conduct by April White (#1)

Code of Honor by April White (#2)

Code of Matrimony by April White (#2.5)

Code of Ethics by April White (#3)

Cipher Office Series

Weight Expectations by M.E. Carter (#1)

Sticking to the Script by Stella Weaver (#2)

Cutie and the Beast by M.E. Carter (#3)

Weights of Wrath by M.E. Carter (#4)

Common Threads Series

Mad About Ewe by Susannah Nix (#1)

Give Love a Chai by Nanxi Wen (#2)

Key Change by Heidi Hutchinson (#3)

Educated Romance

Work For It Series

Street Smart by Aly Stiles (#1)

Heart Smart by Emma Lee Jayne (#2)

Book Smart by Amanda Pennington (#3)

Smart Mouth by Emma Lee Jayne (#4)

Lessons Learned Series

Under Pressure by Allie Winters (#1)

Not Fooling Anyone by Allie Winters (#2)

Out of this World

London Ladies Embroidery Series

Neanderthal Seeks Duchess (#1)

www.ingramcontent.com/pod-product-compliance
Lightning Source LLC
Chambersburg PA
CBHW030619310726
48979CB00003B/794
9781959097549